P9-EMF-498

# CRUEL IS THE NIGHT

# CRUEL IS THE NIGHT

Karo Hämäläinen

Translated by Owen Witesman

First published in Finnish under the title


The writing this novel was supported by the WSOY Literary Foundation and the Finnish National Library Funds Board.

Translation into English was supported by a grant from the WSOY Literary Foundation.

Robert borrows some of his thoughts and the aspen forestry example from *Markets and Democracy: Exiting the Tyranny of the Majority* by Björn Wahlroos (Otava, 2012).

Reijo Salminen borrows his quiz questions and related anecdotes from *Suuri tietovisa* 2008 by Reijo Salminen (Gummerus 2007)



Soho Press
853 Broadway
New York, NY 10003



Library of Congress Cataloging-in-Publication Data

Hämäläinen, Karo, 1976–
Witesman, Owen, translator.
Cruel is the night / Karo Hamalainen ; translated by Owen Witesman.
Ilta on Julma. English
ISBN 978-1-61695-681-3
eISBN 978-1-61695-682-0
1. Married people—Fiction. 2. Murder—Fiction. I. Title
PH356.H358 I4613 2017 894'.54134—dc23 2016034461

Interior design by Janine Agro, Soho Press, Inc.

Printed in the United States of America

10 9 8 7 6 5 4 3 2 1

# CRUEL IS THE NIGHT

# PROLOGUE

*WHEN LUDWIG VAN Beethoven composed the theme for his famous Bagatelle in A minor, he scarcely could have imagined that it would be playing more than two hundred years later in a luxury flat in London. Even less could he have envisioned the sound coming from a tiny box used for speaking to people on the other side of the world. Beethoven was probably just thinking of his lover, Therese Malfatti, to whom he dedicated the piece.*

*Tenaciously the phone repeated the snippet of melody with the precision of a computer—perfectly, flawlessly, without any personal interpretation. Each time it repeated, the volume grew. The iPhone, only two months old, vibrated on the brown lacquered surface of the chest of drawers. The buzzing caused by the vibration mingled with Beethoven's notes, creating a combined sonic experience familiar to anyone whose co-worker has ever left his phone behind in his open-plan office pod when going to a meeting, the toilet, or the coffee machine.*

*And then didn't come back to answer it.*

*The caller was persistent. When the call dropped, he tried again, and the classic Viennese melody started from the beginning, quiet at first and then gradually growing louder.*

*From farther off another melody chimed in, this one originally a part of the "Gran Vals" by Francisco Tárrega. During the previous millennium, a Finnish mobile phone company had converted it into the call of the urban jungle, a series of sounds heard murmuring in overcoat pockets, making tinny echoes in subway cars, and breaking the tension of climactic moments in theaters everywhere.*

*No one answered the call.*

*The airy, relaxed progression of notes, amplified, drawn out, and sharpened in post-processing, completed the indiscriminate orchestration, although it was only audible when Beethoven was resting, since it played so softly coming from the back of the apartment.*

*No one was there to hear the noise and do what anyone would do after being forced to listen to half an hour of telephones ringing: go and switch them to silent or shut the blasted things off.*

*This was the result of no one being in the rooms.*

*No one alive.*

# Mikko

THE FLIGHT WAS unpleasant.

A family with two children sat behind us, and somewhere over the North Sea, the boy decided that the armrests of the aisle seats would make excellent parallel bars. Using them to swing himself along the aisle was great fun. The fact that some of the passengers—myself included—were resting our elbows on his play equipment did not hinder the boy in the least. He simply grabbed hold of each perfect stranger's wrist and continued on his way.

When the boy's game began, I knew it wouldn't last long. Temporally limited discomfort was tolerable.

It went as I had assumed. After ten minutes of running amok, one of his many falls left him crying, which was followed by soothing and caresses from the mother. For the remainder of the journey, the parents succeeded in keeping the boy's attention on an activity book.

On the other hand, the party of five young women sitting two rows ahead of us granted no such mercy. Their horse-faced hahaha's pummeled my auditory canals, and the blondest of the quintet frequently ejaculated admiring and horrified uh-ohs. Thanks to my daughter, Julia, I had learned the dialect of today's youth relatively well, but this was my first time hearing someone use the acronym OMG in speech. No principle of economy could justify the expression, as it could in a text message, because pronouncing the three letters took just as much effort as three one-syllable words. So it was nothing more than a corruption of the language.

The women were talking about their plans for the future—one was nursing hopes of marrying an American exchange student and moving to Ohio to be a housewife ("or was it Orlando?"). They went through what each had packed—one had three blouses, another was going to make do with two, but the latter had a dress with her that was pretty blouselike and could also be worn with jeans, but not the one with stripes that the third one thought was so delicious.

This endless recitation didn't even stop during the meal. Each glass of champagne—"it's already one o'clock and we aren't even drunk yet"—raised the volume level as if someone were clicking a remote control.

I tried to focus on *Murder on the Orient Express*, but due to the distractions of the environment, I couldn't keep track of the personalities and backgrounds of the characters. My attention kept getting stuck on the Finnish translation, and I found myself trying to guess how each sentence went in the original English. Then I retranslated them. Veera asked whether I wanted to trade places with her. She was sitting in the middle seat, where perhaps all the noise was not quite as audible as on the aisle. I said we shouldn't bother. I had been dealt this tribulation and would bear it with my paperback in my lap, staring at the bright yellow upper half of the seat in front of me.

When the wheels of the airplane touched down on the tarmac at Stansted Airport, I only had one thought: It will all be over soon.

But when I caught hold of that thought, I changed it.

Soon it would all begin.

Carefully I inserted my fingers into the left front pocket of my jeans. With my fingertips I felt the slick surface of the zipper storage bag. Retrieving my backpack from under the seat in front of me, I thought I could feel the warmth of the rye bread through the fabric, although the bread had been baked the night before. I quickly pulled my fingers away from the heat.

I had to take a few deep breaths when Veera turned her gaze away, because Veera was the one I feared the most. She was a strong-willed woman and knew me frighteningly well. If anyone was going to prevent me carrying out my plan, it would be her. I couldn't arouse even the slightest suspicion in her.

I had been preparing this evening for several weeks, but I had really been building up to it for more than thirty years. As long as I had known Robert.

Considering how much I had contemplated the coming hours, I was calm. I wasn't even really thinking about the evening, instead allowing myself to be irritated at my fellow travelers. I acted as I had planned: I would concentrate on the details, allowing them to fill my mind. Suddenly it would be evening, and everything would be done. And then everything could start.

I hadn't spent three hours of purgatory in coach because I wanted to kill my childhood friend.

I didn't want to. I had to, because the alternative would be lifelong regret. I wouldn't be able to cope with that.

# Robert

MANAGING UNCERTAINTY IS a necessary but not sufficient condition for success. You still have to convert that ability to manage uncertainty into a strength, and that requires years of work at hardening your natural resolve. I had the necessary prerequisites and had purposefully trained myself to load the dice in my favor.

Because uncertainty frightened others more than me, I had a competitive advantage. I understood that and used it in my favor.

Success: Locate your competitive advantage. Strengthen it. Make money.

I was evidence that the recipe worked.

A cardboard box decorated in pastel tones from a patisserie rocked against my thigh as the elevator accelerated to full cruising speed, six meters per second.

Of course a courier could have brought the cake, or we could have asked the restaurant of the Shangri-La Hotel to prepare whatever dessert we liked. The restaurant would have delivered the cake directly to our kitchen using the dumbwaiter, effortlessly and at the time of our choosing. However, I enjoyed simple tasks like picking up a chocolate cake. Passing time was my job now. I enjoyed the speed of the elevator. I had enjoyed walking a few blocks in the almost-summer weather of a Saturday in a London just beginning to bring the short sleeves out, and the sun had been shining so brightly that I could justifiably flip open my sunglasses.

The doors of the elevator slid apart in front of me as discreetly as a butler might have opened them. Stepping into my foyer, I stood above London. During my first trips up the elevator, I had felt the change of air pressure in my ears, but I had grown accustomed to that now. People can get used to all sorts of environments.

Italian architects have an eye for detail and they understand the importance of space. What is the Coliseum but arches surrounded by stone? Where else can you feel the majesty of heaven as you do kneeling in contrition under the dome of a Roman Catholic cathedral? Nowhere but on the treeless top of a fell in the wilderness of Lapland—or in the Shard, the ninety-five-story skyscraper towering over the wilderness which goes by the name of London Town.

When he designed the building, Renzo Piano understood that people need air and light, and that success in life is easier if you can see farther than everyone else. With clear skies, I could see sixty kilometers from my foyer.

In the center of this landscape, my wife stood taller than the radio masts of the BT Tower off across the Thames. Elise was dressed in a white bathrobe I had bought her in Paris early on in our courtship. Her shapely calves glistened alluringly below the hem. I knew what came next. I knew what the bathrobe was covering.

That was why I could barely, just barely control myself.

Three years earlier I hadn't ever been able to, so I was pleased with myself.

Elise was a treacherous woman, which was why she was so irresistibly attractive. My classic good looks combined with Elise's graceful femininity. My analytical faculties and intelligence combined with Elise's magnetism and abandon. The superb synthesis of genes our future offspring would receive would make things possible for them that were not yet for us. They would be capable of anything.

When I saw Elise for the first time at an office-warming party for the law firm my company used—in order to emphasize how unconventional it was, the firm had moved out of the City into a nondescript building in Covent Garden—I was conversing with a corporate restructuring attorney about the evening's Champions League match. Elise walked past me, and her bare arm brushed lightly against my bicep through my coat. I stopped her and asked whether she thought Chelsea or Bayern München would win.

"I've always been an HJK supporter myself," Elise replied in Finnish.

We behaved quite rudely, retiring to a quiet side room to talk in a language no one else understood. I found myself searching for words, since I had never had any interest in keeping up with the Finnish circles in London and hadn't spoken my mother tongue in months.

We moved on to one of the picturesque little pubs in Covent Garden and from there to a hotel room for two.

Then we ended up married.

I slipped behind Elise. She was concentrating and didn't notice me.

I kissed her neck.

I smelled the sickening sweetness of cider.

"You've already started," I said.

"Is that a problem?"

I was disappointed, but I couldn't say as much. If I did, Elise would point out that eating and drinking are personal matters. Over the past few months, Elise had begun drinking more and more. Perhaps I was also more aware of it because my own alcohol use had declined since I quit working at Union Credit.

We had agreed that I wouldn't interfere in Elise's personal business. That was black and white. So I didn't.

Taking a glass from another's hand was not forbidden, though, if you were taking it to drink yourself. I forgot the flavor of the cider, because Elise wasn't in the habit of tying her bathrobe shut. "Who's going to see?" she had asked once when I mentioned it.

I had no reason to encourage her to change that habit.

Still, I couldn't help thinking about how Elise avoided belts. About how she had a good reason to.

"That chocolate cake smells good," Elise said.

"So do you."

Mikko and Veera would arrive in a little over an hour. A tingling tension filled my body.

Tonight everything was possible. The course of the evening wasn't completely planned out, which allowed for an intriguing sense of uncertainty. Uncertainty and possibility are the same thing viewed from different perspectives. An opportunity is never a certainty.

I have never been interested in certain stability, only in uncertain success.

This was not going to be just any night. And I truly had no way to guess where it would lead.

# Veera

ONE TICKET QUEUE wasn't moving. So I didn't need to guess at which one Mikko was waiting in. Or at what was causing the holdup. Could the traveler ahead of Mikko be having a hard time deciding where he wanted to go? Was the sale terminal broken? No, the issue was that the person being served was my husband.

Locking the handle of my suitcase into rolling position, I weaved through the lines. As I dodged toes, the toes also dodged me.

"Two adults for Victoria station!"

"Veera, I haven't . . . "

"Yes, return please. Thank you."

"Don't be in such a rush!"

I slapped a fifty-pound note down on the counter. Mikko snapped that he hadn't yet had a chance to ask the price of the Stansted Express train. And did it really make sense to buy round trip tickets? What if we found a cheaper offer in the city for the journey back? Or what if Robert drove us to the airport tomorrow?

The clerk handed us the tickets and pointed the way: the National Express bus would leave from platform sixteen. Scooping up the tickets and change, I placed them in the front pocket of my jacket, where the coins jingled against my reflector and toothbrush case.

Toothbrush case. So that's where it was!

Mikko didn't catch up to me until the holding pen constructed of riot barriers. As he did, a white bus began backing away from the platform. At least we were at the head of the queue for the next one.

"We would have had plenty of time to go ask about competing prices and think things over properly."

"We would have had plenty of time to make the bus if you wouldn't have been going around checking every offer."

I wasn't exaggerating. As I waited for our bags to arrive, Mikko had rushed around the hall where placards from rival companies offered connections from Stansted Airport to the London city center. Each more inexpensive and more convenient than the last! Before passport control there had been ticket salespeople loitering in the corridors. Even on the airplane the in-flight menus peddled bus tickets in amongst the sandwiches, drinks, and lottery cards.

"What did the tickets cost?" Mikko asked.

"Money."

"Veera, I understand that the time always seems longer to the person waiting, but comparing prices wouldn't just have benefited this trip but any other ones in the future!"

"Now we have tickets into the city and back. They aren't going to cost another red cent," I said. "And you already checked the prices online."

"I might have."

"And this bus is the cheapest, right?"

Mikko pointed out that prices changed according to demand. "There could have been last-minute special offers in the terminal. Those prices in the advertisements—"

"The prices in the advertisements are 'starting at' prices, right? But generally this bus is the cheapest, right?"

"Yes, it is. How did you know?"

"You would have stopped me at the counter if you thought you could get them cheaper somewhere else!"

We sat side-by-side in the middle of the bus—Mikko thought

that was a good compromise. Earlier in our marriage I would have sighed loudly and looked at my watch every thirty seconds, but I didn't need to show I was right anymore, unlike Mikko. Knowing that I was right was enough for me.

Out of the zippered pocket of his light jacket, Mikko dug an advertisement from a mobile phone operator with the word "SAVE" covering half the page.

"Should we get a pre-paid SIM?" he asked after a moment.

"No."

Outgoing calls would be considerably less expensive than using a Finnish account, Mikko argued. I replied that incoming calls would be even less inexpensive since no one would know the pre-paid number. Or did Mikko intend to send a text to everyone he knew informing them that his mobile number was changing for the weekend?

"What if we need to call Julia?"

"Julia promised to call us."

"But what if we need to?"

I said that if we needed to call, then we'd call, and we could do that perfectly well with my phone and my SIM card.

Mikko calculated what the per-minute price would come to on a ten-pound pre-paid card. I pointed out that the number of minutes promised in the advertisements most certainly did not include international calls.

"No, a pre-paid card probably doesn't make sense," Mikko stated as if the result of a long process of evaluation. Which it probably was. Mikko doesn't do anything without careful planning in advance. While Mikko weighs and deliberates, I get fed up and handle things. It's a very practical division of labor. Things get done the way I want, and Mikko gets to blame me if they don't go just right.

"You should get a company phone," I said, although we had discussed it before. I didn't catch how Mikko began his explanation this time, but it went something like this: He had calculated that at his salary the twenty-euro tax value of the personal use benefit would come out to an eight-euro net cost ("you have to calculate it using the marginal tax rate"). His current bill was less than that, just the monthly connection fee and a few calls and text messages. Mikko's phone was about five years old, a basic model without a camera or data. The kind of device you don't dare remove from your pocket in a public place. Teenagers thought he used it for a retro vibe. Julia was just embarrassed.

The explanations also included that a cell phone heats up your ear, potentially throwing your entire system out of balance, unlike a landline, and that with a mobile phone, you're always reachable. He did add something I hadn't heard before, though.

"And it's wrong for an employer to pay for an employee's personal calls."

Mikko said the practice treated employees unequally: the ones who gabbed the most and bought soft drinks from vending machines and paid for parking with their phones received more benefit than the ones who used their phones properly.

"And then there's you, who doesn't benefit from anything. You could do with buying a bottle of soda every now and then."

"But that's just the sort of moral decay I'm talking about."

"Moral decay! It's approved by the Tax Administration and at least a million Finns do it."

The East Asian man sitting across the aisle must have thought we were a squabbling married couple. But we weren't squabbling. We were conversing. That was what Mikko would have said, and I had learned to think that way too.

"That was a sloppy decision by Parliament. They made it back in Y2K when Finland was the Silicon Valley of mobile technology. The sponsors said it would promote the development of an information society . . . "

"It's terrible for workers to be the ones who benefit for once."

"It's the telecommunications companies who benefit. It's nothing more than corporate welfare. The workers know the company's spigot is open, so they go around carelessly using their phones to buy snacks from vending machines at prices they would never pay out of their own pockets."

Mikko questioned, investigated, and cogitated. That was who he was, but the even crazier thing was that the largest daily newspaper in Scandinavia paid him a monthly salary to do it. He could dig into the minutest of details with a patience no one else could match. Which every six months led to a full-page exposé that reshuffled ministries, indicted CEOs, and spurred the passing of new laws. Then every year he would attend the investigative journalism society's back-patting event to collect his engraved snow shovel to line up in the corner of the garage next to all the others. But we couldn't use them for snow removal or even spreading salt on the driveway.

Mikko's bosses didn't dare lean on him, because they were afraid what sort of exposé he might write about them. They feared Mikko, as did the rest of the establishment. That was why Mikko didn't have set working hours and why they had violated the dictates of modern interior design to build him his own office on the periphery of the open-plan editorial floor. His office had no windows, just fluorescent lights and walls hung with framed diplomas and clippings from the high points of his career. I had visited once and had no desire to go again. The place stank of everything I hated about Mikko.

They were also the same things that made me love him, though. And I do love him. I love Mikko. There's no one like him. He's special. And he's obviously sick. I work as a clinical nurse specialist, but at home is where I keep my truly special case.

When the invitation came from Rob for us to visit London "to see the new flat," I was surprised that Mikko suggested we accept. Usually just luring him onto a cruise to Stockholm was difficult.

You have to take food to avoid the expensive fare on board, and the whole thing messes up your normal routines—you can't even take a proper walk on a boat. Plus it takes up vacation days.

Mikko wanted to live by routine. Routine brought him safety, and who was I to torment the man I loved? Once a year Julia and I took a quick jaunt to Central Europe.

Of course I suspected that this London trip had something to do with Mikko's work. But because we had reserved our outgoing flight for Saturday and our return for Sunday evening, the reason couldn't be an archive Mikko wanted to visit or an interview he wanted to conduct. If the reason for the trip was work, that meant the victim had to be Rob or his girlfriend, whom we had never met.

What kind of woman had Rob chosen? That was the thing that most interested me.

Every seat in the bus filled up. When the driver announced the journey would last an hour and forty-five minutes, I started reading my travel paperback. I had already made it more than halfway through: On the train from Pasila to Tampere, on the bus to Pirkkala Airfield, in the waiting room in the corrugated steel terminal, and finally on the plane. Of course we had flown Ryanair.

"If we take the Tube, we'll have to change trains. We could walk partway, though."

"Our invitation is for five o'clock."

"A Tube ticket costs four and a half pounds."

"It's already past four."

"Let's take the Tube."

As we were transferring from the bus platform to the Victoria Underground Station, Mikko remembered that we needed to buy flowers.

"Isn't the rye bread enough? And the salt?" I asked, even though I knew my questions wouldn't get me anywhere. We had actually packed rye bread and salt, the traditional Finnish housewarming gifts. Mikko had pointed out that Robert probably didn't have very many Finnish visitors. This might be the first rye bread in the apartment. We could have brought *salmiakki* licorice on the same grounds, but Mikko had always noticed how Robert picked the fruit-flavored candy out of any bag they bought to share. So rye bread, because you couldn't take Finn Arabia mugs or Toikka glass birds or any of that Marimekko rubbish as a gift from home.

But none of the normal brands of bread were good enough for Mikko. No, Mikko had come home the night before with a sack of rye flour. After spreading out the rye bread recipe he had found online on the counter, he began rummaging for the kitchen scale, a plastic mixing bowl, and a wooden spoon.

I had retreated to the bedroom to read a crime novel my friends had been raving about on Facebook. Later I heard from Julia that Mikko had sat in front of the oven door watching the bread baking like it was *Inside Job* or a Michael Moore documentary.

"Don't eat any of it!" Mikko had said as he swaddled his baked creation in a linen cloth.

I never ate rye bread. It upset my stomach, especially fresh.

"So keep on not eating it. This isn't for us; it's a housewarming gift."

As if that would have even crossed my mind.

I parked myself with my suitcase on a bench that circled a pillar in the passenger hall while Mikko set off to find a flower shop. I figured this could take some time due to the required comparison shopping, so I opened my paperback. Harry Hole was just exiting a tram in front of the Holbergs Gate Radisson after visiting his office for the last time and walking home, where the mailbox contained a pizza advert and a collection letter about an unpaid parking ticket.

Hole made it to Schrøder's, ordered food, and read a story in the newspaper that would undoubtedly have some significance for the plot because the author recounted its contents for nearly a page. Soon it was the end of February and the Norwegian hero was in his new office. That was how long it took for Mikko to reappear wearing his dark blue rucksack and carrying a bouquet of white lilies wrapped in cellophane.

We stepped onto the escalator side-by-side like a newly married couple.

"Two stations on green or yellow, change at Westminster, and then three stops on the grey Jubilee to London Bridge Station," Mikko said resolutely.

# Mikko

LIFE HAS MEANING.

Of course it's possible that my premise is wrong. Maybe life has no meaning and the universe has no purpose, but would that matter? If I believe that life has meaning, doesn't that create meaning for me?

Every individual influences humanity, the world, and future generations. It's natural to think that each life has a purpose.

Which is why I think that's a valid starting point.

I'm speaking openly now about something I've never discussed with anyone before. I don't talk to Veera about the really important things. I don't dare. I find it much easier to open up in lecture halls and the cloying interviews young reporters give. Laying myself bare publicly is easier than with Veera.

I know I'm going to tell more than I should.

I will tell the whole truth and nothing but the truth, but in places I may be a bit wordy. Being the center of attention tickles me since thousands of times I've been the one asking the questions.

Regarding the meaning of life. First: biology, the most materialistic of all explanations. My genes have been propagated to Julia. Julia will continue my life indirectly just as I continue the lives of my forefathers and foremothers, which imbues them with meaning. But is that all? I wasn't born simply to reach sexual maturity and conceive an offspring. If that were the only meaning of my life, I could die right now. I could have died fifteen years ago. So the meaning has to be something bigger, something more than me and my direct descendants.

I have a responsibility to the entire human race and its future. Just like every other person does.

I contribute to a better world in the ways that fit me best, and what I'm most suited for is working for justice. I call attention to the evils of the world and cause change. I reflect the good in society by telling my readers about it.

I am moral where my readers don't have the energy and the establishment doesn't bother.

Caring about how wrongdoers feel isn't my job.

Of course Robert's life has a purpose too. He was independently wealthy at thirty-seven. He had more money than he would ever have time to use if he didn't get mixed up in gambling or inordinate excess. But it was perfectly clear he might become entangled in both and die with tens of millions in debt.

That was how Robert was. And I knew him better than anyone else.

After serving in the army he applied to the Helsinki School of Business, earned a master's degree in finance, and then left for postgraduate work at the London School of Economics. Later he only visited Finland sporadically.

The information I received about his career came through random emails: an invitation to a dissertation defense, an updated phone number, a new address.

Robert's dissertation dealt with options pricing. Really it was a loosely connected collection of essays, which is common in academic finance. Researchers are in such a hurry to make money that monographs are well beyond their attention span. Rather than staking out a specific territory, they flit around the field reporting what they see, complete with covariance, standard deviation, and confidence intervals at ninety-five and ninety-eight percent.

Equally rushed advisors urge them on, and money-hungry dissertation opponents heap praise on them over expensive drinks at the graduation reception.

I downloaded Robert's dissertation as a PDF right after he defended. I read it with a math encyclopedia and still only understood that somehow he was using what he knew to make money.

When I say "money," I mean "a lot of money." Robert was on a runway that would launch him soaring to excess. And soar he did.

When he was still a doctoral student, he received a minor management position with the derivatives unit of Commerzbank in the City of London. A couple of quick career moves, each bringing more power, responsibility, and a fatter pay package. By the time he ended his career—or "temporarily stepped back to focus on person interests," as he wrote in an email last August—he was the deputy managing director of the Union Credit's Markets Unit and a member of the board.

Robert had served many masters, but their names were always the same: money. And those who serve money well receive their reward.

The "stepping back" occurred soon after Union Credit was found guilty of LIBOR rate manipulation. That was big news. Union Credit was a megabank, the second largest financial institution in Europe, and a whole raft of other heavy hitters in the industry such as Barclays and UBS had participated in the maneuver.

At home in Finland we only heard the basics from the news wires. The initial revelations hit during summer vacation, so no journalist had much desire to dig deeper into the topic. Despite the fact that interest rate manipulation was a perfect distillation of the moral failures that had led to the collapse of the US and European financial systems—as well as to the constant visits of those same bankers to the public trough.

At the Tube station there weren't any signs for the Shard.

This clearly wasn't a building guests used public transportation to access. Near the tourist entrance was a blinking display telling what times were still available for tickets to the viewing platform on the top level. The sign was completely green, and no wonder since the elevator ride cost £29.95. A couple leaning on each other were buying tickets even though they could have gone out for dinner or been responsible and paid down their mortgage with the same money.

I wanted to see the building before we went inside. To do so I had to back up all the way to the patio of a Starbucks before I could inspect the tapering glass tower. My neck was sore from the flight. Although the top of the building was meant to represent broken glass, I thought it looked like an upside down icicle. The sharp edges of the tip would have hurt if you jabbed someone with it in a winter sword fight.

"It's already five," Veera said, "and I'm hungry."

I replied that waiting would do Robert good. And besides, hunger would make the food taste better.

"What a giant dick," Veera said.

Veera often used indecent language even in situations in which it wasn't appropriate.

This time it was. The tallest building in Western Europe, the Shard was a symbol of plutocracy. Reaching skywards, its glass walls excreted the essence of the elite. It was as ridiculous as the pyramids of Egypt, medieval churches, and royal castles.

The human race had learned many things, but its leaders had never shaken off their megalomania, egocentricity, and need for attention. Rather than gods and kings, twenty-first century monuments were built with other people's money by bankers looking to enlarge their egos. These were just a new form of personal mausoleum.

Building the Shard had cost half a billion euros. In addition to the offices, hotel, and viewing platforms, there were only ten residences in the building, seven of which occupied entire floors. The other three were two floors. I had Googled information about the skyscraper before our trip, and estimates put the costs of the apartments in the tens of millions. Did Robert really have so much money that he could buy his own apartment here? If he did, something must have happened that I didn't know about. Which was perfectly possible.

"Aren't you going to ask?"

"What?"

"Whether I meant that thing or Robert."

"Is that how you think of Robert?"

"What? As a giant dick?"

"If you absolutely have to use that word," I said. I didn't want to visualize the metaphor.

"Robert is a banker," Veera said.

"Those two things are hardly mutually exclusive."

"Correct."

"Do they have a causal relationship?"

"You mean does being a banker make someone a giant dick?"

"Yes, or vice versa."

"No."

I pointed out that Veera still hadn't said what she thought of Robert.

"Yes, I did. Robert is a banker. Come on. Are we going to go in or what?"

# Robert

WHEN THE ELEVATOR doors opened in the lower lobby, my guests were nowhere to be seen.

The receptionist nodded to the right, and there they were, standing in an alcove where no one else would have thought to go to wait.

Mikko looked fifty. His jacket was a size too large and hung limply from nonexistent shoulders. Wrinkles from constant worry surrounded his eyes. However, his gaze was the same as the boy I had practiced multiplication tables and German irregular verbs with. Occasionally an uncanny alertness would flash in his eyes, which said that Mikko had realized something and that he was working through his thoughts like a labyrinth: *if I turn right there, that leads there . . . and then that means . . .*

Mikko did not belong in the lobby of the Shard, unlike the man whose profile reflected in the side of the elevator. Hair carefully trimmed on Thursday, soft, healthy skin and eyes that give an impression of authenticity and authority. High quality clothing that emphasized the youth of their wearer.

I looked good. I had taken care of myself and increased my training volume after exiting Union Credit. My upper body muscle mass in particular had grown, and I had purchased a few slimmer shirts to show off the curves of my triceps and biceps.

Mikko had spent more time taking care of other people and

their problems than himself. His expression was harried and his demeanor that of a hunting dog. I was sure he bit his nails. In high school he had taken the whole world on his shoulders, and he still didn't understand that if you wanted to carry the Tellus, you had to have the muscles of an Atlas.

Mikko was the kind of man other people tried to cheat. This is not a criticism, just a neutral observation, and I have to follow it up by saying that cheating Mikko isn't an easy task. Even though his appearance conveyed a certain carelessness, he was at least as precise as the best bond traders at Union Credit. If a conversation partner formed an impression of Mikko based on his mussed hair and poorly fitting clothing without noticing how his eyes flashed, they would soon find themselves hopelessly trapped. My colleagues in Helsinki feared Mikko.

The sloppy demeanor could have been a conscious choice Mikko made to get the people he was interviewing to underestimate him and let things slip they otherwise never would. If that was the case, Mikko was bloody clever. And in fact, he was the wisest man I knew.

Cautiously I cast a glance at Veera, who was carrying a bouquet of flowers. I was ready for the dinner, but was she? I had formulated the invitation carefully. We would spend a "relaxed couples night" together. Couples night. No going solo. I hoped Veera understood what I meant.

Veera came up to me, hugged me briefly and then turned to Mikko, who raised his hand lamely. Veera's behavior seemed neutral, but she was unpredictable. I had to keep up my guard.

Mikko was having trouble with the suitcase. I offered to help.

"No, could you take this?"

Mikko shoved a faded Fjällräven hippy rucksack at me.

Once we got up to the apartment, he didn't pay any attention to the view. Instead he asked for the rucksack back and started digging around in it. He produced a bundle, but then couldn't decide whom he should give it to, so I made his decision easier by grabbing it myself.

Rye bread.

It really was rye bread.

# Elise

ROBERT WAS DARK brown. Robert was tense. Robert was excited.

Robert wasn't usually excited.

The corn chips were good and crunched nicely. I had eaten half a bag of them.

I was wearing a fun dress. It was from Harrods. Shopping there was always easy and painless. Almost as easy as mail order.

Robert yelled from the living room, "Where is my belt?"

The servant scampered to look. Robert had a lot of belts. They hung from nails pounded in the door of his closet: one for the black belts, one for the browns, and one for the blues. Sometimes Robert left his belt in his trousers, which could be a problem since some belts went with several pairs of pants.

Then there were other belts that could be used for play. You could use a belt to slap a bottom or tie up wrists, if it had enough holes. One of Robert's did, but Robert didn't use that one with trousers anymore. Or for anything else. I couldn't find it in the closet when I looked for it once.

In the dark the hanging belts looked like snakes.

I went into the kitchen. I lifted the lid of one of the saucepans. There was something brown inside, almost like chocolate sauce.

I didn't taste it.

I heard the servant's footsteps. The right belt must have turned up. Robert was very strict about these things. He had a certain system and a certain way of seeing things, and deviating from either never succeeded without shouting. That was Robert's way of keeping the world in order.

I like that the world isn't always perfectly orderly. It's more exciting that way.

I chomped a few more corn chips. When they dissolved in my mouth, they got stuck in my back teeth. There wasn't any point only eating one handful of chips. Just like toffee.

I had to wash the chips down with some apple cider.

Cream liqueur would have been better for toffee.

Robert headed down to fetch the guests.

I like having company.

I waited for them in the foyer. I leaned against the suit of armor. Falling in high heels was easy if you had eaten too many corn chips.

The suit of armor was grey and two meters tall. It stood next to the elevator like a Christmas tree. Robert had received it as a goodbye gift from somewhere he had worked.

Robert was wearing dark blue jeans, a blue and white checked shirt, and a relaxed brown sports coat. His belt was brown, like his shoes. Blue and brown went well together. Robert was handsome tonight.

Mikko's hair was wispy. Mikko was a great blue tit. No, more like a Bohemian waxwing. That bird with the red and the silly crest on its head. On Mikko the red was on his cheeks. Mikko seemed nervous too. Mikko was silly. Such an odd man.

Veera was Mikko's wife. She gave me a flower arrangement with white lilies in it. Lilies are serious, solemn flowers. But this was a fun time, and we were going to have a fun evening. I was sure of that.

Flowers in hand, I gave them each a kiss on both cheeks.

Veera squeezed me against herself a little uncertainly. We girls would get to know each other yet! When they left we would squash each other flat!

Mikko whispered in my ear when our cheeks brushed each

other. I didn't hear what he said. I gave a cute smile. Smiling makes people feel good—other people and yourself. A smile is a gift that comes back to the giver. I'm a smile girl. I'm a lucky girl.

Mikko pulled a brown paper bag out of a backpack with a fox on it and offered it to Robert, then to me, and then to Robert again.

Mikko said, "Congratulations on your new home!"

Robert took the bag, squeezed it, and then pulled out a dark round loaf of rye bread.

I said, "Rye bread is like a Finnish man." The others looked at me. I continued: "It's hard on the outside but soft on the inside."

Veera said, "Rye bread is sour and tough."

Mikko said, "Without any artificial ingredients or coloring."

Robert said, "This one has a good tan. And apparently doesn't use moisturizer."

Robert handed the bread to the servant. Then he said, "Thanks!"

I curtsied and smiled.

So Mikko was dark blue after all. A dark blue Bohemian waxwing. Veera was green. A small silver cross hung from Veera's neck.

Veera asked, "Where can I put these things and change clothes?"

Robert asked the servant to show them to the guest room. He said, "Let's raise a glass as soon as you're ready."

Those glasses would be filled with champagne. That would make us feel good. I smiled at that.

Mikko grabbed the closet door handle and stepped in. Then he backed up and said, "That wasn't the . . . "

I showed Mikko to the bathroom. I opened the door. I turned on the light.

Mikko asked me if I understood.

I didn't understand what I was supposed to understand, so I smiled.

The flowers were cheery.

I smelled them.

They were white.

*THE NIGHT WAS gentle. Rather than striking his face, it caressed and welcomed him as he stepped out of the Shard. He didn't deserve such a warm reception.*

*A taxi stood idling. The female driver had opened the door and wished him a good morning. So it was morning.*

*He said he would prefer to keep his carry-on with him on the seat. He didn't have any other bags.*

*Classical music was playing in the car, probably Benjamin Britten. He asked the driver how her night had been. Apparently a standard Saturday night. He nodded.*

*"They usually are."*

*Then again, sometimes they aren't. He had very recent, personal experience with that.*

*The driver turned the music up.*

*The vehicle joined the almost nonexistent flow of traffic. He watched through the side window as a group of young people returning from a party swayed down the middle of the street without a care. A red BMW sped past recklessly. One of the youths staggered in shock as the others waved their fists and hurled insults after the car.*

*The taxi driver braked and honked. The young people retreated to the sidewalk.*

*The city was a place for wild animals where the only mercy was shown by properly rested taxi drivers.*

*He was some kind of animal too.*

*A sausage vendor pushed his cart. His work day was ending. The day didn't change at midnight, it changed between four and five. That was when some bade goodbye to yesterday as others greeted tomorrow, not knowing where it would take them.*

*The music had changed to Rimsky-Korsakov's "Flight of the Bumblebee." That was a poor fit for the languor of the morning but better for his state of mind. His head buzzed. There was sure to be something he hadn't taken into account.*

*The taxi stopped at a light. Through the window a few people could be seen walking, a few cars moving.*

*Where were these people going? Who needed all of them?*

*Those questions never entered his mind when he was in a traffic jam, only when there was hardly anyone. Especially right now.*

# Veera

THE SERVANT GAVE a curtsy at the door just like in a black and white movie. I dug in my jeans pockets: Did I have something to give as a tip? However, the girl managed to disappear before I even found a pack of gum.

Apparently gratuity was included in the monthly salary.

And our room really was like a hotel suite: beige sheets, carefully made bed, off-white Biedermeier chest of drawers, and a side table belonging to the same set, a chair next to it with yellow upholstery on the seat and backrest. All that was missing was the minibar and price list.

Well, the nightstand did have two large bottled waters, one sparkling, one still. Glasses upturned next to the bottles, under the glasses spongy paper coasters. I opened the sparkling water.

On the ceiling, directly above the bed, was an enormous metal decoration. The grotesque whatsit didn't fit at all with the primness of the other furnishings.

"Hopefully the mounting hardware holds. It wouldn't be fun waking up to that thing crashing down on your pelvis."

Mikko then gave a brief lecture on tensile strength.

"Why would it come loose tonight if it hasn't come loose yet?"

Of course it wouldn't. How stupid of me for even saying such a thing.

Flipping the suitcase open, I hung the next day's clothes in the closet. I had to separate the hangers, which were still in bundles of three. Rob's chick clearly wasn't the housewife type.

SORRY IF THAT sounds demeaning, but that's just what you call women like that. Women or girls—she looked about twenty-five, but their kind uses so much makeup that they all have the same look whether they're sixteen or forty.

Poor Rob. I was so disappointed! I would have expected something with a little more punch than a standard-issue blond. Although Elise's blondness wasn't any more genuine than anything else in her. Her lashes curled with such flourish that they couldn't be her own, and if it didn't take padding for her boobs to fill those D cups, then at least her teeth had been whitened.

Was that kind of fake really what Rob wanted? Maybe you had to have a personal Barbie doll if you were a banker in the City. She didn't seem like the type to catch Rob's eye, and I couldn't believe she satisfied his mind.

Maybe she had other virtues.

Mikko pulled the curtains away from the window that covered one entire wall and stared into the distance. Glancing over his shoulder, I saw London. I wondered what Mikko saw.

"Quite a view."

"But no balcony," Mikko said.

This Mikko who so missed having a balcony here was the same man who had argued that balconies were pointless because they were used so infrequently. People buying new apartments should demand cheaper apartments instead of balconies! Mikko had written a long article on the subject. Which had set off a cascade of letters to the editor invoking smoking, grilling, and the bicycle thefts so common in Helsinki.

I put Mikko's suitcoat on a hanger and left it on the doorknob. My nightshirt and Mikko's pajamas went in the armoire. I remembered the stuffed shelves of our closet at home where you couldn't remove so much as a T-shirt without shifting a whole stack of clothes to the bed.

"It is convenient having a servant."

"I don't know."

"Wouldn't it be convenient if all you had to do was say, 'Would you please start the laundry and hang the clothes to dry? Could you organize the garage and sort the socks? Today would be a lovely time to clean the porch.'"

"You'd end up cut off from normal life. Like Robert is."

"You let other people do things for you, too. You take your car to a garage to have the oil changed. And you go to the barber to have your hair cut."

Snapping the suitcase shut, I took off my jeans and draped them over the arm of a chair.

"We have a pair of clippers, but you just don't want to use them," Mikko said.

My shirt electrified my hair when I pulled it off. Apparently I didn't need to wash my hair.

"When you do it yourself, you know what's been done," he continued.

I tossed my bra and panties into a drawer. Mikko didn't even turn his head. "I'm going to shower."

Of course it bothered me a little that he didn't look, even though I hadn't intended to try anything. I wasn't one for false hopes. But still, sometimes you just feel like a quickie. Hotel rooms seem to trigger it: With everything so shiny and the sheets all pressed and staticky, you have to do something to make the room your own. Rumple those sheets and soften up those towels! Dogs aren't the only ones who mark their territory.

And besides, it was Saturday, and screwing is sort of a Saturday tradition for us.

I knew that with Mikko there was no point expecting anything; I'd only end up disappointed. And yet, I was still disappointed.

The disappointment wasn't so great that it could have had any influence over what happened later in the evening, though. And disappointment is too strong a word. I knew nothing was going to happen. I knew Mikko and had learned to live with him. That's the funny thing about love—learning to live with disappointment can be part of it too. I knew Mikko wouldn't turn around, scoop me up in his arms, and throw me down on the bed. I knew that Mikko wouldn't even turn around and say something that might give me a reason to walk over to him and start fooling with his belt and the buttons of his shirt. I knew it! So I couldn't really be disappointed if I got what I was expecting, could I?

Mikko didn't turn, even though I waited so he could. But at least Mikko understood that he was supposed to do *something* if his wife was standing naked a couple of meters behind him.

So he asked, "Is there a bathroom in here too?"

"Well, this isn't a closet."

The hot and cold water had separate knobs. One lever switched the shower to a cascade, another to a massage setting. The shower gel smelled expensive and glided on my skin like massage oil.

Goddamn it! Even in a place this posh you couldn't get the water to stay the same temperature. Quickly I turned the hot down and cooled off my red thigh.

As I lathered up, I squeezed my arm muscles and my boobs. I massaged my hips and buttocks. I imagined Mikko's tentative hands. Soon I had to pee. Bending at the knees, I aimed at the drain. Dark yellow urine pierced the soap bubbles. So I would mark my territory this way.

From the color I could see I hadn't been drinking enough. I would remedy that mistake shortly.

When I returned to the room wrapped in an enormous towel, Mikko was still standing at the window. It reminded me of one of those picture games where you have to find five things out of place: What was different from when I went to shower?

I didn't find anything.

When I put on the dress I had brought, it was the first time since the fitting room. The red diagonal stripe gave the black dress a dangerous sexuality.

"Have you seen this?"

"No," Mikko grunted, and he didn't see it now either unless the window was working as a mirror.

"I bought this at an after-Christmas sale," I said as I did contortions to put deodorant on both armpits, followed by a little perfume.

Mikko didn't budge.

"Change your clothes so we can eat."

Nothing happened.

In moments like that I wished I could have read his thoughts.

I was privileged compared to a lot of others—although I couldn't read my husband's thoughts as he stared off into the middle distance, at least I could read what he had been thinking later in the newspaper.

And of course that's what I thought—it had to be work. It didn't even cross my mind that Mikko could have been thinking of something else.

"Yeah, let's go," Mikko said when I touched his shoulder. "Oh, wow. You look . . . "

"Beautiful?"

"Drop dead gorgeous."

"Thank you," I said, and slapped Mikko on the butt. "Get your clothes off already."

"Aren't we supposed to go back out now?"

"Yep."

"So let's go," Mikko said, his hand already on the doorknob.

"You aren't going to wear the same shirt you had on the plane, are you?"

Mikko asked what was wrong with it. It was made in Finland after all. He was being patriotic.

"You need a dress shirt and a jacket. That's what you're supposed to wear."

Mikko said he wasn't going to start dressing up just for Robert. I pointed out that Rob was wearing a jacket too.

"Robert is a banker. Are you ashamed of me?" Mikko asked.

"Why would I be ashamed of you?" I asked.

"Because I'm not wearing a jacket."

"But Rob is your friend! Are you ashamed of me then?"

"Is there some reason I should be?" he asked.

Actually, there was, but why would I say so?

# Mikko

THE NATURAL STONE floor of the bathroom radiated heat through my socks. I lifted the plastic cover of the thermostat. The heat was set at 24 degrees Celsius. Robert heated the room through the floor, even though there was a radiator on the wall.

Thoughtlessness? I doubted it. Stupidity? Not a chance. Robert was just shameless.

He had to show that because he had money he didn't have to care. That sins can be absolved with money: just pay, pay, pay! Electric bill—who cares! Raising the gas tax? Well, that must means not so many people will be able to afford to drive their SUVs, and the lanes will stay open for those who can!

In Robert's way of thinking, everything came back to money. Every kilometer you flew was slapped with a carbon tax, and leaving your trash unsorted resulted in a sorting fee. Anyone who could afford the cost was free to pollute. The damage was economic, not ethical or social. A speeding ticket was a payment for the right to exceed the speed limit, not a sanction for endangering traffic safety.

The euro is a universally applicable unit of measure for Robert and his ilk. The euro is better than the meter because the meter can only measure distance. The euro is better than the second because the second can only measure time.

The euro can measure both distance and time: one meter of fabric costs twenty euros and one day in a hotel costs one hundred fifty. What's the hourly rate of a cardiologist, a masseuse, or a hairdresser? The cubic meter price of unstacked firewood—the euro measuring volume. The purchase price of a ten-hectare plot of forest—the euro measuring surface area. The price per ounce of gold, the price per kilo of apples, the price per gram of saffron—the euro measuring weight.

They could normalize anything to euros. And not only could they, but they preferred to. Everything was euros, dollars, pounds, francs, kronor . . .

I turned the floor heating down to eighteen degrees.

The window of our bedroom was a specialty triple-paned glass that resisted pressure, heat, and cold. I rapped the window glass with my knuckles. I tapped it with the tip of my shoe. The city spread out endlessly from my toes. I tried to translate the panorama into a map, but all I could recognize were the Thames and the skyscrapers of Canary Wharf, which I couldn't name. One of them had been the tallest building in London before the Shard. I knew that when Robert looked at it he felt like a conqueror, alone above all the rest.

That thought was repulsive.

It was just repulsive enough to make me angry at Robert. And I needed anger. I was preparing myself mentally. I reminded myself of the what and why.

This was how I thought, and I still subscribe to these principles: I can't imagine a higher duty for anyone than promoting a better world. Each in his own small way, each according to his own abilities and opportunities. This requires both taking a broad view and zooming in to the individual level.

One dimension of promoting good is rooting out evil. Humanity is led not only by genes but also by ideologies. Biological evolution and cultural evolution. Currents in modes of thinking change the human species as prevailing ideas become Truth and bend the world in their direction.

On the other side stands man, the individual person and his actions. Is one person more valuable than another? What rights does each person have? And what of duty?

Total world happiness would increase if there were no Robert.

And what of my personal happiness? I'm not so stupid to deny the significance of that, but I want to emphasize that I was motivated by the common good. Of course I have to admit that I never would have embarked on such an attempt without personal aims.

If the previous is ever quoted, I would like to invoke my right to review my statements.

Veera threw her towel on the bedspread and walked around the room naked. She was humming the chorus to "It's My Life."

How had Veera guessed that I was thinking exactly the same thing?

We raised our glasses in the dining area, which looked out over another side of London. The sun shone in so brightly that the servant turned the blinds. It was a waste of the view.

Robert stood next to a glass display case holding in his hand a sword a meter long, with Elise next to him, small and delicate. Elise was like the flower of a liana vine, which needs another woody plant for support to stay off the ground. She smiled and batted her eyelashes, which curved upwards, long and thick. She was the sweetest woman in the world.

The blade of the sword was wide but the hilt was slender. Three blood grooves ran along the blade. Robert showed off the monogram of Nicholas II on the butt end and explained that the saber was a Russian officer model from 1909. Apparently Marshall Mannerheim had owned the same type when he served in the Russian army before leading Finland's forces during the Second World War. Robert had purchased it from an antiques dealer as a champagne sword in honor of the liberator of the fatherland. I pointed out that Finland lost two wars to the Soviet Union under Mannerheim's leadership. At what point had Robert begun sympathizing with losers? According to Robert, his foreign guests were never as cynical as me.

"So off with its head," Robert said playfully. "Who wants to start?"

The others hummed. I didn't.

Robert ran his gleaming sword along the seam of the bottle before pulling back and taking an aristocratic stroke. The cork and lip of the bottle clattered on the hardwood floor.

*Bong.*

The imposing boom didn't come from the cork but from around the corner on the other side of the open space.

*Bong.*

My mind assembled the sounds as the striking of a grandfather clock.

*Bong.*

I could trust in three more chimes coming.

*Bong.*

White vapor still rose from the neck of the bottle as Robert poured it into the glasses.

*Bong.*

There was no way he could have intentionally timed the opening of the bottle so perfectly.

*Bong.*

Robert had just finished topping off the glasses as the sixth stroke rippled through the air. Veera and Elise applauded.

I knew the brand of champagne and knew how much it cost because I had done a story on fine sparkling wines for a May Day Eve issue of the newspaper a few years ago. People wondered about my choice of topics in our editorial meeting, but they praised the end result. "I didn't know you were interested in champagne," the head of the financial beat had said in the elevator after the story came out. Champagne didn't interest me in the slightest, I replied, but it might interest the readers. "Champagne interests everyone," he said.

Robert portioned out the expensive drink generously. That was part of the show. The most important thing about champagne was in the display, not the utility. It may be perverse but in no way is it an economic oddity. Much of global capitalism is based on the immaterial promises offered by branding.

Most people believe that the essential characteristics of Champagne are properties such as taste, color, effervescence, and alcohol content that can be verified in laboratory tests. They believe that the grapes must have come from a specific region of France. These people are wrong. What creates the impression of a luxury beverage are the shape of the bottle, the cut of the label, and the grandiloquent language used to describe it. Those things have value and are at the root of consumers' willingness to pay significantly more than the substantive value of the product.

And yet the brand value of no champagne manufacturer is anything compared to the seventy-eight billion US dollars of Coca-Cola. Coca-Cola is the world's biggest bullshit operation. The company's gross margin is more than sixty percent. That's nothing but air in the price. Even more than the carbon dioxide bubbles in each bottle. And that's before the store's markup.

Coca-Cola spends as much money marketing its drinks and managing the company as it does making the drinks. Coca-Cola doesn't use those marketing dollars to sell a brown carbonated drink, it uses them to sell the American lifestyle and the Olympic spirit, and those sell even in developing markets. The legend of a secret recipe sells Coca-Cola just as well as Santa's ho-ho-hos. All are carefully premeditated and controlled uses of intangible assets in order to exploit the indigent.

Human irrationality ensures billions in profits for the marketing men. They convinced Robert to pay a thousand euros for a 750 ml bottle for the same reason a Sub-Saharan African black man would use his daily pay to buy a bottle of Coke. The whole point was to demonstrate what you can afford.

As a journalist it was my job to bring sense to the world. I shone light on injustice and defended what was right. That's how a reporter makes the world better.

However, there are areas journalism can't touch. Like love and death.

I hadn't come to London as a reporter, I had come as a person.

# Elise

MY BRAIN BUBBLED. My mood swelled and rose to the surface.

I was sparkling. The party was starting.

Robert ran the blade of his sword between his thumb and forefinger. The champagne sword was so sharp that it could kill, Robert had said.

I hadn't asked what you could kill with it, but it definitely wasn't a fly. Hitting a fly would be really hard.

Robert stored the sword in a locked glass cabinet. Now he set it on the serving table next to the champagne cooler.

Robert had strong fingers. Maybe he could have broken the neck of the bottle without any help, but that would have left a nasty mark. He trained his grip strength with a device I thought was a nut cracker. Robert had kept one on his desk. It was his stress ball. Robert told me that. Not before he squeezed me, though. And not right after, because when I woke up, I was in a private hospital room and Robert was busy shouting, "She's waking up."

I asked, "Who?"

Robert yelled again, "She's waking up!"

Robert meant me. He was talking about me to a nurse who had just come into the room, as if I wasn't even there.

After that Robert got rid of his squeezing thing.

At first I thought that Robert had decided his fingers didn't need exercise anymore. They were already so strong he could choke a person to death.

You never could know when you might need a skill like that.

But that wasn't why. Robert had been worried. He was in shock. Robert was afraid I could have died.

I could have died.

And that wouldn't have been fun because then there wouldn't be anything. Or who knows what there might be.

I could have died, but Robert wasn't upset by that as much as by the fact that he nearly killed me.

Robert wanted to make that up to me. He wanted to make everything right. That was my chance.

In the hospital we wrote up a *letter of intent*. We finished up the details the next week before Robert could change his mind.

That would provide for me for the rest of my life. I became a lucky girl. I would never need to write another LOI again.

That was how I got Robert. Nothing would ever separate us.

Except death, Robert said.

So I had started being afraid of that, too.

A champagne glass clinked on the table.

Veera said, "Wow, that hit the spot."

I quickly emptied my own glass so Veera wouldn't be embarrassed. Keeping her guests happy is the duty of a hostess. I was a good hostess.

Robert laughed. It was the servant's turn to pour the drinks. Keeping the guests happy was also the servant's job. I didn't know what the host's duty was.

To Mikko, Robert said, "We'll have to hurry to keep up with the girls."

Mikko was full of energy. He tilted his head back and let the glass rest on his lips. Not a single drop could go to waste.

Mikko was a serious guy. When his type gets embarrassed, it's really funny. I've seen it.

Maybe I gave a little laugh.

Mikko smiled at me. He probably couldn't guess what I thought was funny.

Veera said, "Good bubbly."

Robert said, "What is this?" He inspected the label on the bottle.

Veera was dressed in black. I was wearing black too. We were two thrushes, one with a red stripe across her breast. I had white accented pocket flaps and a silver rose on my lapel. Robert had given it to me. He'd said that the rose would last as long as our love. Oh how it glittered! The servant had shined it with silver polish.

Robert said, "I'm glad we could arrange this."

Mikko said, "We've been busy."

Veera said, "Mikko has been busy. My patients aren't going anywhere. The names and social security numbers change, but the diseases and symptoms remain the same. You never run out of sick people by healing them."

Their voices were music. Mikko was a clarinet, Veera a violin. Robert was the Champagne sword.

Mikko picked up the sword and hefted it in his hands.

I knew it was pretty heavy. Weapons are. It isn't just the metal of a weapon that's heavy, there's also the responsibility.

People are sharp like swords. That's why we need suits of armor. Robert's suit of armor was in the foyer. My suit of armor was on me, between my bones and my skin. It wasn't very strong armor, but it was stronger than what protected my brain. A body is easier to protect than what's inside of it.

I asked, "When did you last see each other?"

Mikko said, "Sure is sharp."

Blood was running from his finger.

I said, "Oh no!"

Mikko said, "Why does it have to be so sharp? I thought you

could open a bottle like that even with a dull one as long as the blow was hard enough and you hit it in the right place."

Robert said, "Even the Russians make cars that will get you where you want to go, but a Mercedes is more fun to drive."

Mikko took a paper tissue out of his pocket and wiped his finger. Along with the tissue came a tiny plastic bag, which remained peeking out of Mikko's pocket.

A couple of red droplets shimmered on the sword blade. The servant brought a Band-Aid.

Robert said, "Let's put that away before things get any more bloody."

Squeezing his finger, Mikko said, "It isn't fatal."

Veera said, "Elise asked when you last saw each other."

Robert said, "It's been a while."

Mikko said, "You visited us in Herttoniemi right after we moved. That was probably 1998. You haven't seen Veera since then."

I asked, "Why didn't you keep in touch?"

Everyone thought hard.

The bubbles ran out. The glass was empty.

# Veera

IN HIS NEWSPAPER articles, Mikko presented the facts he had verified and left the drawing of conclusions to others. He let his boss write the column that would run alongside his report, describing the results of the revelation instead of Mikko doing that himself. Afterwards the rest of the news media would start deconstructing the incident and present even more pointed interpretations, until they were far afield from Mikko's words.

Still, when he wrote the piece he would be perfectly certain how the dirty facts he had dug up should be understood. The self-assurance was apparent in the turns of phrase and what order he presented things in.

When Mikko discovered through his sources that a business leader was suspected of insider trading, he would work his way through each and every one of the CEO's stock trades, sitting in his office surrounded by stacks of paper. But he wouldn't write that the CEO was guilty of insider trading. Mikko would only lay out the CEO's purchases and sales, and report what negotiations the company had been involved with at the same time, on which dates the board had met, and who had been present.

Mikko built his story so the reader would connect them like the dots in a child's line drawing. According to him, a conclusion a person drew themselves was more convincing than anything a reporter underlined.

I had learned how to see from my husband's expression when

the hunt was over and it was time to shoot the decisive shot. During the writing phase he would mull over sentences for the article at the dinner table and in the sauna on Saturday. He wanted to perform the execution with style, and he always did. He would hold off publishing to make time for an extra round of fact-checking. He took pleasure in gloating over what he knew his article would bring to pass. He enjoyed knowing that he would astonish first the news bosses and editors and then all of Finland.

In journalism if not in the bedroom, Mikko was a foreplay kind of guy. In the past few weeks, the signs had been in the air again. I had learned not to ask.

Mikko's artless writing style exuded absolute certainty and frigidity. The same attitude that rang in the words, "You haven't seen Veera since then."

He left no alternatives: there was no use arguing, and no one would even think to try.

And yet Mikko was wrong.

My husband stood next to me with an empty champagne glass in his hand not knowing that he was wrong. There had never been any reason to tell, and I was good at keeping secrets. We approached secrets in different ways. I didn't derive the same kind of joy from exposing secrets as Mikko did. For him a secret was something that had to be revealed. For me a secret was something to keep concealed.

If my husband had ever happened to ask whether I was screwing Rob, I would have answered without evasion. I wouldn't have let myself get caught treading the same endless quicksand as the victims Mikko hunted and slaughtered for his job.

My husband hadn't asked. He didn't suspect a thing. He had no reason to suspect because he had never thought things through from my perspective nor paid attention to anything but himself, his own work, and saving the world.

Mikko was perfect. He was right and everyone needed to live the way he did.

I don't say this ironically.

If everyone lived the way Mikko did, he would be horrified because he wouldn't be able to experience moral superiority anymore.

Mikko was never wrong.

The possibility that he could be never even entered his mind.

*THERE WAS NO point glancing around. He was certain to be surrounded by security cameras at Paddington Station. Some camera or another had probably caught him the moment he exited the taxi.*

*It was only 4:50. The first Heathrow Express on Sunday morning was scheduled for departure at 5:08.*

*He would have plenty of time to buy his ticket from the machine.*

*One-way, of course.*

*He didn't know when he would return to London. Would he ever? That thought hadn't occurred to him until now, but it didn't move him at all. He didn't start trying to commit everything to memory because this might be the last time he would ever visit here. This place had no particular significance to him. How many places had he left forever without thinking a second thought?*

*He didn't know what awaited him. He only knew what he had left behind and that he could not return to it. The only option was to go forward.*

*The first thing was to exit the country quickly.*

*He would have all of Sunday. No one would miss him enough to check the security camera hard drives until tomorrow morning. No one would miss any of them.*

*One day was a lot of time.*

*Not so long that there was time to waste, of course. The farther away he got, the safer he would be. The greater the head start he could get, the harder catching him would be.*

*Onward!*

*The yellow nose of the airport train stared from platform six.*

*The coffee shop opened at five. The shopkeeper arranged sandwiches in a Plexiglas display case.*

*He didn't feel like eating. He couldn't if he'd wanted to. For something to do, he bought a smoothie.*

*His thoughts were clear and straightforward. Inebriation had simplified his thinking. He could only hold on to one thought: he had to get away. He wondered at how easy making decisions was. As if he had planned everything from the start.*

*Maybe he had.*

*Behind the glass wall of a shop stood a line of gentlemanly teddy bears with blue coats and a happy expression that seemed to say the whole world was a fairytale.*

*He turned back to the platform, marching past the first class carriage and taking a window seat in another, empty car. An elderly woman entered, and a lone businessman who was looking at his phone. Just before the train left, a young American couple took seats right next to him and left their hard-sided transatlantic suitcase in the aisle even though there were luggage racks at either end of the car.*

*He mentioned the luggage racks to them as a point of advice, although he really meant it as a complaint. The man moved the suitcase to the space between the next two seats.*

*He realized he was attracting unnecessary attention. He had to act as normal as possible even though nothing was normal. He was on the run.*

*He was trying to escape. He looked at himself in the third person, as a character in a video game that he could control but wasn't him.*

*The young couple continued their conversation in their broad American accent. The train smoothly glided into motion. It was April, and it was morning. The summer and the day were just about to begin. He had time for everything there was time in life to do.*

*There was a touch of hope in that thought.*

# Robert

SO SOON AND already Maarit was on everyone's mind. I could see it in Mikko and I could see it in Veera. We didn't say out loud what we were thinking: *We haven't really seen each other since Maarit . . .*

No one's thoughts completed the sentence. I could also see that. One of my professional skills was sensing what others were thinking.

I was one of the best in Europe at my job. Everyone in the profession knew I would be free for new work at the end of the year once my extended non-compete term ran out. Once summer came my inbox would fill with invitations to lunch. There was no room to let a talent like mine go unused. I could set my own price on my skills because I had papers stamped by a judge to prove that I knew how to make money in every possible way.

Just as I got Maarit out of my thoughts, Mikko brought up the international financial crisis. "International" sounded more threatening than just financial crisis.

In the meantime we had sat down at the table and been served prosciutto and something green that looked like pickles. There was green salad in a bowl.

I sat with my back to the window like the hosting negotiators did in Union Credit conference rooms. The purpose wasn't to give the guests a better view but to give the hosts the first sight of anyone entering the room. When you have the home field advantage, you should use it. We were professional about it. We chose the food according to how we wanted our guests' blood sugar to react. The air conditioning system filled the conference rooms with a carefully controlled cocktail of smells.

When you sit with your back to a window, no one can stab you between the scapulae.

Danger doesn't come from outside, though. You had to remember that. Danger comes from within. And even I was not immune to that. Inviting Mikko and Veera to visit was one symptom.

It isn't healthy to be away from working life for more than a three-week summer vacation. You end up being with yourself too much and find out what an unpleasant person you're dealing with.

I tasted the wine and nodded. Hungarian. From our kindred Finno-Ugrians. Elise revived the conversation. She asked what plans Veera and Mikko had for Sunday. That was a better topic than dredging up the past. The purpose of this evening was both an interim settling of accounts and a new beginning.

Of course it bothered me that Elise reminded me of Maarit, not to mention that she reminded Mikko and Veera. Elise didn't do it intentionally—I hadn't told her any of the story. Why would I burden her with old things like that? Why would I remember them any more often than I needed to? People shape their surroundings with their thoughts and their thoughts with their surroundings. Life is what you make it. Some people looked to the past and others to the future, but only the future matters. In an investment portfolio there is no reason to keep any position that you wouldn't open at this moment and at the current price. Purchase price, purchase logic, or other historical facts only have anecdotal value. It is irrelevant information that you can't let confuse you. That's why you have to forget it. There are no unrealized profits or losses, only open positions.

Just as an investor should always be asking whether this

portfolio is the best for his future, a person should always be asking himself, "How do I improve the life I have left?"

Markets are accused of being unconscious of history. This is the humanists talking. They have studied history and think that all that matters is what is known. Wrong. All that matters is what we don't know, because knowledge focuses on the past, and the past is past.

"We'll see tomorrow what we feel like," Veera said.

Elise mentioned that there was a Vincent van Gogh in the National Gallery. Actually there were dozens of them there, because the exhibition consisted entirely of van Gogh self-portraits: There were two whole halls full of ginger-bearded vagrants. We had gone to see it during opening week. The paintings were arranged in chronological order. A couple of the paintings included an easel, and most had the yellow straw hat that covered the hair slicked back with the grease of stress. In the final four years of the 1880s alone, van Gogh painted thirty-seven self-portraits. The following year he died at thirty-seven years of age.

Elise had seen something mystical in that. She completely bought into the dramatization of the museum assistant who had written the exhibition brochure, even though I reminded her that the choice to look at the number of works completed in a four-year period was completely arbitrary. Why not count the total number of self-portraits he did in his life?

Elise also reported this detail to Veera and Mikko. She probably didn't realize that besides her, we were all thirty-seven.

"Must have been a narcissist to paint himself all the time," Veera said.

"Maybe he just lacked inspiration."

"Wasn't van Gogh the one who cut his ear and never sold any of his doodles?"

"Couldn't sell," I said, correcting Veera, and then Elise corrected me by saying that he sold one.

That was also in the exhibition brochure. I should have

remembered it. There was also a picture of the painting in the brochure, with peasants bent over working in a vineyard.

"Maybe he should have painted something besides a dude with a scraggly beard."

Mikko pointed out that numerous works by van Gogh had sold for tens of millions. Only Pablo Picasso had more entries on the list of most valuable paintings in the world.

I said that based on that, the problem must have been in the marketing, not the product. Van Gogh didn't know the four Ps: *price, promotion, product,* and *place.* Price couldn't have been an issue, because he was always cash-strapped, and people like that never overprice themselves. And it wasn't the product either, because now there were no end of willing buyers. Promotion and place—had those been any good? Not likely. Van Gogh should have hired himself an agent to handle the mundane aspects of marketing if he preferred to spend his time standing in front of a mirror duplicating himself in oil.

No one disagreed, so I didn't confuse the theory by adding any facts that didn't fit. As a young man Van Gogh worked for a Paris art dealer, and his brother Theo was instrumental in launching Claude Monet and Edgar Degas toward international fame. Why didn't Theo put his shoulder to the wheel and get Vincent's work out on the Paris and London exhibition scenes?

"He was a prisoner to one style," Elise said.

"If he was the best in the world at it, why should he have changed his style?"

"Maybe we shouldn't go there," Veera said.

"I want to experience the city with my senses, and the best way to do that is out with the common man," Mikko said, changing the subject. "At Tesco, not Harrods. I like walking city streets and looking at the buildings."

Veera nodded, because she had just taken a large bite of salad and her mouth was full.

Mikko continued, saying that cities aren't tourist sites, they're places where people live. There were loads of interesting things in cities besides what the travel guides highlighted.

"I want to walk through the City and gaze on its temples of greed. I wonder how they look on Sundays."

"The same as on any other day."

"You mean they leave up the façades? They don't hang a 'To let' sign in every door?"

"I wish more of them said 'toilet.'" Veera said. "Which reminds me. Tell me honestly: Do you two feel comfortable using a restroom that says 'Gentlemen?'"

I pointed out that business was going quite well in the financial industry nowadays. The turbulence of 2008 had been cleaned up by spreading out the losses unavoidably incurred by a few in the industry. At the same time operations were streamlined and the fat that had built up during the boom was trimmed.

"Privatizing profits and socializing losses," Mikko said.

"Yes, which has been shown in practice to be an extremely effective counterbalance to income redistribution," I said.

Murder flashed in Mikko's eyes. There was a new energy to the evening, and no one remembered Maarit anymore.

# Elise

VINCENT VAN GOGH saw the world in yellow. Yellow liberates. Yellow inspires. Yellow invigorates.

The sunflowers were yellow and so was the wall behind them. Van Gogh's self-portraits also emphasized the color yellow.

The artist didn't suffer from jaundice, though. He suffered from xanthopsia.

Poisoning drove him to madness. Poisoning drove him to death.

Vincent van Gogh suffered from mania, for which doctor Paul-Ferdinand Gachet prescribed digoxin. Digoxin is made from dried digitalis leaves. It was easy to take too much.

Paul-Ferdinand Gachet was a perfectly real doctor. He used the medical techniques of his day. That was what the exhibit brochure said.

Digoxin is a white, crystalline powder. A few milligrams is enough to kill.

In smaller doses it can cause symptoms such as vertigo, confusion, hallucinations, and disturbances in color vision.

In the nineteenth century it was used for treating epilepsy and mania.

They had to start with small doses so the patient wouldn't die right away.

A dead patient was a bad patient for a doctor. That was why they poisoned their patients gradually.

Doctor Gachet poisoned van Gogh into one of the greatest artists of all time.

What would the sunflowers be without their bright yellows? What would the self-portraits be other than the face of a tired man grown old before his time? No one would display them in museums. They would hang them in rehab clinics as cautionary examples. That was what Robert said.

Vincent van Gogh saw the world in yellow. Yellow did not free or inspire or invigorate him. Instead he grew darker.

How dark would he have been without the yellow? How would the world have depressed Vincent van Gogh if he had seen it as it was?

Artists see the world differently. That's why they're artists. That's why people stop and gaze at their work. Century after century.

Van Gogh painted Doctor Gachet twice. In both pictures Gachet was holding a digitalis plant. That was where they got the digoxin. Sometimes more of it, sometimes less.

I said, "Van Gogh wouldn't have been a great artist if he had been healthy."

Robert said, "He could have taken digoxin if he was healthy too."

I asked, "Who would poison themselves on purpose?"

Robert said, "Well, for the sake of art. Put a price on the sacrifice demanded. Put a price on the benefit gained. There are a lot of people out there who would be willing to shorten their lives by twenty years if it meant giving their descendants hundreds of millions of pounds."

I asked, "Would you?"

Robert said, "Everything is for sale. The only issue is the price."

I said, "I think it's noble that artists make sacrifices for other people."

Robert said, "Van Gogh didn't make a sacrifice."

I said, "He sacrificed his health."

Robert said, "He didn't make a conscious choice. He didn't weigh the costs and benefits and then decide to take the digoxin."

I asked, "Isn't that even nobler?"

Robert asked, "What?"

I said, "That he made his sacrifice unknowingly."

Robert said, "But van Gogh didn't get any benefit! He didn't sell his paintings, and he didn't have any children who could collect the money when they gained value later. He didn't make a sacrifice and he didn't receive any benefits."

I said, "He was altruistic."

Robert said, "Amateur mistake."

I said, "It's beautiful that suffering can produce beauty."

Robert said, "Don't glorify coincidence."

# Veera

THAT YEAR MY husband devoured forty credit hours in addition to completing his military service. He was in the summer batch of recruits to report to the Karelian Brigade Garrison. I don't remember why he served there, since I didn't have the patience to listen to his musings on the topic. Was there a communications unit? Was there good running terrain? Had the barracks been remodeled recently? At least I know those were a few of the things on the list of pros and cons he made in his graph paper notebook on the way to his call-up.

He had also carefully planned out his service schedule: first one year at the university to get through the introductory courses that had required lectures. Next a year in the army, during which he could also take exams. That was a double bonus: he would keep making progress on his degree and get leave for test days. Now that was efficiency! Not a moment wasted!

At the time I was just a freshman because I had taken a gap year and earned some money sending faxes and making copies at the Nokia head office in South Espoo. Nokia was a crumbling company that had decided to start manufacturing televisions in Germany. The Germans hadn't succeeded at it—but they had succeeded in selling their junk company to the gullible Finns. The Soviet Union had collapsed, and Nokia was in trouble because they couldn't sell their reels of cable to their eastern neighbor anymore.

Rob and I were freshmen together, Rob fresh back from reserve officer candidate school and me a middle-weight double-sided Xeroxing champion.

My sixteen-square-meter dorm room was cramped, and when Mikko came to visit on his first weekend of leave, my roommate's dishwashing made him fume. He always had a textbook with him, which he gazed at sadly when I suggested that we go out for a walk in the park on Sunday morning.

Mikko started spending his weekends at the barracks. His explanation was that he couldn't concentrate on his reading on the bus since it was so crowded. It was an inefficient use of time, so it was wasteful. He only visited Helsinki for tests and Christmas.

New Students' Night was in mid-September, but it wasn't until the bar crawl after the next freshman social that I ran into Rob. I was waiting in line at the bar with a twenty-mark bill between my fingers, hoping that the bartender would finally pour me a big glass of the cheapest beer they had on tap, when Robert's tanned arm wrapped around my neck.

"Did you order a tequila sunrise?"

That night I didn't think about Maarit. And I didn't think about Mikko either. What kept thumping behind my forehead was, *Robert is trying to hit on me. Finally!*

I was easy pickings, even though I wasn't very drunk or particularly hard up. I was a reasonably good-looking, witty woman who had spent the first two years of high school crushing on Rob. And occasionally moaning on my crocheted bedspread with my eyes closed thinking of him. I was infatuated with him. In my diary I called it love.

And I called masturbation moaning. After that night I did it before and after most lectures, until on the third day I called Rob and announced that, by the way, he wasn't a one-night stand.

With Rob everything was possible. He was a business school alpha-male and behaved accordingly. There was no question of his dominance, and he protected his territory aggressively. We fucked in the bathrooms at dance clubs, in the bushes at the beach, and under a slide at a waterpark just because it was possible and there was a hint of danger.

Mikko didn't suspect a thing. He wasn't interested in how I met my desires. And I didn't ask how Mikko met his own. If I would have asked, he probably just would have started talking about his grades.

I spent more time in the two-room apartment Rob's parents had bought him downtown than in my own dorm room.

When Mikko got out of the army, he and I moved in together on the east side of town across the bridge. Rob soon left for London. A few years later when Rob sent me a plane ticket from Helsinki to Heathrow for the first time, I told Mikko I wanted to take a shopping vacation. I bought Mikko a kilo of English licorice at the airport.

Mikko was shocked I would fly to a foreign country. He took the licorice to his office and rationed it. And he advised me not to pay the airport price at Bassets since you could get the same products cheaper in town. Apparently Tesco had a store brand you could buy in bulk. You want to pay for the taste, not the packaging, was his argument.

I remembered that every time afterwards.

# Mikko

A COUNTERBALANCE! A counterbalance to income redistribution!

Because the bankers didn't make enough, not only was it right, it was our duty to use the taxpayers' money to deal with the catastrophe they caused with their boundless avarice. This idea was so brazen that I demanded Robert explain himself.

"It was society's own decision to save the banks," Robert said. He waved a thin slice of prosciutto on the end of his fork before sucking it silently into his mouth.

What arrogance!

I felt like diving over the table, grabbing his neck, and strangling him right then and there.

Under the table my hand moved to the pouch of strychnine. I gave a start when I noticed that part of it was out of my pocket. No one had noticed, had they? I glanced at each of my companions in turn. No.

I shoved the pouch back in my pocket.

Its time had not yet come. I still hadn't prepared Robert for his death. First he had to understand why he had to die. He had to regret his mistakes.

"The politicians don't have any choice, and the bankers know it. They don't have any other options. I think that sounds like taking advantage of someone in distress."

"If the politicians act unwisely, that isn't the bankers' fault."

Robert bit off half a slice of ciabatta and used the rest to clean his plate. Damn it if he wasn't right. The banks knew the politicians' weaknesses and remorselessly used them to their advantage.

The banks were playing a multi-billion-euro game of chance that always led to one bank racking up more Old Maids than its balance sheets could bear. Before then the executives and shareholders had plenty of time to cram their pockets full, though.

If a megabank failed, it would be like a volcanic eruption. Ash and burning rock would rain down destruction, but the worst thing would be that everyone knew the volcano was only a symptom. It was a sign that continental plates were colliding and soon the whole financial system would shudder with fear.

And if the financial markets froze up, that would mean a trip to the ICU for the entire world economy. With the economy crippled, political chaos would ensue, with opposition parties going for the jugular as cash-strapped corporations began furloughing workers and moving factories to China. And then from China to whatever country offered the most favorable operating environment next.

So the politicians poured taxpayer wealth into the banks in order to enable their own re-election the next time they had to stand.

"So you think that's right?"

"If nations decide to prevent their banks from failing, that is the will of their democratically elected parliaments."

"And you think that's right?"

"The system of representation in each country sets the laws, so it should know best how to follow them."

"Morally, I mean."

"Isn't it morally right to help those in distress?"

"That's obscene!"

"On the contrary, I think it's downright noble."

"Mikko, don't get started!" Veera's knife clanged on the edge of her plate.

"How do you even look at yourself in the mirror?"

"That's easy."

"And nothing is so serious that you can't joke about it."

Robert carefully placed his utensils on his plate. His tongue ran between his gums and upper lip.

"If I was deciding about my own money, of course I wouldn't give to the banks as freely as the politicians do."

"You admit it!"

"Is it news to you that politicians make stupid decisions?"

"Democracy is the worst form of government. Except all the other forms of government that have been tried."

"I think the best is enlightened despotism," Robert said.

"Just so long as the despot is you."

"No, no. I think you would be an excellent dictator."

"Why not you?"

"Because I would act like a man. And an enlightened despot has to act like a benevolent deity, not a man. Justice must prevail. That's why I would want you as a dictator. Out of all the people I know."

# Robert

THAT'S A GOOD question. Why did I invite Mikko and Veera to visit? So Mikko could take jabs at me? So he could pounce on every thought I expressed imperfectly and quibble endlessly?

Of course that wasn't why. And it also wasn't so Mikko could show off his own brilliance. I know how brilliant he is.

And if I had only wanted to see Veera, I would have invited her alone. Besides, I had Elise now, as much as anyone ever had anything.

You don't open the door of your home to just anyone. If you wanted to get to know a colleague after hours, there were restaurants and cafés. A trip to the theater, a three-course meal, and cigars.

But Mikko wasn't a colleague. He was a friend. He was the only friend I had ever had.

Given the fact that we had been so close for nearly twenty years, Mikko and I hated each other with amazing intensity. I don't find that strange, though. You can only bear true spite for those you're closest to. You can only hate your friends and loved ones with this kind of fire.

Why would I direct my feelings at someone I only knew from the television or the flickering pixels of a computer screen? You can only hate people close to you, and you can only love those close to you. Everyone else are merely clients, a public image that needs keeping clean.

I'm only spiteful to those closest to me. I tell them that. I say it's a sign of belonging to my inner circle. That's all. Nothing personal.

I needed Mikko. To measure my own success? That too—yes, of course that—but most of all because he was Mikko. I had never spent as much time with anyone as with him. He was the one person who really knew me.

Mikko had a habit of expressing his views by belittling everything other than what he valued. He did it so the belittling felt like the only sensible way of approaching it. He's ruthless to the extreme. He didn't strike head-on, he dissolved like hydrochloric acid, gradually from every side.

I discovered his method for the first time in the context of soccer.

I was playing for the HJK Helsinki juniors team during the period when Mikko began isolating himself more and more in his room. He would sit at his desk for hours taking notes from books he borrowed from the library. Mikko didn't criticize soccer or HJK directly, but he never let an opportunity go by without making an indirect comment about the general uselessness of the game.

When someone tore an ankle ligament in PE class during a tackle executed with more enthusiasm than skill, Mikko wondered out loud at the number of absences caused by soccer. When I mentioned that Albert Camus claimed he learned everything he knew about morality from soccer, Mikko said that he found Camus's work rather narrow minded. But he didn't think that was Camus's fault.

"There aren't bad students, only bad teachers," Mikko said.

At the time I didn't have anything to say to that.

The point being that I was fully aware of the risk of spending the whole night listening to Mikko nitpicking and ridiculing everything I said. So it's perfectly justified to ask why I invited Mikko and Veera to visit.

I wanted to show Mikko. Not how much money I had. Not that I had succeeded. That I already knew.

I wanted to show Mikko that I had been right in that dilapidated hotel room twenty years ago. That was how petty I was.

Is that a good enough answer? Have we covered it well enough not to have to come back to it again?

# Veera

THESE KINDS OF arguments were exactly why I fell in love with Mikko.

In high school Mikko devoured pearls of wisdom more appropriate to the 1970s, constructing a theory of the good society and condensed his thoughts into carefully formulated principles that he was constantly revising and improving.

Rob didn't have a system, just thoughts. He didn't read books, he read chapters, pages, and paragraphs. Sometimes he only read the sentences that worked best as slogans. Rob sucked these in with a passion and then lobbed them around at random. He would take any thought out for a spin, debating and refining his opinions on the fly. For Rob an idea didn't exist until he said it out loud. He thought by talking.

Rob's idols changed monthly. He had a bright red Che Guevara shirt, and he quoted Milton Friedman, John Lennon, and the Sex Pistols. With the fervor of a religious convert he criticized his previous gurus. You could never know what Rob thought about anything, but he could always back up his opinions with a strong argument.

Mikko was dependable, Rob unpredictable.

Even at the dinner table it was a show. It had always been a show. Maarit and I looked on in admiration, as did our entire private school, except the boys who were jealous of Rob and Mikko, and of course the ones who refused to envy or admire anything because they thought there wasn't anything to admire anywhere in the world.

The pace of their game had grown so quick, there was no way to join in. The ball was already in motion, changing direction and crisscrossing the net like an Olympic ping-pong match.

If I had the chance, I would have thrown in that God might be good but not just. Mikko would have explained the problem of evil in terms of free will. But what would Rob have said? Would he have proclaimed that justice was an illusion because our sense of it is subjective? Would he have asked what reason we had to assume God was good? He wouldn't question the existence of a personal God, though, because that would be too easy a solution to the argument.

I wasn't tired of watching Mikko and Rob's sparring matches. I had been missing them. My husband thrived on them.

Twenty years ago I had thought Mikko intended to go into politics.

"I could never do that," Mikko had said, followed by an impassioned monologue: he wanted to serve truth, which was something politicians couldn't do.

Politicians can serve goodness, I insisted, even though what I really thought was that politicians served their constituents. Mikko became agitated. It was wrong to separate the true from the good.

"A politician who wants to accomplish good has to lie. If a politician wants to change the law three degrees to the right, he has to proclaim how blissful the world would be if the law were moved six degrees," Mikko explained, showing the distances with his hands. "Politicians have to make themselves stupid."

"Isn't it okay to lie when you're fighting for something good? Isn't the good more important than the true?" I showed my interest by interrupting before Mikko could get bogged down in the exceptions and the exceptions to the exceptions.

Mikko considered for a moment and made a swirl in the surface of the gravel playing field with the tip of his canvas shoe. "Maybe in some circumstances, but over the long run I couldn't pretend to think something different than I do."

Mikko knew himself well. I should have realized then too what an unhealthy sense of justice my husband had and what it might lead to.

He went to study law, but it was perfectly clear that he would never be a lawyer. Mikko said so himself: Lawyers only abuse and exploit the law.

So my husband chose to fight for a better world by reining in evil and catching criminals whose fingers stank of money, not gunpowder. He dispensed justice, becoming a sort of scarecrow for the thieves.

That time in the schoolyard—I was wearing a Scottish plaid skirt which I remember was not only stylish but beautiful—I asked Mikko why he still intended to vote and supported democracy. It always led to exactly what he had described: making laws was like an auction with everyone yelling offers and counteroffers.

"What's the alternative?"

Rob walked up and lit a cigarette. He had smoked back then, but only for a few months, working at it diligently until he got bored and stopped.

"An enlightened despot," Rob suggested, then walked away.

Mikko hurried after Rob, raving about democratic oversight and the net sum of good and evil.

I didn't hear the end because I stayed where I was. I wasn't nearly as interesting as social theory. The clouds started drizzling.

*THE DEPARTURES BOARD was full of faith in the future. All these screens of flights would lift off, and once they were all in the air, it would only be midday. The world would continue at least until then, and not one of the flights was marked cancelled.*

*He scanned the list in order. Frankfurt wasn't until the second board. An LH-coded flight would leave just after eight.*

*Wasn't there anything earlier? He started again from the beginning.*

*LH2485 to Munich at 6:40.*

*He could make that easily. Munich would do. There was no point throwing away an hour and a half.*

*Going and purchasing the ticket, he received instructions about check-in, security, and the departure gate.*

*He stopped at an ATM on the way.*

*The machine spat out his card and a bundle of cash, which he shoved in his jacket pocket. He inserted the card again, this time taking out the largest amount the machine would allow. He repeated this operation until the ATM would not give him any more money.*

*He squeezed the credit card between his thumb and middle finger and let the plastic bend. Wait. Not quite yet.*

*His information would be in the airline database anyway, which would be easy for them to find. It wouldn't matter even if he left tracks in Munich.*

*He had to think, he had to plan more thoroughly.*

*When he found an open currency exchange, he traded the pounds for euros.*

*The exchange rate could have been more favorable in Munich, but there was more money in the bag, much more than he had received from the ATM.*

*As he boarded the plane, he selected a copy of* Die Zeit *from the rack, even though he guessed he wouldn't read it.*

Die Zeit. *He smirked. Now he had time.*

# Elise

MIKKO AND ROBERT were talking about God. I don't know whether they were talking about lower-case G "god" or capital G "God." Sometimes people pull a prank and say "god" with a small g even though they mean it with big G.

God is surely good. A good thing or a good person or a good . . . spirit. That's the conclusion I've come to. Big or little, one or many.

God created the heavens and the earth. Maybe it was a DIY job or maybe he was more like a building contractor. God created humans, too.

God created good and evil. If there weren't evil in the world, it wouldn't be perfect because it would be missing evil.

The servant returned. She was talented. She knew when everyone was ready. She had to have a sixth sense. She was black and white like her clothing. Together those made grey, which is inconspicuous.

Or maybe she was standing at the kitchen door listening to the clinking of the silverware: fork, knife—now!

Seeing the servant reminded me of the bread. I asked for it.

Robert and Mikko's conversation broke off.

The servant turned. She handed me the basket of ciabatta.

I said, "The other bread. The black bread."

Mikko said, "That's your housewarming gift! We shouldn't all eat it. Veera and I get rye bread at home every day. And besides, Veera can't . . . "

Veera said, "No, I can't, but do we have to announce it to everyone? Or should we talk about how your farts smell next?"

Mikko said, "Come on, we're at the dinner table!"

Veera said, "They smell the same at the dinner table as in the bedroom."

I asked, "Couldn't we at least taste it now?"

The servant said, "Excuse me. Ciabatta was requested for the meal."

Robert said, "There, you heard her. She did exactly as she was instructed."

I had made a mistake. That bothered me.

And I don't even like hard bread.

The servant had gathered the plates on her arm. She asked, "Would anyone like some of the dark bread?"

Robert said, "No. Everything is fine."

To me, Mikko said, "But could someone show me the facilities."

I said, "Go to the foyer, second door."

Mikko said, "Maybe it would be better if you showed me."

I understood. I stood up. My napkin fell to the floor. Why hadn't I set it on the table? Was I a little tipsy? Maybe I was. All the edges were soft. Nothing was hard.

I showed Mikko the first door next to the elevator. I said, "This is the closet."

Mikko grabbed me by the arm. He said, "Elise, didn't you understand?"

I showed Mikko the second door, which was farther from the elevator. I said, "This is the WC." I opened the door.

Mikko shook my arm. He said, "Don't touch that bread! That bread is for Robert. You can't eat it."

I said, "Okay."

Mikko asked what I was supposed to remember.

I said, "The rye bread is Robert's bread."

Mikko asked, "And what does that mean?"

I said, "It's like a Finnish man."

Mikko ordered me to remember. He said, "Elise, I'm doing all of this for you."

I said, "Gotcha. April fools! Of course I'll remember. I'm not allowed to eat the bread."

Mikko asked, "And the servant?"

I said, "She can't eat Robert's bread either."

Mikko asked, "Have you told the servant?"

I hadn't, because I didn't know it was Robert's bread. I asked if Mikko wanted a little kiss.

Mikko said, "Elise, what did I already say!"

I looked at Mikko with an expression that meant, "I'm sorry."

Mikko said, "You'll remember now, right?"

I said, "The rye bread is for Robert. I'm not allowed to eat it. And the servant isn't either. The bread is a special treat for only Robert."

# Veera

ROB ALWAYS CAME to meet me at Heathrow in a taxi. In the back seat we would talk loudly in Finnish, enjoying that the driver couldn't understand. Rob wanted to live on the edge. London was anonymous to us. No one in the city knew me except Rob, and when one of Rob's colleagues walked up to us in Kensington Park, Rob introduced me as a Finnish friend who was visiting and wanted to see the sights. It was so easy and so true that the colleague never guessed what the sights in question were. Still it was always possible that Mikko would find out. He knew a lot of people, both in the financial world and in London, and his job was information gathering.

Every time my plane approached Helsinki on the way home, I wondered whether I should feel like a whore. Once or twice I had stumbled across threads about cheating in online forums, but I could never stand all the moralizing. The situations were never the same, so why would the same morality apply? "Morality" was just a word nauseating people used to place themselves above the rest of us.

Sometimes I wondered whether I should tell Mikko. But that thought always vanished before I made it through the jet bridge into the Sunday afternoon bustle of Helsinki-Vantaa International and headed to wait for the airport bus with my carry-on packed with panties and wrinkled dresses. Mikko never met me. Why would he? I had a monthly bus pass.

How would Mikko have reacted if I had told him? That alone was interesting enough to me to keep me thinking about telling every time I came home.

He might have acted like the people on the forum, throwing some dishes and then marching down to the magistrate on Monday morning. He might have withdrawn to his office for two weeks and then returned a changed man. He might have said he was going out for a jog and then come back two hours later with a bouquet of roses to offer me his freshly scrubbed body with champagne and a good movie on the side. He might have begged me to go to couple's therapy—and everything might continue as before, except that Rob and I would have to come up with a new meeting place.

Rob was actually helping me maintain our relationship! He was giving me what I couldn't get from Mikko. Without Rob I would have suffered, or we would have divorced. Because I don't live for suffering, we would have divorced. Thanks to Rob I was able to live with the man I loved.

The servant brought me a steaming plate. Dark brown marinated beef tenderloin with creamy mushroom sauce dribbling off. Potato polenta. Some green herbs and a small orange fruit with a name I didn't bother guessing at.

The spring Mikko was researching the election funding activities of a foundation aligned with the Center Party, I visited London every two weeks. I fed Mikko a story about a cooperative project between British and Finnish nurses. Information exchange, best practices, on weekends because during the week everyone was too busy for anything extra. I hadn't put much work into the story. Mikko could have caught me easily, but he was only interested in the old meeting minutes and accounting files he was studying.

Mikko had the slender body of a runner. He always jogged at a steady pace, just to maintain basic fitness. He avoided any stimuli, abnormal exertion, or overcompensation. When he ran,

Mikko held his hands at the seams of his pants to avoid wasting energy.

And now Mikko rotated in his chair and said that Julia hadn't called.

"It's still early . . . "

"At home it's two hours later."

"She's probably just chatting online."

"Don't try to frighten me!"

Mikko thought rapists would use the internet to contact our daughter, who would then take her clothes off in front of the camera. Unregulated environments were always full of criminals, like cockroaches, and they would take advantage of Julia if not physically then at least emotionally.

"She's just watching a movie. If it's *Schindler's List*, it'll still be a while."

"We arranged that Julia would call."

I saw it as my duty to protect Julia from her father, who was protecting his daughter from the world. Julia needed to have an opportunity to grow up straight, not twisted. When Julia asked if she could have a party while we were in London, of course I gave her permission. If she lived like Mikko, she would go through life without ever having a party. And she would never forgive herself or us for the regret that would follow. At Julia's age, I had already tried every drug I could find. I bought Julia and her BFF Anna six half-liter ciders. We hid the bottles in Julia's closet and I explained that she had to clean everything up afterwards well enough that Mikko wouldn't notice.

"So you mean straighten all the sneakers and make sure there aren't any empty bottles on his desk?" she'd said.

"Fair point. So clean up so that *I* wouldn't notice," I'd replied.

Rob suggested that Mikko call home. I asked if Mikko wanted to send a text from my phone.

Mikko remembered that his phone was in the guest room. Rob and Elise had also been served now, but Mikko left.

I said that the rest of us should go ahead and start.

But we didn't. I told Rob and Elise that Julia had chosen French as her elective language. German was her A-language, and she had started English in the fifth grade. Trivial information.

"Interesting," said Elise.

That was when I decided that I would bang Robert that night. What he had planned didn't matter.

And yeah, you can bet Rob had planned something. Rob was like that. He always has some kind of plan, even if it doesn't show or he won't admit it. Rob's antics could look like he was just following his gut, but he sure as shit thought things through. He always knew what the next step would be. At least. Otherwise he never would have been able to waste so much money.

But what Rob had planned didn't matter. What mattered was what I decided.

That thought made my armpits sweat and put a teenager's flush on my cheeks. I savored the titillating taste of the game and breathed in the scent of danger, both of which felt out of place on the upholstered seats around the white tablecloth as I held a designer fork in my hand. Bored by the drone of conversation, my brain began hatching a plan to get my former classmate Rob the millionaire banker under me crying out and licking—well, you can imagine for yourself.

When I brushed Robert's leg with my foot under the table, the grandfather clock began striking seven. By the third stroke I had ensured that Robert would understand I hadn't touched his leg by accident.

What I was offering Rob was risk, not sex.

# Mikko

WHEN THE AROMA of the food hit my nostrils, fear and uncertainty rose in my throat.

The main course. That meant we were one stage closer. Every stage increased the probability of completion, and one hundred percent was approaching with a grim inevitability. Once we reached the final stage, Robert would die.

I had divided the evening into stages. The first was entering Robert's flat. The opening toast was the second, the hors d'oeuvres were the third. The main course was the fourth of eight total stages.

Robert had made his fortune analyzing probabilities, and that fortune was his life. That was why it was fitting that probabilities would also determine his fate. It was the right way for him to die.

I had left my phone on the nightstand. It was on silent. I had received but not opened the text messages that told me the prices of calls and data while roaming, and the separate message that informed me how to prevent further pricing messages.

Julia hadn't called.

So I called her. The phone rang for a long time.

I stood at the window, clenching my fingers into a fist. My pulse was well above resting, which was as expected. I had assumed I would feel similarly to how I felt at the end of an investigation, that final phone call I would make to nail down the scoop. At first I would stammer as I moved from general questions toward the crucial details, gradually revealing how much I knew and allowing my interviewee unwittingly to confirm the facts I already possessed. And then came the release when the call ended, and I began reviewing my notes for key quotations to add to the article. Perhaps something juicy for the title or lead-in.

But Robert did have a right to the view from this window.

No, I couldn't think things like that. I couldn't retreat.

I called again. After another long wait, Julia answered, irritated.

"What?"

"Is everything all right?"

"Yeah."

"You didn't answer before."

"I was in the middle of a game."

"What are you playing?"

"Ski jumping."

Julia had a game console with a board you used to control the games by jumping and shifting your weight from one leg to the other.

"What was that sound?"

"Anni just biffed it."

"Is Anni there?"

"Yeah."

"Do Anni's parents know?"

"Yeah, of course."

"What are you going to do next?"

"Maybe ice skating. Or tennis."

"Make sure you go to bed on time."

"Come on, tomorrow's Sunday."

"Sunday is a good day."

"Uh, yeah."

"No point wasting it sleeping."

"When else am I supposed to sleep?"

"Is there a boy there?"

"Here? That was probably the news."

"You have the TV on even though you're playing Playstation?"

"Wii."

"While you're playing."

"Yes."

"Isn't it usually hooked up to the TV?"

"Of course."

"How can the TV be on then?"

"My TV."

"You brought your TV downstairs so you could watch the news while you were playing?"

"Yeah. Is the interrogation over now?"

"This isn't an interrogation. Will you please call later before you go to bed? That's what we agreed. These calls from here are expensive."

"Yeah. Okay, I gotta go now. It's my turn to jump."

"Have to. 'Gotta' isn't a word."

"Was that all?"

# Robert

"IF YOU WERE murdered, how would it happen?"

Elise changed the subject casually. She had a skill for that, and it was smart. No subject should ever be completely exhausted—one should leave an appetite for it. Unless you're talking to a terminal cancer patient. But a negotiation with the living should leave a spark alive for the next contact. That's one way to keep a grip on a customer.

"How would I be murdered? Can I even answer that? And what if one of you is plotting something?"

The question wasn't the most common small talk opening, and that was why it was so ingenious. I would definitely have to start using it. Clients like being surprised. You could hear the standard platitudes in any conference room. If you want to make it big, there has to be something more. You have to offer a premium.

"It's important to remember our mortality, but murder? I don't consider that a probable scenario."

"If I could choose how to die, being murdered would definitely land in my top three ways. The downside is that murder ends your life earlier than it otherwise would have ended. Being murdered means being worthy of murder."

This was an interesting topic to consider, because murders were exciting. They wouldn't fill prime time television programming every night on multiple channels otherwise. If I were to write a book, I wouldn't do an investment guide, I'd make a half-drunk Swede solve homicides.

Or maybe I would be the victim. If so, my death probably wouldn't be terribly dramatic. No assassin was going to shoot me through a car window. I didn't have an ugly Rolls-Royce or a cramped Ferrari. A guy who drives a Mercedes may be a bastard, but not the kind you'd waste bullets on or whose front wheel well you'd fit with a bomb.

Mikko walked back into the dining area and asked what we were discussing so intently. I said that it wasn't a discussion, it was a brief lecture I was delivering on the subject of "How I would be murdered."

"Ah," Mikko said.

"Some murder victims have become great heroes. You don't get the same postmortem glamour if you choke on a peanut. Which, by the way, would be one way to murder me. As you know, I'm allergic to nuts. No, dear friends, please at least don't murder me with a peanut!"

Mikko pointed out that nuts wouldn't be enough to rub me out. "If your allergy were so bad that exposure to nuts could kill you, you'd have a syringe full of adrenaline around here somewhere for anaphylactic shock, and if you didn't, we'd still have time to rush you to the hospital."

Mikko was right: I did have an EpiPen, just in case, even though my allergy wasn't as bad as it could have been. Of course I should have noticed how quickly Mikko was able to analyze the difficulties involved in murder-by-nut, but I was so caught up in the topic that I wasn't paying enough attention.

Veera added that if there weren't any adrenaline available, they could try asthma medication or even cortisone for first aid.

I swallowed my potato polenta. Mikko said the food was delicious. Veera suggested that he taste it first. Elise asked that we not get distracted by such a boring subject as food since we had just been talking about murder.

"The safest bet would be a gun or a bomb," I said once I got my mouth mostly empty. "Relative to the effort required, a high caliber firearm would probably be the easiest way to bump me off. And if you want to be sure of the victim's death, of course you need to do it yourself," I said.

Elise sighed. "So much work."

"A hitman would be ready to kill for you but not to die. If something goes wrong, he'll protect his own skin regardless of whether the job is done. You can only count on yourself."

Other means similar to firearms included sharp-edged weapons such as knives and swords, and improvised blunt instruments. These required strength and precision, and preferably both. I couldn't recommend their use while intoxicated. At least not to kill me. I might hold on for a while. Nasty way to die.

"Many people still use them," Veera said.

I pointed out that many murders failed. They acted like amateurs.

"As a murderer, I would definitely consider the risk of getting caught. Olof Palme's shooter is still free. However, sniper attacks require careful planning and exceptional skill with a rifle, so I wouldn't recommend that either for the hobbyist. Shooting for year after year at the range to develop the skill for one single pull of the trigger? Would it be worth it?"

Then of course there were the poisons. They got used a lot in books, but significantly less in real life.

"Maybe poisoners are just skilled enough they don't get caught," Veera suggested.

Of course that was possible.

"Poisoning would be a classic murder death. Or what about a dagger? Now that would have style! At least so long as the newspapers could have their photographers there to witness the police pulling the slender blade from my carotid artery by the jeweled hilt. No point having my death go to waste. Better to delight and astound the public if I can!"

Veera pointed out that if the dagger hit the carotid, it would spray an awful lot of blood.

"My noble aspect would not be handsome to behold?"

"Death is not beautiful."

"You see so many of them."

"Yes, I know what death looks like. It's messy and ugly. You can't show the family the real pictures. They would pass out on the floor of the morgue."

Next Elise asked how I would carry out a murder. I said I wouldn't. If I hated someone enough that I could kill them, I wouldn't let them off so easily.

"Torture?"

"Absolutely. I could be a Bond villain who builds a secret underground lair with a torture chamber designed specifically for that person. Megalomaniacal. Flamboyant. Grandiose."

"Not very spontaneous though."

"Is spontaneity desirable in murder? Is it even murder if it's spontaneous? Isn't that manslaughter? Just the word manslaughter reeks of knives. Manslaughter victims stink of stale booze. Pathetic."

"Plans can be made quickly."

"For example after asking the victim how best to approach killing him."

Veera nudged my leg—she had done this several times during the evening even though I had shifted my legs—and showed the tip of her tongue between her lips. Her lips extended from the left edge of her mouth to the right. Veera had a wide mouth that all manner of things could tumble out of.

Such as: "Good murder. Sounds like a plan."

"Not all plans need to be implemented."

"If you leave a good plan unfulfilled, isn't that a sin? Doesn't God want us to do good things?" Mikko asked.

"You're usually good at predicting movements in the markets,"

Veera said to me. "Doesn't that mean you know which plans to follow and which to scrap?"

"Tisk, tisk, I don't need to know where the market is moving. Just so long as it moves."

"If it doesn't move, it can be helped along," Mikko said.

The others had nearly cleaned their plates. I started catching up. I asked Elise to tell about our vacation in Budapest.

Before doing so, however, I pointed out that there was still one more way to kill me. I promised to come back to it after the main course.

# Elise

MIKKO IS LIGHT blue. Not like the sky in the morning, more stern than that. I can't describe it. Words aren't colors.

Robert asked, "Dear, would you tell?"

I asked: "What?"

Robert said, "About our trip to Hungary."

It wasn't a nice trip, even though the sun shone yellow like in van Gogh's flowers. There was where I realized I was a prisoner. In bed we had been cops and robbers and nurses and teachers, but in Budapest I realized that my ring was squeezing my finger. Rotating it off and cleaning it didn't help. It was a collar and handcuffs even though it was so much smaller.

Robert wasn't a playmate anymore. He wanted to be a father. He took care that I didn't fall and hurt my knee on the asphalt.

There wasn't anything about that in the agreement, but Robert was exceeding his obligations. So shouldn't I be flexible? The phrasing of the agreement was imprecise. Those paragraphs were supposed to ensure my future, but now they turned against me.

I said, "We went to a lot of vineyards. There were a lot of grapes in them."

Mikko asked, "When did you go?"

I said, "It was the fall before we . . . "

Oops. Then I didn't know what I should say. Mikko had said that I couldn't tell Robert and Veera that we knew each other. Not before everything was done. It was quite a demand. When would everything be done? Never!

Robert said, "Elise means that we were in Budapest before the futures contracts had been made for the next year's grape harvest."

What I was thinking was before Helsinki, where I met Mikko. I flew directly to Helsinki form Budapest.

When I recognized Mikko in the hotel in Helsinki, I knew immediately what I should do. I should tell Mikko about my trouble with Robert. But before then I should use my talents on him. Then I could get him on my side. Mikko could convince Robert to set me free. He could use words to break my cords and unlock my handcuffs.

Mikko was a silly boy.

He still makes me laugh. He was so serious and concerned about me.

I said, "The wine was good. There was one we liked especially. This red wine is made there."

I lifted my glass and swished it around. Mikko and Veera did the same.

I said, "The white wine is from the same vineyard, too."

Robert asked, "Would you tell Veera and Mikko why?"

I said, "They were the best wines, of course!"

Robert said, "That must have been it."

Mikko slammed the table hard enough to make the dishes ring. Mikko said, "How can you treat Elise like this! Let her speak for herself. Stop grilling her!"

Veera tried to calm Mikko down.

I said, "It's good for Robert to remind me."

Robert said, "Let's keep things civil."

Mikko yelled, "You think that's civil? You're treating your wife like a little child! 'How old are you dear? What did we do next? Was it fun?'"

I said, "It was fun."

It wasn't completely true though.

Mikko started laughing. He said, "Excuse me. I got a little over excited."

Veera said, "So you did."

Robert asked, "Work stress?"

Mikko said, "Yes, I've got one big story in the works."

Robert said, "Someone's head about to roll? Whose?"

Mikko said, "Of course I can't say."

# Veera

MIKKO WAS THE first of them I noticed, but Rob noticed me.

I was a shy girl with a backpack who had just moved from Lahti to Helsinki. I spent my time riding the buses and exploring the metro library system.

In my first class in my first year of high school, Mikko sat in the second desk in the row by the window. He had a short-sleeve T-shirt and was concentrating on organizing his pencils in order of length along the left edge of his desk.

I didn't know anyone in the class, but when I saw Mikko, he immediately felt familiar. He would have been the easiest person to approach if I had dared. He obviously wasn't putting on an act or pretending to be anything. He was the kind of boy it would be easy to be friends with, I thought.

Then Rob came to talk to me right after that first class. His polite behavior felt overly slick. The boys in middle school had hung around outside the wood shop with their mopeds, spitting and smelling of cigarettes and sweat concealed with deodorant, wearing chains around their necks bought from the hardware store. Rob was completely different. I figured he was trying to hit on me, even though school had just started. It felt insulting. With that, Rob disqualified himself.

And I disqualified myself.

I made friends with Maarit, who had moved from Kotka. We made food together at each other's houses, rode bikes to hunt for mushrooms, and when the other room in my dorm unit opened up, Maarit move in. We started getting invitations to house parties at fancy places as far away as Espoo and Kirkkonummi. Together we studied the bus routes and split the taxi home.

After one house party as we were eating white bread straight from the bag, Maarit said that Rob was interested in her. I asked what she thought of that, and Maarit said that of course she was interested in Rob too.

Maarit and Rob started dating soon after. That was right at the beginning of our sophomore year. Because my best friend had found other company, I needed a new relationship too. Because my best friend had started dating, I wanted to try out how it would feel too.

The conditions were favorable, and I did like Mikko. I had spent time with him during free periods since school started, because Mikko was alone whenever Rob had something else to do.

Still I was horribly nervous when I asked him over after school for tea at my apartment, where he had been many times before. Mikko grabbed the tea bags from the pantry as he was accustomed to, meanwhile lecturing me about Kant's Clock. I remember because it was a long story and I was nervous. There were all sorts of things about *a priori* and dialectics and representation and Königsberg and on and on. Transcendental idealism. That was a sufficiently difficult concept to seduce Mikko.

"Mikko, can I ask you something?"

"You don't need to ask that."

"If you were Immanuel Kant, how would transcendental idealism analyze an idea such as you and me starting dating?"

Mikko analyzed the idea carefully. After this consideration, he said that it would be practical now since Rob and Maarit had started dating, and Robert was his friend and Maarit mine.

I pinched his cheek and kissed him on the mouth. Not because of the content of the response but because of the way he presented it. That was what I loved about him then and what I have loved ever since.

# Mikko

"WHAT ABOUT IT?"

"What about what?" Veera asked.

"About transcendental idealism. That's what you just said."

"Me? Why on earth would I have said something like that?"

"There are three of us sitting here and we all heard you say 'transcendental idealism' just now."

Robert and Elise didn't back me up, so Veera claimed I had just imagined it. Why on earth would she have started philosophizing when we were talking about murder and Hungarian wine? But I was sure of what I'd heard. I trusted myself, not anyone else. That is a skill you must have if you want to succeed in my job. People say things in interviews without considering them. They claim to have seen or heard something that they haven't seen or heard. Maybe they actually smelled it: If a person smelled fresh coffee, based on that observation they might be sure they heard the clinking of a coffee cup. You have to notice things like that when conversing with people. Corporate communications officers go to a lot of work to craft phrases that look like other than what they are.

Robert and Elise could have a social reason for avoiding lining up on either side in a controversial issue. But in this case they sided with Veera because they didn't do anything, although passivity is a smaller act than active admission or denial. Also note that they didn't claim that Veera didn't say "transcendental idealism." And

Elise wouldn't dare do anything that Robert didn't do. So this was not in fact a case of weighing the word of two people against one but simply the discrepancy between my testimony and Veera's.

Veera said the words quietly enough that they weren't necessarily audible on the other side of the table.

Looking at Elise, I wanted to whisper, "Hold out for just a few more hours. Then everything will be good."

That was what I hoped. The call to Julia had been a premeditated trick to give me a moment alone to refine my tactics. I hadn't figured out how to proceed. At the dinner table I wasn't going to have any opportunity to slip the strychnine onto Robert's plate or into his glass without the others noticing. It would arouse too much attention if I demanded Robert try the rye bread. I had to wait for a better opportunity to present itself.

Instead of placing my trust in Elise, I asked Veera to say "transcendental idealism" again.

Veera again denied ever saying it. So I asked her to say "transcendental idealism" for the first time. Just to humor me.

When Veera said the words, sounding slightly tipsy, I immediately remembered the first time I had heard her say them. Our second year of high school had just begun, and Veera had asked me to her dormitory to go over some physics problems.

Small details could bend the course of world history and human fate. Sometimes they're insane coincidences, sometimes moments of weakness for strong people, sometimes simply carelessness or complacency. Some inflection point occurs and then nothing is as it was before.

This is what you hear if you ask historians, who lump facts together in order to dramatize events, selecting individual points even though history isn't points with straight lines connecting them. Points are landmarks and symbols. The first landmark in my life is "transcendental idealism" as pronounced by Veera in September, 1994. That afternoon significantly changed my life.

An imprecise popular historian, novelist, or news editor seeking to keep the story *in the cycle* would write it without any further problematization: "That day changed my life."

Of course literally that was true. Every day has an effect on the rest of a life.

Inspecting my life up to this point, that day changed my life more than any other day afterward. Until this night.

The next point would be death, because life is mostly a steady progression without room for many twists or turns, and if there are a lot of twists and turns, they become insignificant. Death, a couple of turns, and death. That's it. Beginning, middle, end.

Before that afternoon in that tiny apartment in Helsinki, I had been a student focused on facts. Participating in my classmates' socializing was difficult for me. In middle school I had spent most of my time with Robert or with books. In high school, Robert's social circle expanded because he was an extrovert, and I became isolated. I kept company with great thinkers more than high schoolers. I went to some house parties. When I said something, I heard my words twisting. Whenever I made some small move toward the girls I imagined might be within my realm of possibilities, they quickly removed my hand from their leg or waist. Placing it there had required a great deal of boldness.

In the bathroom, I looked at my hands as I washed them and wondered what was wrong with them.

I gave up because I didn't want disappointment. I could live without dating, even though everyone else was pairing off around me, exchanging glances in the halls and kisses outside the school fence. I had long since understood that I wasn't exactly like most of my other classmates. Most of my classmates weren't exactly like people their same age on average either. Our community supported difference, even encouraged it. I didn't feel at all uncomfortable.

When Veera asked me how transcendental idealism would analyze the idea that the two of us start dating, I was confused because I had never considered such a thing. Not that Veera and I could be anything but school friends, a little like Robert and me before. Nor that I could be good enough for Veera. I knew that even Robert had pursued Veera without success. "Snob. No one is good enough for her," Robert had said to me a couple of days before rumors had started circulating in the halls about Maarit and Robert dating.

The damp linden leaves were slippery under my deck shoes as I walked in the drizzling rain toward the bus stop. My legs were working fine. My knees weren't buckling. I examined my feelings. I stopped by an R Kiosk to buy a chocolate bar because I was hungry, even though it would have been cheaper at the K Market across the street. In the bus I took a window seat and wondered if this was love. Was this how it felt?

It felt good. It felt wonderful. Someone was interested enough in me that she wanted to date me.

But where were the surges of emotion that novels always associated with love? Those words about the life-altering power of love—did they just mean a feeling of satisfaction?

At home I wrote in the oilcloth notebook that served as my diary: "Veera suggested that we go out. Why not?"

I had read that brief entry again a month before the trip to London. I don't remember aiming for a sense of indifference when I wrote it. "Why not?" described my feelings: I was fine with the idea of dating, but it didn't send shudders running through my body.

Despite the implications of the term, dating didn't really change anything about my everyday life. Sometimes at school dances or house parties we would be alone together, and we could go dig our shoes out of the pile by the front door and leave anytime we wanted without attracting undue attention. What before might have labeled us losers now elicited jealous glances. Usually we just both went home, but sometimes, more rarely, we went to

Veera's dorm room to drink tea. Veera held my hand in hers and sometimes I put mine on her thigh.

I was satisfied because I didn't have to feel inadequate, and I didn't think about the issue any further. The relationship aspect of my life was taken care of, and the days passed focused on things other than dating or "being a couple" as the state of affairs came to be called. I kissed Veera when it was appropriate.

When I came home from the army, I suggested to Veera that we move in together. This was a pragmatic move. The rent on our fifty-square-meter one-bedroom apartment was only slightly higher than a thirty-square-meter studio. For Veera it also signified an improvement in quality of life since she could move out of her dorm room with its plastic rugs. My newspaper subscription was delivered to our door and she didn't have to worry about the TV license inspector.

Our days developed a rhythm, and that rhythm developed into routine. Everything ran smoothly. Our love wasn't burning, and I thought that was good. Our relationship was practical.

After Maarit's death—I still lived at home then—for the first time Veera said she wanted children. I took a cautious approach to this. We weren't even married. Veera asked if I didn't want to marry her. I said that wasn't the issue. "Well let's do it then," Veera said. "Would this fall be too soon?"

We didn't make our vows until after my military service, though. We found a free day on the calendar and held a small wedding. Robert wasn't able to come but he sent a pair of Ultima Thule crystal candle sticks in the mail. The card said that every bourgeois Finnish home was supposed to have a set. That wasn't malicious, just a fun way of saying it. For our honeymoon we visited a spa in Pärnu, Estonia. We laughed that we were living like retirees, who made up all of the other guests except for one lone businessman. We observed that it was good that way because old age was getting closer by the day.

When on the second morning of our honeymoon I left Veera sleeping—this was our usual habit since I got along on less sleep—and went out for an easy jog along the beach, I considered whether I was sure of my feelings. Did I love Veera enough? I was prepared to love on the uphills and the down, and I wanted to do so, just as I had promised a couple of days earlier, just so long as no particularly large demands were placed on that loving. But did I love enough for my own good? And what about Veera—did she? I recognized selfishness in my actions—a lot of selfishness—even though love was supposed to eliminate selfishness.

I found it easy to join in with the celebration of the universal and institutional victory of love preached by a recent Eurovision entry about how love would unify all nations and remove jealousy, pain, and a few other negative emotions the lyricist identified that matched the meter of the song. People would stop waging war and the sun would shine and chase all fear away. Discontent would be felt no more. But at the individual level, I didn't experience anything like that. Veera was important to me and we got along well together, but Veera wasn't the most important thing in the world.

I asked myself the same question again sometimes, but not often, because asking it made me think about it, and I had other things to think about. I was getting into my career and was reading eagerly.

Veera said I would be a good, attentive father. I didn't have any counterarguments. A little more than a year later, Julia was born. What I liked most about the baby was her nose. "She has your nose," was what Veera's mother said.

Julia's arrival only made our life more routine, and routine always worked well for us. One's routine needs to be in order because most of life is routine. Reasoning this way quieted the doubts that occasionally entered my mind. We moved into a house with a small garden, apple trees, and black currant bushes. I planted gooseberries. I handled the man's work and Veera the woman's work and sometimes the man's as well. I became an award-winning journalist.

I saw women who aroused greater sexual attraction in me than Veera ever had. I reasoned that a person is a whole of which outward appearance, or, more broadly, habitus is only one part, and not a very critical one. I was infatuated now and then. I investigated the backgrounds of the people I met and identified why they were impossible for me.

I argued that my feelings were part of my natural desire for assurance and certainty. In a notebook I listed the facts that demonstrated that Veera was far and away the best spouse for me compared to all other possibilities. And besides, most of my infatuations—with extremely bold quotation marks around that word—were already taken. That was to be expected, since I mostly saw people my own age.

In any case, all was well since I didn't allow love to interfere with my work or trouble my mind.

CANS AND GLASS *bottles jingled in the airplane beverage cart. He wouldn't have time to visit the lavatory before the flight attendant serving the drinks arrived at his seat. Afterwards returning to his seat would be difficult because the cart would fill the aisle. And besides, his tray table was down with a breakfast biscuit packed in orange and yellow cardboard resting on it, as there was on the tray table of the traveler in the aisle seat.*

*He would have to wait until the meal service was over.*

*Once he was through security he had bought two half-liter bottles of mineral water at a news stand, immediately emptying one of them. He'd consumed so much alcohol during the course of the evening and night that he was still intoxicated, but he could prevent his system from completely dehydrating.*

*Sensible planning. Good. He could still do that.*

*He would ask the flight attendant for orange juice to wash down the roll. Its sharp crispness might speed the clearing of his head.*

*He didn't feel drunk, but feelings could be deceptive.*

*Although, catastrophes could make people act with rare sanity. Stress hormones sharpened the brain.*

*His watch said twenty-five past seven. In the initial announcements, the captain, whose name sounded Polish, had estimated that because of favorable wind conditions, the flight would arrive in Munich according to schedule at 9:35. So more than an hour of flight time was left.*

*He turned his watch to Central European time. To Munich.*

*Carefully considered, Munich was actually a better place than Frankfurt. It was located in the center of Europe. From there, in a few hours by train or car he could easily access the Czech Republic, Austria, Switzerland, Lichtenstein, Italy, France, Hungary, Slovakia, or Slovenia. Munich was one of Europe's best starting points if you wanted to disappear.*

*He took the airline customer magazine out of the seat pocket and opened to the page that showed the flight map of Europe. After Frankfurt, Munich was Lufthansa's second home hub and the number of red lines starting there corresponded appropriately. But he would do best not to fly anymore—he didn't want to feed his information to the authorities investigating those registries.*

*Feed information. Maybe not such a bad idea after all.*

*He would act like Jason Bourne. That was exactly what he had to do even though he couldn't yet think of what he would do that night, what he would do tomorrow, or what he would do ten years from now.*

*Where would he live? What would he do?*

*And with whom?*

*When the plane landed in Munich, it would be eight-thirty London time, but in Finland it would be ten-thirty. In Helsinki couples would be out jogging in their shell suits in the fickle spring weather. In London, corn flakes would be rustling in breakfast bowls.*

*He had the whole day. First he would have to decide where he would go next.*

*The blond flight attendant gave the man sitting beside him orange juice.*

*"And what can I get you?"*

"Weisswein," *he found himself saying.* "Und Orangen-saft, bitte."

# Robert

YOU HAVE TO feel death in your groin! It has to shake you like a doll.

Death reminds you that you are alive. Uniformity breeds apathy, which kills any intense emotion, ambition, or ability to surpass the boundaries of the possible.

Which is why I lob war metaphors at my underlings. Metaphors that aren't really metaphors. The world of finance is a battle where some win and some die. Anyone who doesn't believe that, just let them look at the *Financial Times*. They don't save bank obituaries for the back section, they splash them on the cover page. And no one sends the family a bill, because everyone knows they can't pay.

You have to stay awake to avoid finding yourself in the grave. If you relax, the enemy will rush through your lines. And then it will be everything you can do to retreat fast enough to even catch up with the enemy.

The Second World War is well documented. It touches a sufficient number of different nationalities. Which is why I tend to draw the most comparisons from it.

I've also told all of my subordinates that at home not only do I have a couple of bars of gold bearing UBS stamps, but I also have some cyanide. That's everything you need for living and dying. You can get along in any situation with those two things.

Because no one ever dares to ask why, I ask them what they think the reason is.

"You want to reserve yourself the option to decide how you die?" That was how they always answered, although the phrasing varied. It was the correct response.

Death is a possible state of affairs and deciding to die is a choice. The possibility to choose is an option, and if an option is free or inexpensive, both monetary theory and good sense suggest that you should buy it even if you don't intend to cash it in. If a situation were to arise in which one did wish to decide one's fate, the value of the option would be greater than life, even under future valuations decades from now.

More likely the option would expire worthlessly: the cyanide capsule would remain in the safe and hopefully the heirs would be sensible enough to leave it untested.

However, I hadn't acquired the capsules because I believed I would use them; rather, a cyanide capsule reminded me of the proximity of death and forced me to live with strength.

Mikko was stuck on his last pieces of beef. Excusing myself, I retired to my office. At the safe I punched in my six-digit code, which had originally been based on the model numbers of my first two cars registered in Finland. Whenever the keypad's microchip demanded that I change the password, I had increased the number by one. So it reminded me of the passage of time.

I picked up a small box that contained three ampules bound with a leather thong. I had purchased the box and its contents from a consultant with whom I had reviewed the security arrangements at my previous apartment. Taking the leftmost of the ampules, I closed the safe.

I flipped the glass capsule from one hand to the other on my way back to the dining area.

"This might be completely unnecessary."

I remained standing. I allowed myself a performance. This could be the evening's show. I hadn't booked a magician, a juggler, or even a flashy chef. "One of you could have put poison in my wine while I was away. No, not one of you—all of you. The others would have seen."

"Like in *Murder on the Orient Express*," Mikko said.

"No spoilers!" Veera exclaimed.

"Although Mikko was so lost in thought that he wouldn't necessarily have noticed if someone had done something. And I don't believe the women are up to it."

"Are you saying women are incapable of murder?" Veera asked.

I pointed out that poison was precisely the woman's way of killing. The history of murder demonstrated as much. "No, I don't wonder every time I step into a room whether my wine was poisoned while I was elsewhere. Life can't be the constant avoidance of death."

"People who can avoid death forever are pretty rare."

"Death is good to know. Remember death. Mikko could say it to us in Latin."

"Yes, I could."

"*Memento mori*, right?"

"Right."

"*Memento mori.* In order to remember to live, sometimes I have to hold death on the tip of my tongue."

Revealing the ampule, I purposefully held it carelessly between my index finger and thumb.

"As you see, this is cyanide, perhaps familiar from Nazi films. This is the kind of ampule Hermann Göring broke between his teeth on the night preceding his hanging. This is also glass," I said and tapped the ampule with a fingernail.

"The shards lacerate the mucous membranes of the mouth and assist in the absorption of the cyanide," I continued, explaining how Göring took three cyanide capsules to jail because he anticipated what was coming. The first he hid in a jar of ointment. The second he kept in his sock during the trial in case he wasn't able to visit his cell after the judgment.

"The third ampule Göring hid poorly enough that the guards found it."

"Idiot."

"Clever. When the guards found the poorly concealed ampule, they believed they had robbed the prisoner of his opportunity to choose his own day to go. Afterwards they never looked again. Göring did it on purpose."

I showed the ampule to Veera, Mikko, and Elise in turn.

"This poison kills as quickly as it does in the movies. In the capsule is a solution of cyanide in water, hydrocyanic acid, also known as prussic acid. It halts cellular respiration and causes death almost instantly."

I placed the ampule between my front teeth. Carefully biting down, I removed my fingers.

"Oh my God! Stop it."

Talking without moving my teeth was difficult. I ordered everyone not to make me laugh. I could die if I did.

That made Veera laugh. Mikko was bewildered. Elise poured back her last drops of red wine.

I spat the ampule in my hand.

"You aren't getting rid of me that easily."

"Don't play with death."

"If life is a game, then why can't death be, too?"

"Could we talk about something else besides death?" Mikko asked.

"What are we talking about when we talk about death? We're talking about life! We talk about death so we can remember to live! People, dear friends, Veera, Elise, Mikko, this night is one of a kind. Let's live it like it's our last one on earth!"

As if by command, the servant appeared to pour the cognac.

*"Mein teurer Freund, nach deiner Art, nur vivere memento!"*

We slightly raised our snifters. Veera shoved hers out for a clink. This was a stylish breach of etiquette and fit our group nicely. We weren't stuck-up adults; we were childhood friends who made our own rules.

The evening was going wonderfully. My performance had stopped and reassured the party. I was in control. It was hard to remember when I had last been as satisfied as when Veera's cognac glass gave a solid chink against my own.

# Elise

THE BOTTLE HAD small breasts and wide hips.

Mikko asked, "Is this from your vineyard too?"

I said, "Now I don't have any room for dessert."

Veera said, "Thank you. That was good."

I said, "Let's have dessert later."

I said that to the servant.

Veera told the servant the food was good.

Robert said, "No, this is French."

I said, "Let's have a taste."

Robert raised his glass to a night that was one of a kind.

Veera said, "To a lovely evening!"

Veera clinked her glass against Robert's. I followed suit and toasted with Mikko. Soon all four glasses were touching.

Mikko said, "To a night that could change everything."

Veera asked, "What do you mean by that?"

Mikko said, "Just a toast."

Robert slapped Mikko on the shoulder. I imagined that they had done the same as young men.

Robert suggested that we go through to the library. It was the right time. The sun was just setting, and the library had the best views of the evening sky.

As we stood up, Mikko banged his knee on the table. Robert's glass capsule rolled across the tablecloth and onto the floor. Robert didn't notice the tinkling sound. The capsule didn't break.

The servant picked it up and placed it on the buffet beside the champagne sword.

The library was another world. Not another place—another time. We could travel a hundred years back in time with a few steps.

Robert had bought the furniture for the library from a gentlemen's club that had shut down because all of its members died.

That sounded like a valid reason for ending a club.

The bookshelves were dark wood and skillfully decorated by a carpenter. Sometimes I just sat in an armchair and traced the patterns. The small panes of the glass doors bent the light in crazy ways because they were so old and had lived so much. The backs of some of the books twisted, as if the viewer was tipsy.

The high-backed chair was from the same set as the bookcase. It had leather upholstery. The springs bounced nicely when you sat on it. The two couches and two other armchairs matched each other. They had hefty lines. As if Rubens had turned furniture designer. Sometimes I felt like I was sitting in the lap of an ample matron.

Between the bookshelves was a fireplace. A light burned in it. It looked like a perfectly real fireplace. There was a poker and a shovel.

The most attractive object in the room was the grandfather clock, which was tall, dark, and handsome. The dial was the face and the pendulum a tie. The clock had its own voice. Sometimes, when I was alone, I talked to it. It never argued. It just nodded: yes, yes, yes, yes.

Sometimes I jumped when the clock suddenly started chiming. Even though that shouldn't have been a surprise. The clock always rang at the top of the hour, and it kept perfect time because a clock surgeon had installed a new mechanism in its brain box.

The clock had just struck eight. Next it would strike nine. Then it would strike nine, even though we were only four. Or five, if you counted the servant.

The clock would be the strongest of all.

Mikko sat down on the couch on the foyer side and said, "That's a lot of books."

Veera said, "People remember the strangest things about books. Completely irrelevant things."

Mikko said, "Nothing is irrelevant. Otherwise the author wouldn't have written it."

Robert asked, "Who reads books all the way through anymore? You can open a book, read a bit, get some energy, ideas, impulses—whatever you want from it. Then you can close the book and put it back on the shelf."

Veera chose a book from the shelf. She read aloud. Like a bedtime story.

*"In the spring of 1917, when Doctor Richard Diver first arrived in Zurich, he was twenty-six years old, a fine age for a man, indeed the very acme of bachelorhood. Even in war-time days, it was a fine age for Dick, who was already too valuable, too much of a capital investment to be shot off in a gun."*

Mikko said, "You have some unique books."

Robert said, "There are Elise's books, too."

What Robert didn't say was that most of the books had come with the shelves.

I had the feeling a lot of people were leaving things unsaid this evening.

Robert asked, "Do you remember *Buddenbrooks*?"

Mikko said, "It has very clear capitalistic overtones. An artistic son destroys the family business. He is too sensitive and humane for it. He needed to be a hard-nosed social climber like the competing family's—what was their name?"

Robert said, "Kleinesohn . . . no . . . Schneider?"

Mikko said, "Yes, Schneider."

I thought the family's name was Hagenström. Maybe I remembered wrong.

Robert said, "That is definitely a well-founded way of reading

*Buddenbrooks*. But for me, I see *Buddenbrooks* through one particular scene. What is it? Is it the one where a loveless marriage that looks good on paper is arranged for Tony? When I read that, do I think, 'Money can never replace love?' Or is it the one where Consul Thomas Buddenbrooks decides to build a house—the moment when the Buddenbrook empire is at its greatest power and the book at its climax?"

Mikko said, "Of course the latter."

Robert said, "No, it's neither, and it also isn't the workers' uprising in Lübeck, or Tony's odyssey in Bavaria, or the word they avoid saying for so many pages. For me, the most important scene in *Buddenbrooks* is the death of old Jean Buddenbrook. What does he think in the moment before his death? Does he wonder whether he lived his life right? Did he make the right decisions in what he did and left undone?"

Veera said, "At the moment of death people usually think about pretty everyday things. Can they reach the call button? Will the nurse arrive in time? Will the pain end? If only the pain would end. Am I alive? Or, where is that urine bottle?"

I said, "In books people don't think about urine bottles. Books shield us from death."

Robert said, "I'm definitely not claiming that when Thomas Mann was writing *Buddenbrooks* he was thinking anything like that or that Jean Buddenbrook would have thought that way. I think the whole novel is condensed in that one scene."

Mikko said, "You're doing violence to the book."

Robert said, "Since I bought the book, it's my property and I can do whatever I want to it."

Mikko said, "You're destroying your own reading experience. The author has created a polyphonic score that you're destroying by reading it randomly."

Robert said, "Books are handy precisely because you can open them at random."

Mikko said, "You don't understand the details if you don't understand the overall picture."

Robert said, "Life is details, not overall pictures."

I said, "Life is dying. Death is the teleological purpose of life."

I made it to the end of that difficult word without stuttering.

# Veera

THE BOOKCASE WASN'T designed for browsing. I opened the glass doors and flipped through books at random. They were in various languages, business books the size of floor tiles and worn-out paperbacks, old and new all in a jumble. Apparently the servant's duties did not include organizing the books.

There was a copy of *Buddenbrooks*. The glued binding crackled. At least the pages weren't stuck together.

"Hey, should we start the sauna heating?" Rob asked.

Pulling out his phone from the breast pocket of his jacket, Rob tapped, growled, and then pressed a button, seeming satisfied. Of course it would have been too much bother to go turn on the sauna heater himself.

"This heater is pretty powerful. We'll be able to start in fifteen minutes. Who wants to go first?"

"Won't we all fit?"

"It's actually a bit small," Rob said. "You can imagine how hard it was to get in here at all . . . "

"Yeah, and this will actually be safer. We'll all be alive tomorrow," I said.

In plain Finnish, Rob's glance said, *What the fuck are you doing bringing up old shit like that?*

Elise asked what we were talking about.

"One of our old friends."

At the time were weren't old but we also didn't think we were young anymore. It was almost graduation, and we had just received our college entrance exam results. Rob had rented a cabin in the woods for the weekend before graduation. I don't know why that ever occurred to him—Rob wasn't a cabin-in-the-woods kind of guy. The plan was to do the traditional cabin thing, so we loaded the back of Rob's car with a grill, a bag of charcoal, sausages, and some other grillables. The name of the game was clear: Time to get drunk because tomorrow we don't have to get up for anything.

The boys set up the grill and debated like they always did. Maarit and I made hamburger patties and salad so we didn't have to live on sausages alone. From the beginning everyone was operating on the assumption that this party was going to be neither tasteful nor refined. The music was loud, and we played drinking games to get our blood alcohol levels up. Not only was this the fastest way, it was also perfectly respectable for straight-A students like us. We weren't boozing, we were playing games! Intoxication wasn't the ostensible goal, simply a result of acting according to accepted norms.

That was how Mikko put it, and I've never seen him as drunk as that. Nowadays Mikko bought a 24-case every twelve weeks at Lidl and drank two each Saturday during sauna: one between sessions and another afterwards while we were watching the ten-o'clock news.

After food the boys went to heat the sauna. Maarit and I dumped the paper plates in the trash and talked about our boys. Maarit said she was happy, and I didn't doubt it. Rob took good care of Maarit. Sometimes I was jealous because Mikko didn't act like that. I had to make the first move, and it was still awkward.

I said I loved Mikko.

"Is Mikko . . . good?" Maarit asked.

"There isn't anyone better."

Rob came from the sauna and said that the previous occupant had used the stove wrong and now they couldn't get it lit. Mikko followed him and suggested that instead of sauna we go rowing. He had read some directions left on the mantle and memorized the route on the map to the dock half a kilometer away.

I popped the top on another beer and marched past the boys into the sauna. Little twigs lay in a messy pile in the firebox with burned paper ash all around. The damper was almost closed. Taking out the kindling, I shook the extra ash down into the pan. With the kindling I built a log cabin and then put some crumpled newspaper in the middle. Finally, I ripped some dry bark from the birch firewood and sprinkled little bits on top. I opened the damper as wide as it would go.

There were only two matches left in the box, but one was enough. The flame caught the newspaper, setting the bark on fire, which licked the kindling until it also burned with tall yellow flames. I added some small birch logs. Hot air hummed in the flue.

"Oh, so we can sauna?"

"How did you do it?" Rob asked.

"It was almost ready. I just had to put on some finishing touches."

Maarit made me a sauna champion medal out of bottle caps.

We all fit on the top bench. We sang Finnish pop songs. Mikko was surprisingly good at the eighties ones. The lake was a good walk away, and the water would be cold, so we just cooled off on the deck. No one was up for any more sausage. And no one wanted to play strip poker either, so we started a game of couples Trivial Pursuit. Mikko knew the answers but Rob knew the questions. We agreed that the game was a draw.

After sauna we had to help Maarit walk. The evening was calm and bright. Maarit wanted to go rowing. With me. I wouldn't have let her go with the others.

We walked barefoot along the forest path to the boat. Maarit thought we should wear life jackets. We didn't have any other clothes.

I sat Maarit in the back and told her to hold on to the sides while I pushed the boat into the water and jumped in. I banged my knee on the end of an oar. My curse echoed across the still water.

Once I had us out past the reeds and turned the boat, Maarit admitted that she was a virgin. We defined what she meant by that. The words were difficult for Maarit and she giggled after each sentence. There had been groping and hand jobs.

"Have you taken him in your mouth?"

"Yeah."

"I guessed."

"From what?"

"I can imagine Rob wanting a girl on her knees in front of him."

Maarit got embarrassed. I apologized. I didn't realize until the next morning that Rob did have an overriding purpose for arranging the trip to the cabin. Their first intercourse was supposed to happen here. And Maarit knew it too.

"What is Mikko like?"

"Mikko is sweet."

"I mean in bed."

"I like how awkward he is. That's my Mikko."

I said that Mikko liked to guide it in with his hand so it wouldn't go in the wrong hole.

That made Maarit laugh, but it also scared her. I comforted her, saying that Rob would be even more nervous.

"You can be the helpless maiden in the tower, but Rob has to be the knight who knows how to do everything."

Maarit watched the swans who had parked themselves next to the reeds. Everything was perfectly still. I realized that our conversation could have been heard at every cabin along the shore.

"Rob has probably been with other girls before," I said.

"Probably."

Maarit was contemplative. I rowed to shore. The night was

cooling quickly. We visited the sauna to warm up again before going inside.

"How was the lake?"

"We saw some swans."

Mikko started singing "Swan Song," another eighties Finnish pop song, accentuating his vibrato to make it ooze pathos. We sang until we went to sleep. In the morning we compared our memories of the previous night and then started again. We would have even more to remember the following morning.

# Mikko

AFTER THE WOMEN went to the sauna, Robert wanted to show off his office.

The exterior wall was all windows, with the City of London rising beyond. Rising—but not reaching the level of Robert's apartment even though the cranes continued piling additional stories on the skyscrapers of the opposite bank.

"Big savings with no need for drapes."

The smoked glass desk was parallel with the wall of windows, with Robert's chair behind it. He turned his back on the City and the view he paid millions for, but I was sure that he often rotated his chair to behold what he had achieved. Off by itself next to the window was a leather chair standing with open arms. Probably a Mies van der Rohe. I sat down in it.

Robert woke up the computer by wiggling the mouse. Typing in his password, he gazed for a moment at the three LCD monitors that dominated the desk.

We were alone. It was time to increase the probabilities.

I dried the sweaty creases of my fingers on my jeans. Inserting my thumb in my front pocket, I felt the packet of strychnine. I had to get Robert to swallow it. Even a small amount would be enough to kill.

"This is where you listen to the music of the markets," I said.

Robert disagreed. "The markets don't make music. They convey information. Information helps us make correct decisions and target resources."

Robert was brazen in his defense of the night-watchman state. He questioned public health care ("people would take better care of their teeth if filling their cavities didn't just result in fifteen minutes of drilling but also an economic sanction"), social insurance ("people would use safety harnesses on construction scaffolding without regulatory requirements if the result of falling wasn't three months of guaranteed paid leave—that practically invites accidents") and free higher education ("university students should understand that their schooling is an enormous sacrifice for society, with them receiving the lion's share of the benefits, which doesn't sound terribly fair from the perspective of all the cleaners and auto mechanics"). His message was clear: the market solves all problems. It even clears blocked nasal passages and makes German pop songs tolerable listening.

I reminded him that unregulated markets had been tried in many industries with poor results.

"And good results," Robert said and asked why I hated the free market. What evil had it ever done to me? Why did I vilify the market when it was just another human activity?

I said I thought it looked pretty inhumane. Almost as inhumane as a host sitting his guest down without a drink.

Robert apologized profusely as if I were a millionaire client and asked if cognac would suffice or whether we should move on to something else. I assured him that cognac would be perfectly satisfactory.

Of course it was all the same what Robert served just so long as he brought something for himself I could mix the strychnine into. Strychnine dissolves poorly, but the amount needed to induce death was so small that Robert wouldn't notice it. Of course in terms of covering the taste of the poison it would be good if the drink had a strong flavor of its own.

Robert left. I looked around. What could be the trick to get Robert's attention focused somewhere else while I placed the poison in his glass? The room was sparsely decorated. Next to my chair was a small round table. On the wall facing the window hung a Cubist painting. Next to the door was a squat safe and a coat rack from which hung a single necktie. Otherwise everything was focused on Robert's enormous desk.

If I asked Robert to show me the view, I would have to stand next to him and pretend to be interested. I wouldn't be able to get at his glass. Same with the painting.

"A company is its owners," Robert said when he returned. Between the fingers of his right hand he held two cognac glasses. "Ultimately they are people."

"A company is workers, machines, raw materials, and products," I said and watched him set his glass down carelessly next to his mousepad as he sat.

*The safe.* How could I get Robert to look for something in the safe? What did he store there? Securities were all digital now. Did Robert keep a list of passwords locked up? Real estate contracts? Champagne recovered from the shipwreck of the *Jönköping*? Spare keys to his car and summer house?

*We just got new Abloy locks for our doors at home. I think Finland has better lock systems than the rest of Europe. Should we compare keys?*

Wouldn't work.

"No way. A company is the physical manifestation of its owners' will. If the owners of Coca-Cola suddenly decided that the company was giving up colored soft drinks and started making car tires, that's what it would do."

"And the workers would be fired?"

I sipped my cognac. Robert did the same and placed his glass back in the same place from which he had taken it. I wouldn't be able to get at it.

"Probably," Robert said, leaning back in his chair and turning himself toward the window effortlessly. "The workers manifest the will of the owners of the company, which is transmitted through the board and executive leadership, and if they don't, they don't have to be paid. I think that's pretty simple. Just as simple as the fact that if the company doesn't carry out the will of an owner, that owner will relinquish his ownership. And that can be handled in a fraction of a second. So the owners of companies are always in agreement about the direction of those companies. Votes aren't necessary at shareholder meetings because the owners who don't agree have already left. If there has to be a vote at a shareholder meeting, the board should be dissolved immediately. A board that has to hold votes is not viable."

Robert then extended this idea to nations whose parliaments were constantly voting. I pointed out that diversity of opinion was the cornerstone of democracy.

"Leaving a country is much more difficult than selling stocks, but it is getting easier all the time. Increasing language skills, good communications and transportation infrastructure, the changing nature of work—people have the freedom to choose where they live."

Robert sprang up and walked to the safe.

My chance had come with so little warning that I lost a few seconds before I realized I should act. As Robert punched the code into the door of the safe, I snuck over to his desk. The cognac glass stood aristocratically on the transparent surface. Next to it on the mousepad, a bull charge with its horns up. *Bull market.*

When I pulled out the packet of strychnine, my elbow banged the desk lamp.

The noise made Robert turn around. Pushing the packet back into my pocket, I left my thumb hanging on the edge of the pocket as if I were leaning casually.

I explained that I wanted to look at the mouse pad. "Nice picture."

"It's from Barcelona," Robert said and shoved the safe door with his foot before slapping down two burgundy colored passports on the desk. One of them was from Great Britain, and on the other a Finnish lion roared with sword raised overhead.

The serious expression in the pictures was the same, even though the photos were from different years.

"These are what you need," Robert said as if the passports were entry tickets. And so they were for him. "Dual citizenship is easy to get."

Returning to my chair, I verified that the pouch of poison was completely concealed.

"Maybe families of the future will decide how many public services they want to buy from their country and what kind of tax structure they support. Maybe there will be more Monacos and more Swedens," Robert said.

I asked how the Swedens would collect their tax revenues if all the highest earners moved away.

Robert said that was precisely the question that every voter—including me—should consider in the next parliamentary elections. He compared the situation to corporate taxation ("on that side things have developed faster"): nations compete by lowering corporate taxes and improving conditions for generating profits.

"Within a decade nations will begin competing for good tax payers in the same way they compete for businesses now."

Robert asked if I wanted another and pointed to my glass, which to my surprise was empty.

Without waiting for an answer, he left.

When his footsteps were far enough away, I opened the strychnine pouch. A dash of cognac remained in Robert's glass. I drained it before sprinkling in the powder. Then I sprinkled in some more.

The white powder was inconspicuous but deadly.

Closing the bag, I shoved it back in my jeans pocket. I had

reserved enough strychnine for several doses—probabilities don't always play out.

When I heard Robert returning, I calmly sat down in my designer chair and looked at Norman Foster's Swiss Re skyscraper, now known as the Gherkin, which hadn't belonged to the Swiss reinsurance company for ages. I followed the black lines that spiraled up the building like tinsel strands on a Christmas tree.

We would have time for one more conversation.

# Elise

THE BATHROOM WAS bright. The tile sparkled. I could see my reflection in it. I was a princess. I tried to remember who had said that, but it was hard. Had it been Mikko? But wasn't Veera Mikko's princess?

I asked Veera, "Are you Mikko's princess?"

Veera laughed. Veera was happy too. We were both happy. What lucky girls!

Veera laughed again. Words escaped between laughs: "Mikko only says 'princess' ironically."

I wondered whether that was true. Maybe it wasn't.

I poured Finlandia vodka into tall glasses. Quite a lot came out because we were so patriotic. There was still room for juice though. Alcohol is like ice cream. Ice cream fills in the spaces in the food in your stomach. Alcohol fills in the spaces in juice. It's chemistry. Or physics.

Veera said, "To friendship!"

We touched glasses.

I said, "To cooperation!"

We drank.

Veera said, "To aiding and abetting!"

We laughed. Our glasses emptied. We went in the sauna. It was small but warm. Like a human heart.

That sounded like a bad pop song. Life is a bad pop song.

The stove was smooth and black, just like a flat-screen TV.

I threw water on the rock. My aim was pretty good. The floor was tile. Under it was waterproofing. It didn't matter even if you missed the rock. In life you miss sometimes.

The light in the sauna was under the benches. It was like moonbeams. But it couldn't be the moon, because the moon doesn't illuminate. The moon only reflects the light of the sun.

The moon is like a person.

Veera raised her feet onto the upper bench. So did I. Our toes touched each other. Veera had painted her toenails bright red. So had I.

We could have been best friends. Getting to know people was easy for me. And it did me good. The smile you send out into the world comes back to you. A person is like the sun.

Veera asked me to tell about myself. Occasionally we threw more water on the rocks. Our big toes rested against each other. It was nice. We were a little like one person. If an ant would have started walking at Veera's neck, it could have walked all the way to my neck without leaving skin.

Yikes. I brushed my neck. There wasn't an ant on it.

Veera went out to cool off. It was quite hot now. I went after her. We didn't have a room with a fireplace. The apartment was so small. The bathroom was big. Silly. How can a bathroom be big if an apartment is small?

I stepped onto the lower bench. It wasn't straight. Or maybe it was straight but the world was tilted. Oops. I lurched. Veera turned around. I fell against her bare skin.

Sweat squelched.

Veera held me up. She was a strong woman.

Veera said, "You I haven't been with yet."

I asked: "Do you want to be with me?"

Veera said, "No, no. It was a joke."

For me it wouldn't have been a problem.

Veera said, "Those last shots were strong enough we should probably slow down."

I asked, "Should I ask the servant to bring more orange juice?"

Veera asked, "Is there beer?"

Veera steadied herself on the wall, and her necklace tinkled against the tile. It made a happy sound. I hummed along a little.

*AT FRANZ-JOSEF-STRAUSS IN Munich, the passengers leaving on the morning flights were too tired to buy anything but coffee and triangle sandwiches. The travelers disembarking the arriving planes didn't pause as they marched quickly to the baggage carousels.*

*He was an exception. Rolling his suitcase behind, he walked to an electronics store located on the international side of the security checkpoint.*

*"Excuse me."*

*The young man behind the glass display case was listening to music on black earbuds so loudly that the noise floated around him. The clerk was focused on his computer, so he had to knock on the counter before he gained the young man's attention.*

*"Could I have an iPad like that?" he asked in English and pointed at an advertisement on the wall.*

*The clerk took the key to the display case out of the register drawer and retrieved the device.*

*"Don't you want to try it first?" the clerk asked when he offered his credit card.*

*He didn't. He just wanted the device. The clerk explained that he couldn't sell the display model. He had to get an unopened one from the stock room.*

*"Do you want it with 4G? Sixteen or sixty-four gig memory?"*

*He wanted the best model. There was plenty of room on the credit card, and he wasn't going to be able to use it after this anyway.*

*"Would you like to set up a wireless account? You can take a SIM card now and the device will be fully functional."*

*"Yes, please."*

*"Can I have your ID card?"*

*"Can't I get a prepaid account?"*

*"We only have monthly accounts available. You must have a passport or driver's license since you're coming from a flight."*

*"Let's not bother right now."*

# Robert

MIKKO BLAMED THE markets even though he should have blamed people. Markets only conveyed information. They didn't have opinions.

"You say that markets are immoral, but that's not quite right. They're amoral. Markets have no morality because markets neither think nor feel. Markets just are," I said.

I gave him an example: a man who grows aspen trees, a specialty tree farmer. Even though his wood gets used in all sorts of products, he doesn't have to watch the news in the matchstick industry or the ups and downs of sauna bench manufacturing. All he has to keep track of are the cash and futures prices of aspen. He doesn't even need to know whether the price has risen because of increased demand or some other reason. All that matters to him is that the price is now higher than before and appears to be staying high in futures quotes, so he should buy more land and plant more saplings. What matters is the price now and the price tomorrow.

"So the euro is the measure of everything," Mikko said with disdain, but he seemed perfectly content to drink distilled alcohol that had been aged for years and then purchased from capitalist markets by capitalist means.

The communist leaders of the Soviet Union and the party bosses in North Korea seemed to have refined beverage tastes, too. Everyone did who was able to buy them. The communists distributed their champagne and cognac through a system of hierarchy.

Markets created opportunities for whoever was smartest and most talented. Which was a fairer way of deciding whose snifters would be filled with minimum-six-year brandy? The choice had to be made somehow. If all the world's XO cognac was divided equally, would anyone even get enough to wet their tongue?

I raised my glass. I let the golden brown liquid rise and flow over the inner rim.

The warmth was pleasant. It was Richard Hennessy, which I didn't serve to just anyone. The price of fine cognac had gone up faster than the value of gold in recent years as a result of China's demand for higher quality. As long as the elites in the developing markets continued amassing wealth, my small alcohol collection would continue churning out money with little risk.

I asked Mikko if he didn't think effort should be rewarded. If I weren't rewarded, why would I try? Why would anyone try? Why would anyone have ever tried? I reminded him that not only the middle class but also the poor were better off now in absolute terms than kings had been a few centuries ago.

"You're proud of your achievements," Mikko said. Or maybe it was a question.

I acknowledged that I was. Above all I had freedom. I had the freedom to act or not to act. I also had the freedom to do good. I was quite sure that I donated more annually to charity than Mikko had in his entire life. Didn't that show that I wasn't completely selfish, as Mikko seemed to think I was?

Not according to Mikko.

"You always think of yourself first and then about the bigger picture. Even if the slight benefit to you from a decision is outweighed by significant losses for the rest of society, you will still make it."

Mikko brought up the example of the LIBOR maneuver. Finally.

I was prepared to answer this. I made it clear that what I was going to say was deep background. This wouldn't be an interview, and nothing I said could be used against me.

I took the motion of Mikko's head as a nod.

"We're friends," Mikko said.

I explained that I couldn't have acted any differently. I worked for Union Credit and as such, I represented the incarnation of the will of the bank shareholders. They had expressed their will with very clear economic goals. My task was to maximize the quarterly profit of my division.

"With greed," Mikko said.

"Just so."

I did a hell of a job. We exceeded our budgeted EBIT in eight consecutive quarters. The analysts following Union Credit made our unit the centerpiece of their reports and gave us higher multipliers than the competition in their valuations because we had a proven track record.

"You could reasonably ask whether it was worth it for us to start manipulating the LIBOR. I've calculated it. The answer is unequivocal. Yes, it was absolutely worth it."

"It was worth committing fraud? Getting caught? Being forced to pay fines? Sending your share price into a nosedive? Getting fired?"

"Yes. At the parent company level, we can determine with reasonable accuracy what the net benefits were from the cheap LIBOR value. On the other side, we know what the direct sanctions were, and we can also make some estimates about the short and long-term client losses and discount their value. Then there are some smaller factors, including performance bonuses paid to Union Credit employees through our incentive system."

"All together, the sanctions, client losses, and bonuses are slightly larger than the benefits reaped by Union Credit. So it definitely wasn't worth it. Right? Wrong! You shouldn't just look at the end result. What I ask myself is whether I would initiate a similar maneuver now. The answer is always just as unequivocal.

Yes, I would. The probability of getting caught is five percent at most. The expected value of the maneuver was clearly positive. We just had bad luck that we were exposed."

I took a deliberate pause. Effective speech is made up of the pauses between the words. This was also training. When the headhunters started sending me invitations, I would deliver the same presentation to them. I would make them drool like bulldogs.

A sip of cognac gave a good excuse for the pause. At the same time, I moved my previous glass between the monitors so I wouldn't bump it while using my hands to emphasize my words.

"When the manipulation came out, Union Credit's market value fell by one fifth. That was unfortunate for the stock holders who had purchased just before the bank regulators' announcement. The stock price is still lower than it was then. So, what's happened? Our anchor investors have bought even more! Their investments seem even better if you look at the derivatives market. Our three largest shareholders went short about a year ago when the company's share price was at its all-time high."

"They knew!"

"How could they have known? And if they knew, what should they have done? Just wait? In today's regulated markets, nonpublic information is such a rare delicacy that if you can get it, you should immediately use it to your advantage. And besides, if they already knew what we knew, they couldn't know that we would get caught. Or if they knew that, too, they would have had to figure it out somehow. And that sounds like work, and isn't it normal to receive compensation for work? To me it looks like it was worth it from everyone's perspective that we manipulated things a little bit."

I moved my passport to the corner of the desk.

"Everyone's perspective except the majority's," Mikko said.

I pointed out that the losses were spread out over such a large group of investors that they didn't matter. "No one has gone bankrupt over the collapse of Union Credit's stock or the LIBOR rate. Or if they did, they weren't looking after their risk management."

"You got to leave."

"I forgot all about myself. Maybe I'm not so selfish after all since I was thinking of others more than myself."

Mikko sat in my guest chair with his lips pursed. I thought about when I had seen Mikko smile, when I had heard him laugh. How many times in the past twenty years?

"Who likes remembering being fired? You were fired, right?" Mikko said.

"Yes, of course! The official documents included all sorts of official sounding language. That was a must. We had to calm the markets. Of course my severance package is a private matter with the company, but between the two of us, I can say that the number had seven digits. Which was insignificant compared to how much Union Credit's market value increased when my departure was announced. The market mechanism demonstrated that it works. Corporate executives don't have many legal protections, so we have to have contractual insurance against arbitrary decisions."

Mikko said that the episode I had described was a good example of why banking regulation should be tightened and sanctions increased. That kind of gaming of the system shouldn't be possible.

His speech was oddly slow. The intoxication wasn't making Mikko boisterous, it was making him tired. Still Mikko asked if there was any cognac left. "We can drink the rest out of these glasses," he said.

I stood up. The bottle was in the library bar cabinet and wasn't even half empty.

"Why do markets have to be based on greed?" Mikko asked, staring straight ahead.

"Markets are based on humanity," I responded over my shoulder from the door.

# Veera

THE SERVANT BROUGHT pint bottles of Danish beer. There was no opener. I figured it would leave a mark if I tried to open it on the sink edge, or on the soft teak of the benches.

Then I remembered Rob's Champagne sword. My feet left half-moons on the hardwood floor. The boys were talking loudly in Rob's office.

The sword was still on the side table. Next to it was Rob's bluish ampule. I wondered if it was real. Maybe someone had just capsulized caramel-colored water and sold it to gullible buyers at a high price. Who was going to authenticate the product in a sale like that?

I certainly wasn't going to test it. And I didn't pick it up, either. I was naked after all. Where would I have hidden it—in there? Or was that more a Number Two sort of job? At that point I didn't have the slightest inkling I would have to go looking for it in Rob's safe later in the evening. That early I didn't have any intention of killing anyone. Why would I have taken the ampule?

The sword was heavier than I had imagined. The dark brown blood stain was still visible on the blade.

I took a practice swipe in the air. I saw my reflection in the window. Not exactly Uma Thurman. Before going back in the bathroom, I had a little practice bout with the suit of armor.

Elise set a beer bottle on the shower grate. That was the most level spot.

I counted to three. And swung.

The sword swished past the bottle and banged against the wall.

The next stroke I aimed more carefully. The bottle broke at the shoulder, and it didn't spray like Champagne. Warm, well-shaken beer might have worked. Some of the glass shards had fallen inside the bottle, so I threw the glass in the trash and then dropped the bottle in after.

Elise had found a swag bottle opener somewhere. With a practiced flick of the wrist, I opened the other bottle. I offered it to Elise.

"I'm good with this," Elise said and poured more vodka in her glass.

That woman was a sponge. I had at least ten kilos on her and a lot of it was muscle—I did Body Combat classes twice a week—and my liver wasn't exactly a novice distillery, but I was starting to feel the drunkenness. Opening a beer bottle with a saber may not have been the first thing to come to mind if I had been sober.

We went into the sauna again. I compared Elise's pert D cups to the post-nursing boobs I was carrying. I wondered what a body like hers cost and who had paid for it. There were long red marks on her back and sides that had been covered with makeup. At that point I didn't think about them much, but of course they were the result of Rob and Elise's bedroom sessions.

Elise had a Brazilian wax. Did Rob like it bald? I could definitely do that too!

If someone had asked me what Elise's story was, I would have guessed she was a girl who had met an English boy during a language course and then followed him to Britain. That she liked drinking more than eating. She was beautiful, not your run-of-the-mill whore you could fit three of in the backseat of your Toyota. Her body didn't show the effects of street walking or shagging on sperm-stained mattresses.

She was pretty even without the improvements.

Since she didn't ask me, I asked her.

Elise said she had come to Oxford to study law. She has specialized in finance and gone to work at a firm whose name didn't say anything to me but apparently said a lot to the people it was supposed to say something to, because Union Credit was one of its clients. She had been offered a permanent position. She liked London, and her responsibility and salary had grown.

I didn't believe a word of it.

"You aren't doing that anymore?"

Elise said she had had enough. The office had moved, and the café downstairs didn't sell the cute little cakes she was used to getting when she had to work after hours. And her new boss wasn't as nice as the old one had been.

Elise was beautiful. That is if you like that sort of thing. Rob happened to, but I still thought it was odd that Rob had gotten mixed up with a high-class whore like this.

Elise threw more water on the rocks. Every third ladleful actually hit the soapstone stove. It hissed.

We drank vodka, which didn't taste like anything anymore.

Rob lived a nice life, but I wouldn't have wanted it. I just wanted Mikko. Mikko, who jogged the same route every Saturday morning and then carefully watched the sauna firebox as it heated to make sure there was enough wood but not too much, checking the realty company swag thermometer as if it were the instrument panel of a car.

I didn't want an easy life. I wanted a full life.

I poured more for Elise and myself, and we said *skol*. I asked what Elise wanted to sing.

"'Heroes.' Not David Bowie, J. Karjalainen."

When we finished, we looked each other in the eyes and hugged like hockey fans whose team just won the world championship.

When Elise moved past me to shower, she steadied herself on my thigh and squeezed.

I threw more water on the hot stone until the tips of my ears burned. Through the glass door of the sauna, I watched as water ran across Elise's lithe skin.

In the bathroom cabinet I found scissors, which I used to trim my bush. I finished the job with Rob's razor. The Gillette gel left a manly scent.

I wondered how I would explain the stubble to Mikko the next Saturday.

If Mikko even noticed.

I checked my new look in the bathroom mirror. Okay, well maybe this was one of those things you just had to try once in your life.

When I returned the razor to the cabinet, a bottle of pills fell out into the sink. It shook like a maraca. I didn't recognize the brand, but it seemed to be diazepam. A twenty-five tablet bottle at ten milligrams—the most powerful you could get from the pharmacy. The bottle didn't have a prescription sticker. Which of them suffered from anxiety? Did Elise have an alcohol problem? Or did Rob? Or had the pills been prescribed for insomnia?

While I was there, I checked what else was in the cabinet. The women's products were on one side and the men's on the other. Expensive-looking creams, nail scissors and clippers, probiotics, pills for headache, diarrhea, and exhaustion, two gels for muscle pain.

The bottle had fallen from the men's product side, so the pills were Rob's. Nothing about that was surprising. More surprising would have been if Rob hadn't suffered from any psychiatric issues. I had a hard time imagining him depressed, but that didn't prove anything. I'd seen plenty of guys who kept themselves going in public by popping pills at home.

As I put the diazepam bottle back, what I thought was a pretty clever practical joke came to mind. Emptying the diazepam into my hand, I grabbed the one with caffeine tablets from the other end of the row of bottles. I dumped the contents of this into my other hand. The diazepam went back in the caffeine bottle and the caffeine in the diazepam.

The next time Rob went fumbling for his sleep in a bottle, he was going to get an invigorating surprise.

# Mikko

I SAW ELISE in the lobby of the Kämp Hotel on the 25th of November, and after then nothing was the same. Today was the culmination of what had started there that day.

Elise had been wearing a white evening gown. She was on her way to an art auction arranged by a charity Robert supported. Elise had begun a cautious return to working life by helping out their foundation.

She was beautiful, so beautiful that I had never seen anything like her. All the women I had ever compared Veera to in hotel restaurants and swimming pools were mere moths next to Elise. Elise was a butterfly. With her shy smile, she wasn't a girl but she also didn't have the cynicism of a world-worn adult. She was descending the stairs from the second floor as I put my pen and notepad back in my shoulder bag. I had been interviewing a former board member of an American investment bank and had stayed behind to pay my bill and arrange my notes. Seeing Elise blinded me.

She looked straight at me and smiled.

Then she walked over to me.

"Are you Mikko?" she asked.

Stammering, I replied that I was and asked who she was.

"I've seen a lot of pictures of you. You're always twenty years younger, though. I'm Elise. You know my husband, Robert."

The thought didn't even cross my mind that the woman

standing in front of me dressed in pearl white might have been some sort of nutcase. Occasionally I'd been accosted and had to alert the police. I didn't consider that possible. I wouldn't have even if I had been capable of thought.

I asked how long she was in Helsinki, and said I'd be happy to chat if she had time. Elise gave me her embossed calling card, and I gave her my own more modest one. We arranged to meet the following evening in the same place.

That night I had to go out for a run. My pulse raced even though my legs felt weak. I slipped on a muddy, leaf-strewn path. I ran past intersections where I had turned hundreds of times before. Veera asked if I'd received some sort of shocking news. I said I couldn't talk about work, and she didn't ask any further.

The next day I went to the Kämp well in advance, but Elise was already there and had ordered me a gin and tonic.

Elise told me about herself, her work, and about Robert. She had moved to England to study law. Finance was her specialty, and she had landed a job in one of the more prestigious law firms. More responsibility came quickly, and when one of her colleagues defected to the competition, her work load doubled. Delicate young woman that she was, she had buckled under the load.

"Robert saved me," Elise said, but I knew she meant precisely the opposite. Elise was sick, open to manipulation, and without a job. In this helpless state, she had been an easy target for Robert. Just looking at her it was obvious Robert was keeping her drugged.

Elise was silently screaming for help. She asked that I speak to Robert, because Robert might listen to me. I asked what she hoped I would talk to him about.

"About our contract," Elise replied.

Her words were disjointed and ambiguous, as if she were afraid to tell the truth, but I understood enough to know that she wanted to get away from Robert. But a divorce would leave her out in the cold financially. She still wasn't able to work, and it wouldn't be easy for her to return to law—in order to succeed as a lawyer, you had to be strong, but Elise was weak. Elise hoped that I could negotiate with Robert to protect her.

That wasn't at all unreasonable. It was brutish of Robert not to do it on his own initiative. Robert had bought her. Robert was holding her hostage!

I had to save Elise.

But first Elise saved me.

I hadn't been able to eat all day. I was poorly hydrated too, and by the time I started my second gin and tonic, I was already dizzy. I tried to take deep breaths, but it didn't help. In the lobby was a noisy flock of Germans whose voices transformed into the outlines of multicolored feathers.

Before my eyes they slowly melted from the ceiling to the floor.

When I came to, I was resting on the right side of a queen size bed between the sheets. The room was beige and everything looked expensive. Elise had removed my jacket and shirt, loosened my belt, and opened the button of my trousers.

The mirror frame was decorative, and the fabrics heavy. The energy efficient light bulb peeking out from under the lampshade appeared to be trapped in the wrong century. The room had to be one of the hotel suites.

Elise put an enormous wine glass to my lips and gave me uncarbonated mineral water to drink.

Whenever I cracked my eyes, I quickly closed them again so I wouldn't wake up.

"Easy," Elise said. Stay calm."

"What happened to me?"

"Everything is fine. Would you like a caramel?"

Sucking on the soft candy, I absorbed carbohydrates through the membranes of my mouth. I breathed carefully.

Elise moved me into a half-sitting position with a fancy decorative pillow and pressed her hand to my forehead. She had switched her evening gown for an oversized dress shirt. When she leaned over me, her cleavage came near my face, and her lower stomach brushed my side.

I closed my eyes, trying to keep my breathing steady.

I had taken a first aid class, so in theory I knew what to do. This was the first time I had ever been in the situation of being the one in need rather than the helper calmly giving instructions.

"Keep your eyes open," Elise said. "Don't pass out again. You have to relax."

My memories of that evening are fuzzy. I don't have any watertight evidence of all of the events, but this is how I remember them proceeding.

With one smooth motion, Elise grabbed my underwear and pulled it to my ankles, barely touching the bottoms of my feet on the way to my toes, from there to the sheet, and then dropping them to the carpeted floor.

Only the reading lamp was burning, and the shadows moved slowly on the wall, Elise on top of me.

I relaxed, and I didn't think that there was anything wrong with anything.

It was past midnight when I climbed into a taxi outside the hotel. Nodding off in the back seat of the black BMW, I thought about each and every one of the past twenty years. I thought about what I had gained and lost, but before my thoughts were complete, the taxi driver turned around between the seats and said, "Twenty-four thirty."

I brushed my teeth in the small bathroom downstairs. The motion of the toothbrush kept pausing as I repeated words out loud so I could hear my thoughts.

I tried to remember the night. Individual moments were all my mind could extract.

There had been red marks along the sides of Elise's naked body and on her back. She said she got them in Hungary, where they had been riding and she had fallen from a horse. It was a lie. They were marks left by a whip. Who else could have caused them but Robert?

*Squeezing . . . my neck . . . too tight . . .*

Elise's confused, tired words echoed in my head, even though I scrubbed my teeth vigorously. I had to free Elise. And talking sense wasn't going to be enough. Robert was a violent, insane sadist!

Veera slept on her side of the bed, nearer the window. I crept onto my own side, careful not to disturb the sheets. Still Veera woke up.

"Fun evening?" she asked.

"I won't know the importance of the information I received until later."

"You're so funny," Veera said and stroked my cheek. Her hand was safe and gentle, and the touch of her fingers communicated love.

Responding in kind was difficult. As it had always been.

"Good night," Veera said and turned over.

"Good night."

Immediately her breathing slowed. Next to me slept Veera, my faithful Veera, with whom I had grown accustomed to living.

I stayed up and tried to analyze what I knew was impossible to analyze.

# Robert

ELISE KNOCKED ON the door and yelled that the sauna was free. Taking off my watch, I set it on my desk and then hung my coat on a hanger.

"Let's go see if they remembered to open the vent!"

I grabbed Mikko by the shoulder. He snapped awake.

When I had returned with the bottle of cognac, I had found Mikko sleeping in his chair with his head resting on his shoulder. He had his hands shoved in the front pockets of his jeans. His expression was satisfied, blissful. I laughed to myself.

I was a little jealous of Mikko.

As I watched my friend muttering in his sleep, I imagined him tomorrow sitting hunched over his computer at home like a gorilla typing out an article using the information I had just given him. Of course Mikko would use all of it. At some point he would probably even make some obscure allusion to my apartment—something that only he and I would know meant the whole diatribe was directed against me. Otherwise he wouldn't be a journalist. Otherwise he wouldn't be human.

That was why I hadn't told him everything. My method was to feign perverse honesty. I told him things a journalist wouldn't have known to ask. If it was interesting enough, his focus would stay there and he wouldn't be tempted to dig any deeper. Maybe he would even take it easy on me out of a sense of gratitude towards his anonymous source.

*Tell something secret but harmless to keep uncomfortable facts out of public view.* This was a dictum I had applied successfully many times.

I had expected Mikko would ask about the apartment. He could have ferreted out that the flat was owned by a Qatari industrialist—the whole building was controlled by the Qataris. So why would Elise and I be living here? I would have said that the Arab magnate had bought the apartment for his eldest son in case he moved to England to study, and we were just taking care of it until then. That could have sounded suspicious though. Especially because our landlord didn't have any children of his own. Mikko might have realized that Union Credit had significant Qatari clients, and if he would have looked into their investments during the financial crisis . . .

Mikko would have realized that I lived in the Shard because I had kept my mouth shut. And after discovering that, he would have left no stone unturned.

"Let's go to the sauna. Stand up carefully."

Mikko exhaled and bolted upright, which caused his foot to slip. I just managed to keep him standing.

"Careful now!"

Mikko wasn't in the habit of following instructions from me. I hadn't convinced Mikko to put his tongue on the metal pole of a rug drying rack when it was twenty degrees below outside by bossing or coaxing. Instead I told him that star-shaped ice crystals tasted like peppermint candies.

"They couldn't," Mikko argued.

"But they do," I said, and Mikko hadn't been able to prove he was right in any other way than by trying.

"Look, it's the menfolk!"

Veera was brushing her wet hair when we stepped into the foyer. I asked whether Elise hadn't shown her the hair dryer.

"Now I think it's time for a smoke!"

"You've started smoking?"

"I just feel like it now. Grab your coat and let's go get a pack."

From the set of Veera's jaw, I could tell that objections were futile. She had the same look of determination stockbrokers got after making their first eight-figure deal.

"For old time's sake," Veera hissed in my ear. I whispered back that there weren't any old times.

"Oh, go on," Mikko said. "We can sauna when you get back."

I asked Veera if she intended to change into something besides the baggy sweat pants and tank top she had put on after sauna. Veera said she always got hot when she smoked.

In the elevator I asked what she was up to.

"I'm sure you have a standing reservation at the hotel downstairs. How about we go there?"

We had to go all the way down and then back up in another elevator with a Japanese couple. Shielded from view by their enormous suitcases, Veera reached for my crotch.

"The sauna made me feel all nice and warm."

"I don't like this."

"Don't you like me, Rob?"

"Mikko and Elise . . . "

"Mikko and Elise are upstairs. I'm sure they'll be fine for the time it takes to smoke two cigarettes."

We spoke in tones we could have used discussing whether to watch the news tonight or the semifinals of a singing competition.

"This is the last time."

"Of course. Just like every time. The first and the last."

Veera moved closer and put her chin on my shoulder.

"Not here."

"You're already hard!"

"Someone might know me here."

"I might know you here."

The trip up took an excruciatingly long time. The Japanese

couple got out first, their luggage banging as it rolled across the gap. I asked the desk clerk, who must have been nearing the end of his shift since he had already taken off his jacket, for a room for two for one night. Only a superior room was free. I said that would be excellent. I didn't have my wallet with me, but I found a business card from my Union Credit days in the pocket of my coat. I said I lived in the building and asked him to check with the downstairs reception desk.

"I was sure all you would have to do was smile," Veera said. The desk clerk explained the route to our room, which was located five floors above. We made it back to the elevator before the Japanese. Veera asked if I had ever fucked in an elevator.

"No, I haven't."

"Should I push that red button?"

"No, you shouldn't!"

"Of course not!"

Disregarding the traveler at the end of the hallway, Veera wrapped my arm around her neck. Her steps were more faltering than mine from the drunkenness.

"Will it open if I yell 'open sesame!' really fucking loud?"

"Don't yell."

I inserted the keycard in the lock. It flashed green just as "open sesame!" echoed in the hall.

Veera pushed me in and toppled me on the bed. I was only resisting for appearance's sake.

*THE ORANGE LUFTHANSA sign was visible from a good distance. He walked toward it pulling his carry-on and whistling. That was how he knew he was drunker than he had thought.*

*Had he really thought everything through? What he did today might influence the rest of his life more than any day before ever had or any day after ever would.*

*The male employee dressed in yellow and navy blue looked at him, ready to serve, and taking the final steps to the counter was all there was for it.*

"Was kann ich fur Sie tun?"

*It flattered him to be taken for a German. However, he explained his business in English: his travel plans had suddenly changed and he needed to get to Helsinki today.*

*Without any unnecessary questions, the employee turned to his computer and began typing.*

*"Today there are two direct flights, one at three and one at seven twenty-five. Travel time is three hours and thirty-five minutes. The next connection through Frankfurt leaves at twelve and arrives at five-fifty local time. The three o'clock flight arrives forty-five minutes later. All connections have available seats."*

*He wondered what he would do in this situation if he were traveling to Helsinki. Why hadn't he checked for connections in London? What would the police think when they saw that he had flown to Helsinki via Germany and used a worse route for no good reason? Why wouldn't he simply fly to Helsinki direct from Heathrow?*

*What had seemed like a good plan in the air now felt like a shoddy, transparent attempt at subterfuge.*

*Or maybe the police would think that he had taken the first possible flight from Heathrow before thinking it through. That he had been panicked.*

*And wouldn't that demonstrate his innocence?*

*His innocence! As if he needed to prove he wasn't at fault.*

*But of course he was. He was at fault for all of it.*

*"I'll take the first direct flight."*

*Six-thirty Finnish time. The police still wouldn't be on his trail by then. No one would have any reason to be tracking him. There would be no police patrol sent to wait for him at Helsinki-Vantaa Airport.*

*"Eight hundred and three euros."*

*He handed over his credit card.*

*"LH 2464, departure at three P.M. The departure gate will be announced later, so check the boards," the airline agent said and handed him his ticket.*

*Seat 8A.*

*The window seat, he found himself thinking.*

# Elise

PEOPLE ARE LIKE ships. Some leave, some stay. Now it was my and Mikko's turn to stay, but on another day the wind would catch our sails.

After the sauna I felt pleasantly sleepy. I just barely had the energy to put my dress back on.

When you can't make out the details, you see the whole picture more clearly.

Once the front door had banged shut, Mikko came over next to me to sit.

I mixed gin and tonic in two glasses, but I didn't add anything else. This time I didn't need to.

Mikko grabbed me with both hands. Our noses touched. That tickled a little.

Mikko said, "Just hold out a little longer! I'm going to save you."

I asked: "Have you talked to Robert?"

Mikko said, "Talking isn't going to be enough. You aren't yourself. You don't understand your situation."

I asked: "Am I your princess?"

Mikko said, "You are my princess."

I asked, "Is Veera your queen?"

Mikko said, "Veera is my current wife and the mother of my child. That isn't a problem, though. I've thought through everything. We'll move to Helsinki and . . . "

I couldn't think of what to say. I gave a cute smile. Mikko liked that.

Mikko said, “Elise, I love you. I love you more than . . . ”

Mikko fumbled for the words. He said something about swans, sunrises, a spring, butterflies, and a flower bud about to bloom.

I had the feeling Mikko needed help.

I kissed him. I was pretty good at that.

There was a hair in my mouth. It was a long hair. It wasn’t mine. It was Veera’s. I took it out before we continued.

I pressed myself against Mikko. Mikko’s arms were thinner than Robert’s, but under them I found ribs and armpits to tickle.

Mikko laughed.

I laughed.

Mikko said, “We can’t now.”

I did what I knew Mikko liked. The duty of a hostess is to keep her guests happy.

When Mikko undressed me, the silver rose snapped in half. I remembered what Robert had said about it and our love. Robert didn’t know everything, although he did know quite a lot.

# Veera

FIRST ROBERT WANTED to be dominated. Then he wanted to be master of the universe. All present, future, and imagined realities were his to command.

Speed was a major part of the plot for this fuck. Ripping Rob's clothes off, I tossed them around the room. I squeezed him with my thighs and locked his wrists. Only then did I give myself up for him to take me like a helpless girl. I struck, lit his fire, and then gave in to him. I had simplified the job by leaving my panties and bra off. Rob only had to deal with the elastic waist of my pants.

Rob got to feel like he was in charge even though he was just acting out my plan.

But the end felt forced, almost like work. The hormones were flowing, but it didn't feel as good as I remembered. Rob banged away like he just wanted to be done. This wasn't the frenzied desire of a banker to quickly reach a goal, it was ticking an unpleasant task off an agenda.

The next time I would put up more resistance. At least it was completely different than with Mikko.

"You've got a new style down there," Rob said once his breathing leveled off.

I said I had copied it from the trendy London girls. "Wasn't I good?"

"You're always good."

"But?"

"I didn't say 'but.'"

"You were thinking it. I could hear it. But I'm old? But Elise is better?"

"Elise is my wife."

"And I'm married to your childhood best friend! I have been all these years!"

"Let's not think about the past."

"You were the one who wanted this! You invited us here."

"Exactly. I invited both of you because this isn't what I wanted. Can't we just let it be? The past is still on the balance sheet, but we don't have to keep carrying it over."

Rob turned on his side to wipe himself on the sheet. I said that at the price they charged for this room he could probably use the curtains too if it gave him kicks. Since he didn't get them with me.

Dragging myself out of the bed, I went to the bathroom, where there was a whirlpool tub in the corner. As I started the water running and dried off my sweat, I wondered if Rob was serious about leaving the past behind. We had never talked about the future before. Or that I would come visit again. Or that I wouldn't.

It was all the same to me what Rob thought.

"Now I could go for a whiskey."

Rob was sitting on the edge of the bed lazily watching the TV news. Tanks were rolling on the potholed streets of some raghead country, and the carcass of a bus was on fire. A little global suffering was always nice after sex.

In his hand was a whiskey from the minibar.

"Sorry. This was the last one. There are probably some peanuts and beer left, though."

Rob's eyes stayed fixed on the widescreen panel.

It doesn't always take something big. Sometimes a fifty-milliliter mini-bar bottle is enough. That was enough to release everything I had been holding inside for twenty years.

"Don't you ever think of anyone but yourself?"

"Oh, you mean I should have been thinking of you when I opened the mini-bar while you were taking your sweet time in the bathroom?" Rob switched the war news to snooker on a sports channel.

"You're such a fucking self-centered piece of shit!"

"Come on, Veera. Let's see what we can find for you."

"I don't need your booze!" I slapped Rob in the face.

"Hey, be reasonable!" Rob shouted.

"Reasonable? I'm surprised you even know the word. You've never been reasonable."

"Here, take it and give it a suck."

"Give it a suck!"

"Veera, calm down!"

*Veera, calm down*. That was what Rob had said that night too.

"Getting pussy is more important to you than human life," I said, but I didn't shout. The words were heavy enough on their own.

We hadn't spoken of that night once since we agreed on our story.

On the last weekend of May, 1995, we woke up at a rented cabin to a crapulous Saturday. I left Mikko to continue his restless sleep and went to sit on the porch in the morning sun. I took an ibuprofen and opened a beer. Maarit came and sat next to me, and stared at her toes. I couldn't think of how to ask, but Maarit brought it up herself.

"I couldn't go through with it. Rob was so . . . strange . . . I'm afraid."

I hugged her and let her breathe against my shoulder.

We played croquet on the bumpy lawn, and grilled in our bikinis. Rob kept giving Maarit drinks. And Maarit drank. When we went to swim, I asked Maarit what she intended to do. Maarit was going to try again.

"It only hurts once," she said, and there were many s's at the end of "hurts" even though it was barely after noon.

While we were off swimming, the boys had got in an argument. I tried to get us singing again, but my top ten lineup of Finn rock hits had no effect. Rob fussed over Maarit, and Mikko retreated to our bedroom to read *The Hitchhiker's Guide to the Galaxy.*

While the sauna was still heating, Mikko appeared on the deck fully dressed with his backpack on and announced he was heading back to the city. Hanging out in the woods wasn't his thing. He had checked the map and the bus schedule and found a stop less than a kilometer away.

That was when the evening changed direction. For a while I watched Rob and Maarit, the cooing couple, who wanted to sauna alone.

So I showered and left, too.

I didn't have a bus schedule or a map, but at every intersection I just turned the direction most cars had driven on the dirt road, and found the stop. I made the last Saturday night bus. When I got home to my dorm, I hung my swimsuit to dry in the bathroom and fell asleep on top of the comforter.

I woke up to the doorbell ringing. Rob was in the stairwell, so drunk he could barely stand. He didn't say anything, he just came in.

"Where did you leave Maarit?" I asked.

"Maarit went home."

"Why?"

"She wanted to go home."

Rob sat down next to me on the bed, which was messy from my tossing and turning.

"Do you want something?"

"Yeah."

"Well? Tell me what it is and then maybe I can help."

Rob indicated that I should sit closer to him. Wrapping his left arm around me, he put his hand under my arm and onto my breast, caressing and squeezing softly.

I was still drunker than I realized. I let Rob continue.

"What would Maarit think of this?"

"Maarit is your friend."

I let that explanation be enough. I wanted it to be enough.

I had been dreaming of this for far too long. I let Rob's hand grope me increasingly roughly. Cautiously I stroked his thigh, not wanting to take too much initiative, to be too insistent. It wasn't seduction and there wasn't any emotion. It was drunken pawing, but I didn't care.

When I turned toward Rob, I discovered that he had fallen asleep. Removing his hand, I rolled him down onto his side and covered him with his coat. I stroked Rob's cheek and pushed my fingers inside myself. I didn't think about Maarit or Mikko, just about Rob.

I slept on the floor and woke up when Rob accidentally kicked me in the ribs when he got out of the bed. One word kept repeating in his confused mumbling: Maarit.

Rob was looking for his phone, and when he found it in his jacket pocket, he called Maarit. She didn't answer. I suggested that her phone might be on silent. Rob tried again. I suggested that Maarit might not know how to use her phone. The expensive device had been her graduation present, but her parents had given it to her just before our weekend at the cabin. This didn't calm Rob down. He said something had happened to Maarit.

I asked Rob if he wanted an omelet. There wasn't much else to eat because we were supposed to be at the cabin all weekend, and I lived on a tight budget. Crisp bread, butter, a bouillon cube. In the freezer was a bag of mixed veggies to go in the omelet.

No, he didn't want anything. He just kept calling Maarit's phone, until he stood up abruptly to leave.

I was starting to realize that Rob hadn't told me the truth. Maarit was still at the cabin. Putting my hair up in a ponytail, I pulled on my clothes that I had thrown over the arm of a chair, and rushed after Rob to a taxi.

Rob asked the driver to take us to the bus stop. We covered the rest of the distance to the cabin at a jog, and Rob continued trying to call Maarit's phone.

"Maarit must have it switched off. Or her battery died. Or she doesn't have signal. Or . . . "

My optimistic explanations were all wrong.

We started yelling for Maarit as soon as we came within sight of the cabin. Maarit's yellow towel hung from the line. The previous morning there had been four towels and everything had been fine.

The plastic chairs in the yard were just as we had left them, and on the porch was the tower of empty cans I had built, which rattled as our steps pounded on the deck boards.

The door was closed but not locked. Rob pulled the door open, and I yelled for Maarit. The fluorescent lamp in the kitchen nook was on. The refrigerator door hung open.

The living room rug was crooked, with playing cards scattered on the table.

Maarit didn't respond, and I knew she never would again.

My best friend lay lifeless on the floor.

# Mikko

ELISE WAS SOFT against my side. She presented her dress for me to remove, guiding my hand to the knot holding it up, which just needed a tug. The black fabric fell to the floor. Elise staggered, stepping on it. I heard a snap of something breaking.

I pressed my cheek against Elise's stomach. I hadn't remembered that she wore a silver naval ring.

I saw the marks on her sides—obviously bruises where she'd been hit. Elise had denied it when I asked if Robert abused her. Elise didn't dare admit it, even though I could see with my own eyes what Robert had done.

Elise had said that she was a prisoner. Robert subjugated her emotionally and physically.

Elise deserved better. Through her skin I could hear her heart beating.

*Bong.*

Elise stroked my back and said she wanted to be good.

*Bong.*

I tried to resist, because Robert and Veera could come back at any moment.

*Bong.*

"Later," I said.

*Bong.*

"When everything is different. When everything is good."

*Bong.*

I told her I had already almost succeeded once.

*Bong.*

I promised that after this night she would be free.

*Bong.*

Elise kicked her panties into the corner of the library and said she was already free.

*Bong.*

*Bong.*

*Bong.*

Life with Elise wouldn't be easy. I would have to take care of her, while now Veera looked after the practicalities of daily life. I was ready to take that responsibility. I wanted to save Elise. I wanted to heal her.

Daily life! Always one more day just like the last! I had been living day to day for thirty-seven years. I wanted something more. I was in the middle of my life. The average life expectancy of a newborn Finnish male was seventy-seven years. When I was born it had been several years lower, but since I had already made it this far . . . "To hell with the details. To hell with cohorts and statistics. Isn't that right, Elise? To hell with statistics."

"To hell with statistics."

I had more than half my life left. I didn't want it just to be more of the life I had already lived.

With expert fingers Elise began to undo the metal buttons of my shirt. Stopping and turning one button between her fingers, she laughed before moving to the next.

I had to start getting ready for the sauna anyway—this way I wouldn't have to waste time in the dressing room fumbling with buttons.

I didn't resist strenuously enough.

Elise was having a hard time staying on her feet. She leaned on my shoulder and at the same time pulled my shirt down. I grabbed her hips so she wouldn't fall on the floor.

I sat Elise down in the leather armchair and encouraged her to rest a little. I needed to call my daughter at home anyway. The bar cabinet was within Elise's reach. She poured me a whiskey, neat, to tide me over while I made my call. She also splashed some into her own glass. I took both glasses with me and left Elise's on the glass buffet table out of her reach.

Yes, I noticed that the champagne sword had disappeared. It wasn't in the display case either. I wondered about that, but I didn't dwell on it. Maybe Robert had put it somewhere else. Or the servant—tidying up would presumably be one of her duties.

I don't have any memory of seeing the cyanide ampule. And I didn't need it. I had my strychnine.

I wetted my lips with whiskey. My head was spinning. My thoughts were clear, but there were too many commas in my sentences.

In the guest room, I set my glass down on the nightstand, where Veera's panties hung over one corner.

Why had Veera left her panties on the nightstand? She didn't do that at home. She never even wore the same panties two days in a row. She preferred to run the washer. Washing them didn't take much energy or detergent, so it didn't affect the environment enough for me to point it out.

Why weren't the panties on her person or in the dirty clothes bag?

The phone rang for a long time before Julia answered.

"Yeah?"

"You were supposed to call."

"Yeah. *I* was supposed to call. Not you."

"You didn't call."

"I haven't had time."

"Could you call now? It would be cheaper."

I walked around the room with the phone in my hand and then parked in front of the view. I heard the sighs of London, heard the honking of the taxis, saw the cooing of the lovers better than in the afternoon even though the glass sealed out all the sound.

"There we go," I said when she called back.

"Okay, what do you want?"

The soundscape in the background was different than when I had just called. I heard the droning of cars. The highway.

"Are you outside?"

"Yeah. Everyone's partying so hard inside I couldn't hear anything."

"So everything is fine there?"

"Yeah, except this guy Juha from the other track at school threw up. We sent him home in a taxi. Hey, is it okay if we drink that bottle you got from work?"

"I'm sorry if your father sounds overprotective, but could you please answer seriously."

"I'm so serious I'm delirious."

"Are you drunk?"

"Of course I'm fucking drunk."

"Hey, don't swear."

"You're the one who's drunk. I can hear it all the way here. Maybe it's just echoing. You know, international calls and all."

"Fine. You can get off now. But call if anything happens. If someone tries to come in or if anyone suspicious is sneaking around the yard."

After the call ended, I checked how long it had lasted. I calculated the cost of receiving the call. Julia had a talk-and-text package, so it wouldn't cost her anything extra if she didn't go over her monthly quota. It was well under a euro. An affordable price for peace of mind.

Veera and Robert's smoke break had lasted more than half an hour already. The night was passing, but Robert was alive. Time to raise the probabilities again.

I drank the whiskey and breathed in deep. The sighs of the city were shallow in comparison.

The servant had set out the dessert dishes in the dining area.

But there was no sign of her. Or of Elise. No sounds of anyone arriving came from the direction of the door.

I opened the strychnine pouch. The plastic was slippery in my sweaty fingers. I shook a little of the white powder into Robert's coffee cup. The powder was invisible against the porcelain. Someone with sharp eyes might imagine there was powdered sugar in the bottom of the cup.

Enough strychnine remained for two doses.

This was stage six.

# Robert

"SO I KILLED Maarit now? I puked in her mouth and plugged her nose before I left for the city? Is that what I did?"

"If we're being serious. If we're being serious, yes, you did cause Maarit's death."

"If we're being serious and if that were the case, then it would barely even be involuntary manslaughter. And, secondly, Maarit drank every single beer and every single shot of vodka and every single cider herself that weekend. I didn't pour anything down her throat unless she specifically asked me too. And I seem to remember you doing that, too. I seem to remember you tipping beer cans into Maarit's mouth while she held her head back and sucked them down."

"Sucked them down! What is it with you and the sucking!"

"My choice of words may have been poor, but that doesn't change the fact you're as guilty as me. I didn't kill Maarit. I didn't cause her death. What charge would hold up in court? Negligent homicide? *A person who through negligence causes the death of another shall be sentenced for negligent homicide.* That's what the law says. Abandonment: *A person who renders another helpless or abandons a helpless person in respect of whom he or she has an obligation of care, and thereby endangers the life or health of said person.* That one includes two different points: rendering helpless or abandoning, and having an obligation of care. The first doesn't apply because Maarit put herself in the situation. Perhaps we could quibble about abandoning."

I knew the laws. I had read over them so many times.

"But obligation of care requirement would fall flat because we had only been dating a few months. We weren't married or even living together. I wasn't Maarit's boss or anything similar. And what about failing to render aid? *A person who knows that another is in mortal danger or serious danger to his or her health, and does not give or procure such assistance that in view of his or her options and the nature of the situation can reasonably be expected . . .* "

"You know it section and paragraph!" Veera yelled.

"Who accused me of homicide?"

"For you the whole thing is just a legal problem. If the right clauses are fulfilled, it isn't a problem at all," Veera said. "You're a self-centered shit."

"I'm sure I am. You just said so a minute ago."

"You made her drink until she passed out."

"People pass out and wake up the next morning feeling queasy. They wake up! People don't pass out and die, especially not young people. It never could have occurred to me that Maarit was in any danger."

"You left her and went hunting for pussy."

Veera stood at the end of the bed with a towel hanging from her right shoulder. If I hadn't have been so angry about her accusations, I might have laughed.

Because she was right. Veera didn't know everything that had happened at the cabin. I had destroyed the evidence of our fight and carefully cleaned the vomit from my skin.

When I had finally got Maarit in bed, I was ready to rut. My veins pulsed with aggressive energy. That was the moment I had been waiting for, and I turned all my fear and anxiety into absolute self-confidence. I was like the young stock brokers who react to realizing they have no control by pretending to know everything.

I jumped on her. I called her a whore so she wouldn't smile and try to be all cuddly. I forced her against the headboard and clamped my hand over her mouth. She struggled and tried to breathe, but I was stronger. With my free hand I undressed her. Throwing her down on the bed, I held her in place, but when I tried to get inside, Maarit vomited. The vomit gushed over my hands. The sound was disgusting.

I pulled my hand away and stood up. The lust was gone.

Rage burned inside of me. Everything had gone to hell. I hated myself and took it out on Maarit.

I packed and left. I left Maarit. I was a coward. Like Veera said: I was a self-centered shit.

I left Maarit to die.

"Maarit was so goddamn nervous about it. Did you try to rape her?"

I could have said that what was allowed for women was a crime for men. I could have asked Veera what she would say if I filed a rape complaint about this night and the police confiscated the hotel hard drives and downloaded the footage from the security cameras in the hotel hallways and elevator. Whose version of events would they support?

"You don't know who did what," I said coldly. I forced the memories from my mind.

"Best friends hear more than boys."

Veera couldn't have any evidence, and if she did, it wouldn't matter now because the statute of limitations had run out.

We were both guilty.

That was what I had said to Veera as we cried against each other in the cabin once we understood there was no way to save Maarit anymore. I was hollow from the shock.

"We have to minimize the damage. We can't bring Maarit back to life. But we can save ourselves. Only one person made a mistake, not three," I said as we sat at the kitchen table.

We planned out our story.

We had tried to convince Maarit to come with us to the city, but she had refused. We couldn't force her. We'd encouraged her to be careful and did everything we could to prevent any danger. We hid the matches (we gathered all the matchboxes in the cabin and threw them on the top shelf of the closet in the room Veera and Mikko had been using), we hid the knives . . .

But Veera realized claiming we'd made those kinds of preparations would show that we knew Maarit was in danger. So we returned the knives to their drawer and put the boxes of matches back on the shelf in the dressing room, on the fireplace mantel, and in the middle drawer in the kitchen nook.

Veera was a smart woman. I admired her.

She had cool nerves.

A new plan. As we were leaving, Maarit said she wanted to stay at the cabin to read (Maarit had a Franz Kafka in German with her—she had a flight booked to Prague in July). We didn't have any idea she would start binge drinking. That wasn't like her at all.

"Mikko knows that Maarit was already hammered."

"Mikko left so early, though. I'll tell Mikko it isn't a good idea for any of us to make a big deal about the alcohol. He doesn't want to have to explain that to his parents either. Maarit just wanted to be alone and get really properly drunk for once."

"The Kafka started getting to her. The chair turned into a giant beetle."

"Okay, okay, but why did we go back to town?"

"There was supposed to be rain. We wanted to see a movie . . ."

"We weren't at the movies."

"Who would be able to prove that, though? Why would anyone bother checking?"

"What's even playing now?"

So we checked the theater listings. We assumed that Mikko would tell everything exactly as it had happened. Mikko had had enough and left. Afterwards the rest of us got bored, too—we weren't used to being in the woods. Veera and I decided to go to a movie. We agreed that it was Veera's suggestion, and we chose a showing at a theater where we thought there would be a big enough crowd that no one would remember whether we were there or not. Veera had read a review of the movie and explained the plot.

We had gone into the city in my car, and after I took Veera home, I got a flat tire (I punctured it later Sunday night with Veera's knife, which ended up with rubber on the blade so I threw it in a dumpster full of construction waste at a building having its windows renovated), and because it was late and Veera's roommate was staying with her parents (true), Veera invited me to stay the night.

"But you have to tell Mikko nothing happened between us."

"I certainly will not. It didn't, and Mikko won't assume it did."

The story wasn't completely logical, but we sold it well.

And no one doubted, at least not out loud, that anything different had happened.

MAARIT WANTED TO get blitzed by herself, and we were all just as shocked and confused as anyone else. The three of us, everyone's parents and siblings, our classmates from school. At graduation we observed a moment of silence in memory of our dear departed friend. During that minute I felt everyone's sorrow and knew that I had caused it.

Some people reacted with anger, some with pity, but no one blamed us. Not Maarit's family members, not Mikko.

I reminded Veera now that she was just as much a part of the story as I was. If I was guilty, so was she.

"I helped you. I brought shame on myself. I wanted to help you. You made it all seem so logical."

I pointed out that when we ran into each other in a bar a

year later, it was Veera who attached herself and went home with me.

"And you were the one who called me after that. Once can be a coincidence, but the second times makes it a relationship," I continued.

"Of course I called. I even followed you here to London. Damn it, Rob, don't you know what you do to me?"

"But you've always stayed with Mikko."

"I love Mikko."

The minibar whiskey was gone. Veera turned her back, and a toothpaste advertisement interrupted the tennis match that had come on.

"Those are two different things," Veera said and started dressing.

I found my boxers under the desk chair. Two buttons had come loose from my shirt from Veera's rough handling. I would have to throw it away. For the rest of the night I would wear plain light blue.

As I dressed, Veera did an inventory on the room. She turned the corkscrew over in her hand but then put it back.

"I think I'll take this."

At which she slipped a glass with the hotel logo into her sweatpants pocket. "As a memento of this moment," she said and pulled my head toward her for a quick kiss.

Veera asked for cigarettes at the reception desk. We could get some in the bar. Veera chose Marlboro Whites, which I asked them to put on the room tab. I put the keycard in the front pocket of my shirt. I thought I would come back the next day to check out.

I waited in the hotel lobby bar while Veera went outside to smoke. Smart woman. She had to have the smell of tobacco in her hair. Then we took the elevator down and back up to my apartment. In the elevator mirror I checked to make sure my clothes were on straight enough that the lack of the buttons didn't show.

I let Veera out into the hall first and said, "You wanted to smoke three, and since we were outside already, I decided to show you . . ."

Veera placed a finger in front of my nose, either as a warning or a tease—it wasn't clear, and I didn't ask. When I opened the door, she flashed the cigarette pack, which was missing three cigarettes.

# Elise

ROBERT WAS HEAVY. Veera was heavy. The smoke was still on them.

Robert said, "Sorry, we took longer than I thought. We had so much to talk about."

Veera was a talker.

Veera left the cigarettes on the entry table next to the suit of armor and asked, "Is this the most upstanding man in the building?"

I said: "He's our knight. He protects us. He doesn't smoke cigarettes."

I had many knights.

Mikko came from the dining area. People were coming and going. It was rush hour.

The servant had set out the dessert dishes and coffee cups. I noticed Robert's blue poison capsule on the buffet table. I picked it up and put it in the little pocket of my dress. It isn't good to have poison lying around the house.

I went in the library. Veera came in soon too. She had traded her frumpy pants for a dress. We each sat on our own couch and wasted time.

# Mikko

THE OPPRESSIVE FEELING of guilt had been building by the minute, spreading steadily through my body from my spine, robbing my fingertips of their feeling and making my brain unnaturally light. And the steam of the sauna didn't melt it away.

I told myself I didn't need to feel guilty. I was just aiding fate in its cruel work, assisting the probabilities in playing out.

I was making the necessary possible, moving forward the inevitable.

I would do what I had to do. I would save a person. I would save love. There was nothing greater than that.

The dry air of the electric sauna didn't relax me the way a wood-fired sauna did. My eyelashes fluttered. I couldn't close them.

Robert stepped up aggressively onto the lower bench and started talking before he even sat down.

"That suit of armor you saw in the entryway," he said, "was a farewell gift from BNP Paribas. It's an old Japanese piece, back from their war with Russia. It's ugly. I hate the thing," Robert said as he straightened the bench cover. "Every time I see it, I feel like selling it for scrap."

Robert swirled his hand in the water bucket and asked what I guessed the reason was he hadn't ever sold it.

I prepared myself for a story of gladiators in the bloody financial markets. Clichés about a merciless struggle between life and death. A universal war waged by everyone against everyone. The need for full-body armor because a simple shield couldn't protect you from the back-stabbers. Anything better than the ambrosia anointing Achilles received.

About a career where you always had to be on the alert.

About unreasonable work that demanded unreasonable compensation.

I prepared to turn a deaf ear to blood and death made cheap as motivational metaphors. Take two parts Sun Tsu, add a dash of Clausewitz, deep fat fry, and you could turn any vapid notion into a speech.

*War is an act of violence, which in its application knows no bounds.*

*The military genius of the general is essential.*

*War is an interaction between people.*

*Interaction between people is war.*

*War is the influence of mind on mind, not matter on matter.*

When the markets don't act the way the leader's pearls of wisdom claim, Clausewitz comes to the rescue again: *War is a true chameleon, a constantly changing phenomenon. Every war is different, so there can be no complete theory.*

"Even you need protection. Your skin alone isn't thick enough," I suggested so Robert could get on with his harangue. I would allow him that. It could be his final performance. And then the curtain would fall.

Robert threw half a ladle of water on the soapstone of the heater. The burst of steam made him turn his face aside.

"Yeah," he said. "That's it exactly. I need protection."

"The predators will instantly savage any unprotected gladiator who lets his guard down for a moment," I said.

"No, I don't need the armor against external threats. I need protection from myself. When you're in a suit of armor, you can't tear your wrists open with your teeth," Robert said.

"Ah," I said. "Yes."

"Don't you think so, Mikko? I don't think anyone is interested enough to bother hurting me."

*He that shall humble himself shall be exalted.*

"They might get their hands dirty," Robert continued.

*Hands can be washed.*

"I'm not that valuable," he said.

*The most valuable thing you have is you.*

Robert's outburst was intense and unexpected. I let the rest go without comment, even though Robert implored me to object or agree. He begged for conversation, but I wasn't up for it. I wasn't at my best. I didn't want to lose the last battle, the decisive contest, because that would be what stayed with me for the rest of my life.

"Of course I have plenty of life insurance," Robert admitted.

So it came to money. That didn't take long.

"Don't you think, Mikko, that people are wolves to each other but hyenas to themselves? At least when we attack other people, we leave some remains for smaller scavengers," Robert said, watching the water as it flew onto the stone. The heater hissed. The temperature had risen quite high since the sauna had been empty so long. "All hyenas leave are the hooves and the horns. Did you know that? Of course you did."

I didn't. Robert had obviously learned about hyenas for some speech he had given.

"Their digestive system is so effective that all they leave is lime from the bones," Robert said with a sigh. "The bitter taste of defeat."

I pointed out that lime the chemical might be slightly bitter, but not like the fruit.

"Listen, do you think I'm the most self-centered person in the world?" Robert asked.

I didn't answer, but Robert continued.

"What if I am? Is selfishness a crime?"

These were rhetorical questions.

"I've traveled on so many planes that I've memorized the flight attendants' security routines. If the cabin loses pressure, oxygen masks will fall from the ceiling automatically. Put your mask on like this. Place a mask on yourself before assisting others! First you have to make sure your own affairs are in order. Then you can help others. My affairs are in order. I'm in a very good position, actually. So I can help others. Where doesn't my logic fall apart? Does it?"

Robert rinsed his face with water from the bucket before he threw a ladleful on the soapstone. The hissing rose to a crescendo, and then a wave of searing steam hit. I covered my shoulders with my hands and hunched down.

"Humanity never would have developed if people didn't want to improve their own condition."

I splashed water on my face.

"Oh, sorry," Robert said, and pushed the bucket toward me as he clambered off the bench.

I remained sitting in the heat.

Was I selfish because I wanted Elise for myself? I said I would save her, just as Robert thought he was saving the world in his own selfish way.

Water dripped from the air vent onto the floor. The temperature differences were extreme.

Was I selfish? Was I just doing all this for myself instead of for the world and for Elise?

I rubbed the sweat from my arms. I was just straightening up to throw some more water when Robert yelled my name from the dressing room.

"Your phone's ringing."

Veera had rushed to the bathroom door with the phone. The number on the screen was from Finland. I didn't save numbers in my phone memory, but I recognized it as our neighbor Hannu's cell. The phone must have been ringing for a while because Veera had gone all the way to the guest room to get it after hearing the ring.

"How's it going? Is everything alright?" Hannu asked.

I told Hannu we were in London and that I was a bit busy. And besides, wasn't it one o'clock in Finland? What kind of time was this to be calling?

"Oh, I was just checking to make sure your television is really supposed to be in the front yard and your car is supposed to be revving in neutral in the garage."

*HE GLADLY WOULD have drunk the first coffee of the rest of his life somewhere other than McDonald's. But he couldn't. His new situation set surprising limitations.*

*He had ridden the train to the Marienplatz station in the center of the city, coming aboveground near the neo-Gothic New Town Hall. He had visited three nice looking cafés along the street, all of which were already open, but when he asked about wireless internet, the waitresses just shook their heads and apologized.*

*After the third futile attempt, he asked the waitress dressed in her white apron whether she knew where he could get online. The woman had told him how to get to McDonald's: Go to the end of the walking street and then it's on the left before the intersection.*

*The weather was warmer in Munich than he had expected. His coat was starting to feel hot, especially since he was dragging his luggage.*

*The hamburger joint was quiet, and thankfully it didn't stink of fried oil quite yet—the Sunday lunch rush would start later. He ordered a black coffee and an apple pie, and paid with a twenty-euro bill.*

*On the train he had had some privacy in his half of the car for the first ten minutes. He bent his credit card in two. The tough plastic had taken quite a bit of work to break. With his hand hidden in his coat pocket, he bent one of the pieces in two again. The first of the three pieces he left in a trash can on the walking street.*

*A McDonald's crew member placed the coffee and pie pocket on a red plastic tray.*

*"Also, could I have the code for the Wi-Fi?"*

*The crew member explained that there wasn't any code. All he had to do was turn on his device, turn on the Wi-Fi, and register as a user on the page that opened automatically.*

*"The system sends a PIN to your mobile phone that gives you an hour of free airtime."*

*"Isn't there any other way? I don't have a mobile phone."*

*"You don't have a mobile phone?"*

*In point of fact, he did have a mobile phone, but it didn't have a SIM card. He had flushed it down the toilet before he left.*

*"No, I don't have a mobile phone, but I have to get online. With this."*

*He showed his iPad and turned it on. He searched for the network and the login page came up.*

*"Could I fill this out and give it your phone number?"*

*He inspired the girl's consent with a ten-euro bill.*

*The girl's phone beeped saying a text message had arrived. She told him the four number code.*

*"It worked! Thank you!"*

*"Your coffee!"*

*"Thank you!"*

*Sitting down at the curved window that looked out onto the square, he navigated to the major London newspapers. The news was all about the surprises from the previous night's Premier League games. He did a few advanced searches with names and "The Shard," limiting the results to the past twenty-four hours.*

*There was no information about the night's events online. Of course there wasn't. How could there be?*

*Sipping his coffee, he squeezed the small silver cross that he had found in his pocket. The pie remained on the tray.*

# Veera

I WAS IN the middle of a thought when Mikko strutted into the library with a towel around his waist. On his feet he was wearing Elise's pink sauna slippers, and in his hand he had his artifact of a cell phone, which he was shaking in his fist like a juice box.

*Shake it, baby!*

And then I couldn't remember what I was thinking.

In the other hand he was holding the edge of his towel, because Mikko was one of those men who couldn't keep a towel on his waist. It was a quality like the ability to roll your tongue.

Mikko repeated my name. I said that I was in the middle of a whiskey.

"Veera, Veera," Mikko said. "Julia . . . "

I told him I, Veera, was here, but not Julia. I reminded him that I was his wife and that unfortunately I was indisposed at the moment due to an ongoing decision process related to a box of chocolates.

Then Mikko told me what our neighbor had said to him on the phone.

"Julia isn't answering," Mikko said.

I said she would answer for me.

"So call."

I said I would call very soon but that just now I was in the middle of living my life.

This annoyed Mikko. He stood there next to me dripping water.

Mikko had a few dark hairs on his chest, which had curled from the moisture.

Elise asked if Mikko wanted whiskey or cognac.

Mikko said he wanted me to call his daughter.

"Our daughter."

Mikko said that Julia was also his daughter. I said that that fact was covered by the concept of "our." I asked if he was trying to say that I had raised his daughter poorly. That his daughter had betrayed his trust. Or our . . . fuck it. I could never quibble like Mikko.

Mikko asked whether I intended to call. He said he was worried. We couldn't let anything happen to Julia, he kept emphasizing, as if I might disagree. It bothered me the way Mikko was carrying on. Of course I was worried.

"I said I was going to call, but I was busy."

"Busy?"

"There's always something going on."

Mikko asked why I was irritating him. He clarified by explaining that in asking this question he meant why was I acting in a way intended to irritate. In his mind that was an important point—he needed to demonstrate that he was not choosing to be irritated or that the issue in question was his subjective tendency to provocation.

I said that I didn't have any particular reason for it.

"Is something irritating you?" Mikko asked.

"Oh, dear, so many things! Shouldn't you go back to the sauna so the electricity won't go to waste?"

Mikko shook the cell phone in his hand. Elise poured a third glass of whiskey and carried it to Mikko.

Elise kissed Mikko on the cheek.

"Oh, so you've had a chance to get to know each other."

The towel fell from Mikko's waist.

I looked away and rubbed my neck. My silver cross necklace had left a painful scrape.

# Robert

THERE ARE NO winners without losers. Even though the history of the world is like a stock market where everyone wins on average over the long term, there still have to be losers. If no one was getting poorer in relative terms, no one would be getting richer. If relative winning wasn't possible, everyone couldn't win on average over time.

I looked at Mikko and saw a winner.

Because there was a mirror behind him.

A towel hung from Mikko's hand. Gravity tugged it toward the surface of the earth. Down to zero. If you want to rise above zero, you have to exert effort, fight, and overcome.

I didn't feel like a winner now, though, because Veera had beaten me. Veera was winning, though I didn't even know what we were playing or what we were playing for.

When I looked past Mikko, I was really seeing a loser. It wasn't a pretty sight.

I hated losing, because I loved winning. For someone else a loss might be meaningless. Someone else might think about feelings. Someone else might be irritated that things meant to be forgotten had been dug back up. I didn't think that way. I only thought of the loss.

I'm competitive because I take responsibility.

Mikko looked shocked.

I wanted to talk to him.

I opened the sauna door and urged him back in. I had something important to say.

# Veera

JULIA ANSWERED ON the second try.

"Hi, it's Mom. Is everything all right there?"

"What do you think?"

"I can hear that it isn't—"

"Fuck, Mom, if I don't do this now—"

"—from your voice."

"—when am I ever going to?"

"Maybe you should go somewhere—"

"If—"

"—we can talk."

"—I'm never going to!"

"How about you go in the bathroom?"

The background noise faded as Julia presumably closed the door after her, and then I heard the click of the lock.

I asked about the car. Some boy, whom I didn't recognize from his nickname, had wanted to listen to the Hurriganes but inside all they were playing was Madonna. I understood how he felt.

He had come up with the bright idea that there was a CD player in the car. And it would be lame listening to classic rock if he couldn't press on the gas occasionally, given that he was sitting in a car.

The television—that had been a particular point of amusement. The guests hadn't ever seen a television that wasn't a flat screen LCD. The one we owned looked more like a shot-put. So they organized a shot-put competition.

"Is there anything else?"

"Well, um, how do you get red wine out of a couch?"

Instead of saying, "you don't," I encouraged her to try salt. The sooner the better.

"Just normal salt?"

"Just normal salt."

"Okay, I'll try."

"Is there anything else?"

"Well . . . "

"Are you starting to feel like maybe the party needs to end?"

"Yeah, but . . . "

Julia asked how she should go about it.

"Just say that the party is over. Ask Hannu from next door to help if they don't believe you. Who all is there?"

I still didn't recognize the names.

"Mom."

"Yes?"

"It's a pretty big mess here."

"Are there any bodies?"

"Mom!"

"Once you get the house cleared out and drink a liter of water, call your dad and tell him that a bunch of boys you don't know came in while you and Anni . . . "

"Who?"

"The girl you told Dad is with you. Be careful; he'll remember that."

"Yeah."

"While you were watching a DVD . . . maybe you were watching our *Sex and the City* box set."

"Okay."

"And you couldn't stop them. One of them was a friend of a friend. Then people just kept coming and coming, and two little girls like you couldn't do anything to resist."

# Robert

I DON'T REMEMBER why we went on that bike ride around the lake country or whether it was my idea or Mikko's. It must have been the summer between our first and second or second and third years of high school. Both summers I worked at my uncle's K-Market unloading boxes of frozen corn, peas, and carrots, and building giant swaying towers out of diaper packages. I got to schedule my shifts around summer activities and even take a couple vacations.

During one of them we loaded our bikes on an InterCity train and took the Savo line to Mikkeli. We spent the night in a cheap hotel, and studied the map on the bed because the table only had room for the phone, hotel binder, and a folded cardboard reminder not to smoke.

Those are the kinds of things you remember—like that the strap of one of my saddlebags kept hitting my calf the next day, and I didn't stop to tie it up because I didn't want to be the one to suggest taking a break. Physically I was stronger than Mikko, even though I had traded daily soccer training for a monthly gym pass. But Mikko was as tenacious as he's always been.

Consistent. Tenacious and consistent. Grabs on and holds.

My foot didn't hit the ground until we were through the gates of the campground. I remember the dry pine cones crunching and how soft the sand was. We were thirsty, but neither of us had given in.

When we both had headaches that night, we decided that the next day we would stop every twenty kilometers. We justified this with various arguments that were true but we knew were bullshit. Of course we saw through each other.

The weather was fair, not hot enough to remember, with no significant headwind. For the first two days we slogged away, and on the third we stopped at an art museum in an underground cave. We ate lunch on a nearby hill overlooking the lakes and then swam, since on the previous days we hadn't taken any more than a quick dip. We enjoyed ourselves and were punished for it, as Mikko had warned. A threatening cloud front caught up with us after only another fifty kilometers of riding.

I would have taken the risk and continued on to Imatra, the next large town, but Mikko was cautious. We bedded down in a shabby apartment hotel, which had lemon-scented dishwashing liquid in the soap dispenser, silverfish in the bathroom, and the previous occupant's moldy filter paper and grounds in the coffee maker.

Mikko was the one who wanted to stay there. We would have made it to Imatra before the rain.

The next night I wanted to sleep somewhere with a minibar.

"There's a state liquor store in Lappeenranta," Mikko said.

I explained that I wasn't interested in what was inside the minibar—tiny bottles of alcohol, peanuts, chocolate. What I was interested in was the quality of accommodations a minibar signals. I didn't want to sleep on thread-worn sheets, and I wanted to brush my teeth in a bathroom with a tiled floor and lots of light.

I held on to that, even though the forecast only called for one day of sunshine before more rain would catch us on the road again. Mikko wanted to continue past Lappeenranta to make the most of the weather window, but I won out. So we sat in the concrete courtyard of the hotel eating ice cream cones even though we could have been cycling.

The rain the next day was harder than predicted.

After days of mostly fair skies, this felt like an incomprehensible hardship. The darkness didn't give any hint of passing. The sky was a uniform grey, and the drumming of the rain constant. We didn't have any wet weather gear because it would have weighed us down. We went for thirds at the breakfast buffet and procrastinated leaving. The sky offered no hope of clearing, or even that the rain might let up.

"We could load the bikes on the train. We'd be home by afternoon."

Mikko was so angry I might as well have suggested a flat tax, advocated outsourcing basic health care, and defended George Soros's maneuvers with the pound all at once.

"Give up? Now, when we only have a hundred kilometers left? On our last day!"

I said it was just a suggestion. I was only describing a possible chain of events.

Mikko launched into a diatribe about how challenges were made to be defeated and that sort of thing, but I didn't listen. I just said that of course I didn't want to cut our trip short. If Mikko hadn't interrupted me, I could have completed my thought.

"So what were you thinking?"

"That we should go."

Our tennis shoes were wet through before we even got out of town. The cars on the highway threw sheets of water up as high as our crossbars. We alternated five or ten kilometer stretches of riding point. You had to leave enough space between yourself and the person in front so you could see and veer aside if necessary. The tires of passing semis grazed our saddle bags.

We didn't take any breaks. We covered kilometers. My turns leading grew shorter, but Mikko held on to his kilometers as if to demonstrate his stamina. On the previous days I would sprint, falling back to read a sign and then catching up to Mikko to get some training out of the ride. Sprinting fit my athletic profile better than a constant pace. I had a competitive advantage at that.

"We're getting off this road," I announced after the draft of a passing big rig threw me from the asphalt onto the shoulder.

Mikko tried to calm me down and pulled out the map. The rain soaked it instantly and the colors started to smear under his thumb.

"Right at Savitaipale Road. It's just a couple of kilometers. Before we hit this town, we take a right on Partakoski."

Mikko rode ahead. His tranquility was irritating. As if the conditions didn't bother him at all.

"I think I'm coming down with something."

"Should we take a rest?

I waved the idea away, and we continued on.

The asphalt turned to gravel on my next turn in the lead. We let air out of our tires, and pedaling became even harder. We had to take care not to let our tires slip into any of the cracks in the poorly maintained road. We had to avoid the streams running down the hills. We had to move forward.

After fewer than ten kilometers on the dirt road, my back wheel stopped, propelling me forward and into the mud. The inner tube had burst on a sharp rock or something. At the time I wasn't interested in the reason or really anything at all other than that water was coming from the sky, I was soaked through, and we were still fifty kilometers from Mikkeli even though my strength had run out ten kilometers back.

By the time I got my bike dragged to a nearby milk run shed, Mikko was already stretching a new tube.

"Do you know what I want to do?"

There were many options, and Mikko began considering them as if he were trying to solve a real poser of a problem.

"Call a helicopter and fly somewhere it isn't raining. Leave the bikes here. Buy new ones at home. Go somewhere the sun is shining. Lie in a lounge chair by a pool with a drink with an umbrella."

"Would that be happiness?"

I sat on a crumbling stone road marker and watched as Mikko deftly removed the rim, took off the tire, and pulled out the burst inner tube. He inspected the tire to make sure no rock fragments or glass remained.

"Or we could call a taxi van that could fit both bikes. Then we floor it to the Cumulus, buy us each a bottle of cheap vodka, and fix the world."

This time Mikko didn't reply. Maybe I looked pathetic. Maybe he felt sorry for me.

I ate a slice of bread that had been smashed into an unrecognizable lump in my bag, without the slightest shame that Mikko was fixing my tire. He reminded me that we only had another couple of hours to ride.

"Then we're done. We can say we rode all the way around Lake Saimaa."

"We could say that now."

"Even if we do part of the trip in a taxi?"

"Equipment malfunction. Unanticipated conditions. *Force majeure.*"

"Challenges are meant to be overcome.

"Challenges and victories have to be kept in perspective. We won the war but all the men died."

"No one is going to die."

"We're on vacation! Why do we have to suffer when we have the opportunity to take it easy?"

"It will feel good later. If we give up . . . "

"'Give up' sounds so negative. Making a rational decision when conditions change isn't giving up, it's just a rational decision."

I found a chocolate bar in one of my saddlebags.

"A taxi would cost a lot," Mikko said

"We'll ask him to drive us to an ATM. I'll pay, if that's what it's about," I replied.

"That isn't what it's about."

Mikko started pumping air into the tire.

"Well, at least let me pump it up myself! You didn't let me change the tube. As if I didn't know how."

Ripping the pump from Mikko's hand, I worked the piston until my arm ached.

"You go ahead and start. I'll catch up."

Mikko was waiting for me a few kilometers ahead.

"Did you think I couldn't do it, so you had to wait and keep watch?"

"I was just resting a little."

"If you need to rest, go ahead. I don't like rain enough to stand around in it on the side of a dirt road."

I kept riding. The washboard road rattled the bike. I had filled the tubes all the way to maximize speed even though it meant less traction. After an hour the gravel turned to asphalt, the main road connecting Lappeenranta to Mikkeli. After the sign *Mikkeli 30*, I tracked the kilometers in minutes.

The rain stopped at the Mikkeli city limits.

We had reserved a room at the Cumulus. An optimistic worker was wiping water off of the patio tables and turning the chairs right-side up. I left the bike in the parking lot built on top of the neighboring shopping center and spread my clothes out to dry in the bathroom, on the edges of the dressers, and hanging from the lights. When I came out of the shower, Mikko was knocking on the door.

"They said you took both keys." Mikko pulled two half-liters of Koskenkorva vodka out of his backpack.

My towel around my waist, I drank a plastic cup full and prepared to avoid the question I knew Mikko was going to ask once he had showered too.

"Don't you feel good now?"

That didn't take long.

Denying that I felt good after the suffering had ended would have been ludicrous. Once you've been hanging long enough on the cross, anything else feels like heaven.

"But am I more satisfied than I would have been if we had packed our bikes into a taxi?" I asked. "We would be here in the same place. The surface level in that bottle would be lower but my mood would be higher. Am I more satisfied now than I would be in that situation? Hard to say."

Mikko's opinion was cut and dry: happiness can't just be measured by the hormone levels in your body. It also has an intellectual component. The knowledge of completing a difficult bike ride increases the level of happiness. The knowledge of giving up would lower it significantly. So there was no way I could be happier if we had come by taxi.

"So here's the question: Is my current level of intellectual feelings of happiness greater than the vexation caused by riding in the rain?" I asked.

The value of the contrast was obvious, there was no doubt about it, but did the experience refine me as a person? Couldn't I have felt the same feeling even if we had ridden under fair skies or if we were sitting right now on the shore of Lake Saimaa under silver birches susurrating in a gentle breeze as the evening sun dipped behind the water? Did adversity increase the happiness of my life?

"Are those happiest who are forced to suffer most? Then the starving children of AIDS victims in Africa would be the happiest people in the world," I said.

Between the beds was a battered nightstand, just big enough to hold a bottle of booze and our flimsy plastic cups. We sat across from each other on the edges of our beds and drank as if we had learned to drink from Finnish TV movies. When a furtive ray of sunshine broke through a gap in the clouds, I drew the blackout curtains.

After drinking ten fingers of clear 76-proof alcohol in his long johns the archetypal Finnish man begins talking about life. The rhetorical reservations fall away, with sentences forming in which the slowly enunciated words have more weight than meaning.

That applied to us as well. We were a cliché.

"What do you want out of life?"

"Freedom."

"Freedom?"

"Freedom is independence. It's a requirement for being able to do what you want."

"Is it enough?"

"If there is no freedom, you can't do what you want. You can only decide what you want in life if you are free."

"What do you want?"

"I want what is right. If there isn't freedom, you end up doing wrong. You always have to submit."

"So you believe life is about self-fulfillment?"

"Life is good living and being happy. Just so long as you don't cause others unreasonable harm."

"Infringe on their freedom."

"Yeah. When you're free, you can live right."

The next day on the train we each read our own books and didn't talk except when one of us announced he was going to the bathroom.

# Mikko

ROBERT HAD THE ladle, so he had the power. I wanted to go shower and ask Veera if she'd gotten Julia on the phone, but I couldn't leave.

Robert dosed the steam sparingly. He reminisced about how I had changed the tube on his bike tire during that trip to the lake district. Robert described it as if it had been a divine act of salvation. A miracle. I remembered it too. Robert had been coming down with something, but managed to fight it off. Of course I'd helped him. I would have taken his bags and carried them, too, but he wouldn't give them to me.

I nodded and hoped Robert would throw more water on the rocks. He repeated a conversation we'd had in a hotel room twenty years earlier, recalling it sentence by sentence. I didn't have any memory of it. It must have been an important experience for Robert.

It surprised me that Robert had assigned value to something human. Deathbed repentance—perhaps he sensed something.

Or maybe seeing each other again had just made Robert sentimental.

I'm not naturally impatient. I was then, though. The strychnine was waiting for Robert in his coffee cup. I wished the night was over and the probability had already reached one hundred percent.

At that moment in the sauna waiting for more steam, I understood that I hadn't thought through sufficiently what would happen after Robert's death. I had only dreamed of the future, looking past the immediate aftermath. I had only seen Elise, how she would throw her arms around my neck once Robert was dead. She would shout for joy at being free and proclaim her love for me. I would respond that I loved her too. Veera might be in the room too, but she would know instantly that Elise and I belonged to each other.

At least, she would understand once I explained.

Robert got to the end of the story and emptied the bucket onto the stove. Finally there was steam.

When I got out of the sauna, I showered. Staying on my feet was a challenge. I closed my eyes and nearly fell asleep in the shower.

The towel was new, soft and white. I patted my face on it and breathed in deeply, because there wasn't much time anymore. We didn't have much time. Robert didn't have much time.

Too late I realized I would have wanted to hear him retell the story about our bicycle trip. I wished I had listened. It might be the last story Robert told me. Would that be my final memory—that I hadn't listened? Shouldn't I honor a dying man? Wouldn't it only be decent to give him a little of my time?

When I threw my towel in the woven basket, I noticed the champagne sword leaning there.

Robert had just bent down to lather his feet. His head hung as an extension of his back.

It would have been such an easy swing, sending the blade slicing through his neck from above, or into his jugular from below, or into his vital organs from the side.

Extremely easy.

The opportunity had presented itself unexpectedly. I had helped circumstance along, but now circumstances were helping me. An improbable coincidence, as if a sign from fate.

Or had someone placed the sword there so I would take it up?

What, and perish? Was that it? But who? Robert himself? Veera? No, Elise of course. Elise had understood! Elise had taken a while, but now she understood that I was really going to save her. Elise had delivered me a weapon to kill her husband.

I looked at the saber blade. Neck or side? I considered the amount of blood, the certainty of the stroke. A jab at the liver, or execution style to the neck? Perhaps the heart?

I pulled the sword out of the basket. The blade ran across the jute weave and sliced a furrow in it.

I grabbed the hilt with both hands.

I decided to go for his side.

I raised the sword over my right shoulder.

My reflection was visible in the mirror and the tile.

Robert straightened up. He threw his elbows back and shook his head, stretching his shoulder blades and neck.

I had to dodge so his elbow wouldn't hit my clenched fists.

"Man, that did me good!" Robert said. "The blood is pumping in my veins, and I feel like a newborn babe."

I removed one hand from the sword and slipped it back in the towel basket.

"Life without sauna wouldn't be . . . " Robert paused, pondering how to finish the sentence.

"What's this doing here?" I asked and pulled the sword out of the basket, making a confused face.

"What's what doing where?" Robert asked.

He had closed his eyes so the soap wouldn't get in them. I still could have stuck him then. Robert rinsed his face. Then the moment had passed.

# Veera

THE GUEST ROOM bedspread was slick under my bare legs, smelling of fabric softener. I ran the tip of my tongue along the quilting and imagined it being Mikko's inner thigh.

When I saw Mikko in the bathroom with the champagne sword in his hand, it looked just like he intended to stab Robert in the side.

The thought was absurd, but it burned deep in my gut. Mikko the barbarian! My husband, who would spend half an hour gently shoeing a trapped wasp out of the house. I had seen Jekyll, and now I saw Hyde. Day and night. This was the contrast I had gone to Rob looking for. Aroused by the buzz of the alcohol, I wanted so badly to fall in love with a murderer. I imagined my husband's devious motives, and imagined his face twisted in pain. Then I replaced the pain with a look of defiance, which only took a small change of expression.

Mikko the barbarian. Mikko the murderer!

I developed a theory and invented evidence that seemed to bolster it.

Mikko had wanted to come here. Deviation from a routine always arouses suspicion. All of medical diagnosis is based on that. In accepting the invitation, Mikko acted abnormally.

Second, the flowers. Could it be a coincidence that Mikko, who didn't usually care about anything as mundane as flowers, went to a flower shop and bought white lilies, of all things? Funeral flowers?

And hadn't Mikko been oddly quiet at the dinner table when Rob was contemplating how he might be murdered, even though Mikko usually interrupted him?

Mikko and the sword. Why had Mikko raised it into striking position behind Rob's back if he wasn't planning on hitting him with it? If you find a sword in a strange place, the normal thing would be to return it carefully to the place it belongs.

Why did Mikko suddenly shove the sword in the towel basket as if he'd been startled? Why would Mikko flinch if he didn't have anything to hide?

I didn't remember the last time I had wanted Mikko so much.

When the squeaking of the hotel slippers approached, I didn't leave Mikko any options.

"Good evening, Mr. Murderer!"

I turned toward Mikko.

The dandruff shampoo bottle slipped from my husband's hand onto the floor and rolled under the desk.

Mikko said my name.

I said, "Come here, Murderer. I'm not afraid."

"How did you know?" Mikko asked.

It was a very strange question. Mikko was supposed to laugh and make it a joke. I knew my husband. Mikko was reacting wrong. He only acted this way when I had surprised him.

"Nothing ever stays secret from me," I said. "Or from you."

When Mikko didn't seem to understand what I meant, I pulled him into bed.

*UNTIL HE'D LEFT the airport he'd been leaving tracks. Now he had to become invisible.*

*Of course the Munich railway station was full of security cameras. They would comb through the footage of the transit stations when it turned out he hadn't flown to Helsinki. They would search for him. He would be so important.*

*A line of red Deutsche Bahn ticket machines stood on the outside wall of the station. He chose the last one. The machine offered him a screen full of ticket options.*

*The Schönes Wochenende ticket, of course! With it a party of up to five people could travel as much as they wanted on local trains on Saturday and Sunday. Even though everything that happened at the ticket machine would be recorded on the security camera hard drive and even though they might be able to locate his purchase in the transaction history, the ticket wouldn't reveal where he was going.*

*He didn't even need to know where he was going.*

*As a student he had made a daytrip to Salzburg using the same kind of ticket. A train to Salzburg appeared to be leaving in fifteen minutes. That sounded good.*

*He didn't get on it, though.*

*He boarded the S train, which went to the Munich East Railway Station.*

*At the Ostbahnhof he got off, moved to another platform, and transferred to a local train going to Salzburg.*

# Robert

THE OTHERS STOOD behind the dining table gazing at the city lights. Veera pointed at different landmarks, sighing with enchantment as she leaned against Mikko, who fidgeted nervously and responded tersely. Elise explained enthusiastically where Big Ben, Wembley Stadium, and the London Eye were.

Yes, I remember quite clearly noticing that Mikko was nervous, Veera was besotted, and Elise was excited. Nervousness was typical for Mikko—he was always worried about something—but Veera and Elise seemed abnormal. I had just had a fight with Veera, and I had to work to keep myself composed, but she seemed happy. Had something happened I didn't know about?

Of course I was pleased that Veera seemed to be at ease, but I was overjoyed to see Elise in such high spirits. Lately Elise had been melancholy. I had talked about her to my doctor and asked him to write her a prescription for Zoloft, which I thought she had been taking more or less as instructed, but she still often seemed to be in her own world.

At first I hadn't thought of Elise as a partner. But I also hadn't thought of her as a one-night stand, since I didn't do that. Elise was a woman whom I felt like spending the evening with after meeting her. After that I wanted to spend another night with her. Elise was impulsive. She was young and adventurous. All I had to do that first night was say I was a naughty schoolboy who'd been caught by his teacher, and she forced me down on my stomach and slapped me on the buttocks.

The next time, she turned out the lights, shoved me onto the hotel bed, and took a leather cap and handcuffs out of her handbag before getting on top of me.

Veera and I had role played too, but once when I whispered in her ear "you be the maid" and pulled the rattan carpet beater out from under the bed, she burst out laughing. She swatted it in the air while I tried to get it away from her. This had turned into a chase around my bedroom and then the apartment at large, with some grappling for dominance, but afterwards I never suggested props again. It was fine without them anyway. Veera knew how to subordinate and submit without the toys.

With Elise there were no boundaries—until we reached them.

It was annual bonus time at Union Credit, and traditionally each division celebrated with a plus-one party. The previous year's had been excellent, and the bonuses and party program were commensurate. We held it at the Claridge. After the main course, a man with colorful glasses stepped up to a white piano. "Your Song" was followed by the cheese course.

I had reserved us a room with a balcony overlooking Brook Street—at the time I still didn't want to bring Elise to my home. Elise had started talking dirty to me as soon as the dinner ended, but I still wanted to spend a few minutes circulating among my colleagues. This was always the best party of the year. We were both shitfaced but not just from the alcohol. One of the vice presidents had scored some new pills he said had a special kick.

Elise said that if we didn't leave she was going to climb on a chair and flash her tits at everyone. I was in the middle of a conversation with a young trader, so I just said that good tits deserved to be shown. Applauds and whistles soon followed. When I turned around, Elise was standing on a round table surrounded by empty glasses. Her dress only had one shoulder, and she had pulled it down and was swinging her breasts for the cheering crowd.

We went to our room. Elise was full of energy. She disciplined me like a misbehaving child until we changed roles and I tied her hands to the foot of the bed with my belt. We were on the carpet, and Elise tried to escape to the bed, but I held on to her. I called her a dirty whore and choked her with both hands. Elise groaned with pain and pleasure, closing her eyes and crying out. I squeezed harder, and Elise moaned.

Until she stopped breathing.

I slapped her cheeks and performed mouth-to-mouth. I pumped air into her chest. Then I rushed her out the back door to the private clinic I used.

On the official papers, the incident was recorded as an acute allergic reaction, but unofficially the doctor encouraged us to be careful with unfamiliar chemical compounds. He didn't say a word about the red marks on Elise's neck.

That was the decisive moment. I had to take care of Elise. I had to make up for the trauma I had caused.

I had already lost one woman. I wasn't going to lose another.

We married. Elise moved in with me.

After that Elise changed. It must have been because of what I did to her. She started drinking more. She was late for work, started forgetting things, and got fired.

I should have taken better care of her. My job was to bind us together.

Elise lived with me. She was my wife. I saw us as a family. When I stopped using a condom, Elise asked if she should start taking the pill.

No need, I said. Elise said she might get pregnant. That was what I had been thinking too.

That was the first time Elise ever pushed me off. Once we were sober and discussed adding to our family as we sat at the dinner table, she had nothing against it, but in the fall when we were in Hungary, in her handbag I found a foil-backed packet with a day of the week label for each pill.

"What's so special?" I asked my guests, who were still gazing out over the city and sighing. I was still irritated. Looking at Veera reminded me of our skirmish. "Metal wires surrounded by protective glass and heated with electricity until they glow. More and more LEDs."

"It doesn't matter what it is, only how it looks."

Elise had learned that from me, and she was right. Truth is overrated. Truth can be an object of academic endeavors, but people who are fixated on truth never accomplish anything.

"I've started to get tired of them," I said. I meant the lights, and I meant what I said.

"It makes you restless," Mikko said and asked if the shining of the lights made me uneasy.

On the contrary, I said, the view calmed me. When I glanced out the window, I saw that the world still existed. I wasn't alone.

"Is that what you're afraid of? That you'll be left alone?"

"I get along very well by myself. I like being alone. But I wouldn't want to be alone all the time."

"That would be no different from death."

"There's been a lot of talk about death today."

Elise suggested that we trade places. Mikko and Veera could have their backs to the window during dessert so the lights wouldn't bother Mikko.

"No, no, no. We don't have to change everything for me," Mikko said.

"It's easy though. We can look wherever we want every day. You're only here today."

I suggested that we make these dinners a tradition. "You could come every year. For instance, while the sales are on."

"And arrange everything just like today?" Veera asked.

I responded that we could discuss the details later.

"Well, are we changing places?"

"Absolutely."

"All the cups are the same."

"I think I'd prefer to look at the lights of London," Mikko said.

"Mikko wants a little restlessness in his life!" Veera said and slapped her husband on the behind.

Mikko said the view was like any other view. If you look at the ocean, waves roll in. If you look at the forest, the leaves of the trees rustle.

Veera sat in Elise's place with her back to the window. I sat across from her in the place where Mikko had sat during dinner.

# Mikko

THE SOUND OF my phone ringing came from the guest room. I ran so I could answer before the caller hung up. Calling back would cost twenty or thirty extra cents.

Julia's number was flashing on the screen. I pressed the green button and yelled hi before I got the phone to my ear. I couldn't sit down.

"Are you okay?" I asked.

"Yeah."

"Is everything all right?"

"Well, there aren't any bodies."

"Tell me what happened."

"No!"

"Well, fine, you don't have to tell me everything, but are you okay?"

"Yeah, I already said that."

"Are there . . . ?"

"Any bodies? No, there aren't. And there isn't anything else to tell. I just want to go to bed, but I wanted to call you first."

"That's thoughtful of you."

"Well, you were actually the one who solved the mess. I told them they had to leave right now or I'd sic you on them."

"Me?"

"Maybe they don't know you."

There was the kind of little girl smile in her voice that melts your heart. It was that smile between a father and a daughter, slightly teasing, that reminds you that genes aren't the only thing you share.

Tears started welling up.

I didn't know what to say. I couldn't have said anything.

First the longing came. Then it became unbearable.

I wanted to be at home clutching Julia in my arms. Julia would resist and try to wriggle away. That was our way, a daddy-daughter thing.

And Veera. How had I forgotten how good she was? What else could my feelings toward Veera be but love?

"Can I go to sleep now?"

Julia hung up. I listened to my accelerated breathing through my nose, with the soundless receiver to my ear. Through the door came lively chatter interspersed with laughs, but I couldn't hear the words. The second hand of the clock on the guest room wall ticked, and the grandfather clock in the library boomed.

Together their sounds interrogated me: *Mikko, look at what you're doing.*

The voice continued: *Mikko, you're destroying everything you've achieved.*

It said: *Mikko, you're murdering your best friend.*

That thought ran up my spine into my brain. I understood why I hadn't struck Robert in the back in the bathroom with the champagne sword. That back wasn't the back of a banker. It wasn't the back of Elise's abuser. It was my friend's back, with my friend's ribs curving around to my friend's stomach and chest, and at the top of it was my friend's shoulders, neck, and head.

I loved Robert.

I'd like to point out that over the course of the evening I had consumed alcohol in abundance and was seriously intoxicated. As we know, alcohol alters the personality, weakens coordination, and amplifies emotions. Under normal circumstances I naturally would have been capable of better analytical thought and conversing with myself using logical argument rather than swells of emotion.

Of course I also would have been able to listen to my own thoughts without being moved to tears.

At that moment, though, my analytical powers were impaired and my emotions heightened. I would request that this fact be taken into consideration and not minimized. But of course I'm not trying to explain away anything with alcohol. What would it explain? That I reversed my decision and tried to prevent the murder from happening?

I can't help that by reversing my intention to commit murder I caused even more deaths.

A feeling of love overwhelmed my mind. I loved all of them, each individually and all together. I loved Julia, who wasn't here. These people were my life, all of it that had passed and all that was yet to come.

And I was destroying it all.

All of it.

I threw the phone on the bed still rumpled from our romp. I could still take it back. I could still stop Robert's death and zero out the probabilities.

The chiming of the clock still hung in the air as I stepped out of the guest bedroom. Even though I hadn't counted the chimes, I knew there had been twelve. This was a new day. Today would not be like yesterday.

I dried my tears on the coarse fabric of my shirt. I knew what I wanted. For the first time in as long as I could remember.

# Elise

THE COFFEE CUP incident. What a funny thing to call it. It reminds me of a ride at an amusement park. The one with the giant teacups with enough space for a whole family. Colored lights flash. The cups rotate around themselves and also in a circle around the ride and then in a third way too, so you have to be careful that your cotton candy doesn't come back up.

We had mad coffee cups, though, because the tea cups hadn't been set out. Finns are a coffee-drinking people as long as our stomachs can handle it. Sauna, Sibelius, Moomins and coffee. Black coffee and white snow. Thousands of lakes. Perfect for boiling and making coffee.

Where I sat didn't matter to me in the slightest. I didn't see that clearly anymore. My eyes have this problem that they get blurry as the day goes by. In the morning they're bloodshot. In the evening they get bloodshot again and all the corners turn into grey blurs. I should probably visit an eye doctor.

Robert and Veera were back standing at the window again. I sat in the place that had been Veera's. Funny how a place can belong to a person even though they've only sat there once.

Then I remembered something. When I had been sitting in the library, I had seen Mikko's reflection in the dining area window. He had sprinkled something into a coffee cup. Was Mikko using an artificial sweetener but didn't want to tell the others? Mikko was so healthy and athletic.

Mikko had tried to make sure it was a secret. But even with blurry eyes I had seen. Mikko probably thought no one could see because there was a wall between us.

So which cup was it? Silly question. Of course it was his own! Why would Mikko have put sweetener in someone else's cup? I couldn't think of a reason anyway.

Robert said, "There you can see Kensington Garden."

It would be a shame if Mikko's sweetener went into Robert's cup. Robert's coffee would be too sweet, and Mikko's would be bitter.

Veera asked, "Does that matter?"

Veera and Robert were so intent on the view that they didn't notice when I switched Mikko's and Robert's cups. I even turned the spoons leaning the right way so no one would notice the difference.

Robert said, "We're just able to see it from here."

The Mad Teacups at the amusement park are faster and have more colors. In Mad Coffee Cups, the places only change if someone moves them. Someone like me.

I sat in my place and moved the cups. I was an unmoved mover.

The servant came in with a shiny coffee pot. She asked, "May I pour?"

Robert said, "Our other guest . . . "

Veera said, "Mikko will come when he's ready. And Rob, you go ahead and sit by me. Mikko will sit where we put him. If the lights of the city bother him, let him close one eye."

Robert sat across from me in the same place where he'd sat during dinner. We weren't sitting next to our spouses anymore, because the girls had traded places.

A little variety was nice. Next time we could sit in different places again.

And I didn't remember anymore that I had switched Mikko's and Robert's cups.

# Mikko

I HEARD ROBERT'S voice in the foyer. I wanted to hear my friend's voice again many more times.

I hurried to the dining area. Robert was sitting with his back to the window in the same spot he had during dinner.

In front of him was a coffee cup, which my mind painted red. Anyone who drank from that cup would die within a few hours. Unstoppably and with terrible pain.

"Weren't we supposed to swap places?"

"We'll do it next time," Robert said.

That was a problem. That was a big problem. Coming up with an excuse for returning my own cup to the kitchen would have been easy.

The servant stood next to Veera with the coffee pot extended. So it hadn't been poured yet. I still had time! I was in luck. Nothing would happen now. I could smash Robert's cup. I would stage it as an accident so I wouldn't have to explain.

So I banged into the table so hard that the dishes rattled. The napkin folded at my place fell over. But the cups only shuddered.

"Behave yourself or they won't invite us over again," Veera said.

A glass of water had been set for each of us. I emptied mine.

"Excuse me, could I have another glass of water?" I asked the servant.

The servant left the coffee pot on the buffet table and went into the kitchen. My heart was racing like a sprinter's. There wasn't much time, but now I had as much more as the time it took her to get my water.

"We were just talking about movies," Robert said. "I asked who would want to see a three-star movie."

"Me!" I said, jumping up and banging my thigh against the table, hoping to jostle it. It didn't even budge. The only thing I would get from thumping it was bruises. I sat back down. I had to come up with something else.

Robert thought movie ratings were analogous to investment analysis recommendations: five stars means strong buy, four stars buy, three hold, two reduce, one sell. He did point out that some analysts use *strong buy* in place of *buy,* but that just showed the same sort of over-exuberance as the superlatives used by star-struck movie critics: No movie can be something "you have to see before you die" any more than any stock could be a "bombproof investment."

"Who would buy a stock that gets a 'hold' rating? And by the same token, who would watch a three-star movie? There aren't any other states than buy or sell. There aren't any other states than watch or not watch."

I asked if Robert needed a critic to tell him what to watch.

At the word "critic," I made a grandiose sweep of my hand toward the candlestick, which fell to the table. It was a sort of thin, delicate metal object that had to have been made by some famous designer. Even though the candlestick fell in the right direction, it only bumped against the edge of Robert's cup.

Veera righted the candlestick and said that I needed to be more careful. I felt like asking her which one of us was trying to save a human life.

Fortunately, the candles weren't burning.

Why hadn't the servant lit them?

The servant arrived to check the situation. She shifted the candlestick slightly toward the middle of the table just to show that Veera hadn't put it in the right place.

Then she stepped over to Veera's side and asked her how she liked her coffee.

Soon it would be Robert's turn.

So I stood up.

Veera asked where I was going.

So I sat down.

# Elise

ROBERT SAID, "WHEN someone buys stock, they use money, but when someone watches a movie, they're playing with much higher stakes. They're paying with their time. They're using the most valuable capital they have: their own life."

There were a lot of other things that Robert said. Robert and Mikko were so similar. They liked to talk.

I didn't always listen. If I was listening and didn't understand, I asked. That was what question marks were for.

Robert said, "Using your time is also a way of voting."

Time is not an hourglass. You can't get time back by turning something over.

Time is what is now.

But now it isn't anymore.

Time is like a fly. You have to catch it *now*.

But when you try, it's already escaped from between your hands.

You can catch a fly with a flyswatter. You can't catch time with a flyswatter.

I've learned to bring tomorrow into today. I enjoy this day instead of building for tomorrow. I spent twenty years doing that. A little more actually. For the first few years I was irresponsible just like everyone else, though.

When you live in debt to tomorrow, you'll be a day ahead when you die. No one will make you pay back the extra day.

You never know when you'll die.

The reason for suffering is the thirst for life.

Physical thirst quenches the thirst for life.

Quenching the thirst for life feels nice.

I thought it was nice we had visitors. We didn't very often. We're gone so much that we're almost strangers in our own home.

When Robert was traveling, I watched Agatha Christie film adaptations on the big television screen. I had asked Robert for the complete set for Christmas.

I said: "I like Miss Marple more than that Belgian fatty."

Veera said, "Poirot is better in the books."

Mikko said, "They have a charming, old-fashioned feel."

Veera said, "People certainly were sly back then!"

Robert said, "Maybe movies shouldn't be thought of as realistic depictions of period England."

Veera said, "Upper-class people murder each other because of money. Nasty business."

I said, "They're so safe. Nothing bad ever happens in them."

Nothing bad.

# Robert

I HAVE A hard time understanding how people stand Agatha Christie. The books are just endless tea drinking, and the only purpose for the things that do happen is to create suspicions about each character in turn. By page seven the detective knows who the plotter is and why, but he sits on his information until the author gets her two hundred pages filled and finally gives the little dickhead permission to demonstrate what happened.

"I think Christie crafts a good plot," Mikko said in her defense.

Crafting a good plot sounded just like what Mikko tried to do in his work. He searched for conspiracies and probably even pictured himself as Hercule Poirot—no, it would be Robert Langdon, of course, a slightly shabby and socially awkward academic who in the course of a brisk twenty-four-hour period not only manages to save the world but hangs from a helicopter with a beautiful woman's body pressed against him.

Christie was a commercial success. When she made her breakthrough, there weren't many titles being published. Postwar paper shortages limited production, and publishers only put out books they knew would be a commercial success. Publicity and readers were divided amongst a tight group of writers who dominated the nation's consciousness.

However, Christie pulled one of the greatest publicity stunts of all time when she disappeared in 1926 just before the Christmas sales season. The author left home, drove her car off the road, and checked into a secluded hotel under an assumed name. The police believed Christie had died—had her husband murdered her? The newspapers ate up the mystery, and as many as fifteen thousand people joined the search for her body. When Christie turned up unharmed a couple of weeks later, the British public rushed to the bookshops to buy *The Murder of Roger Ackroyd.*

I knew the plots of Christie's books even though I had only ever read two or three of them back in high school. As soon as I moved to England, I purchased a book with summaries of all of her detective novels. The time it took to read a summary was an appropriate amount of time to spend on a crime novel. The essentials could usually be condensed into a few pages. There was no jingling of porcelain cups, and no one had to listen to an old maid and a gardener with a rustic accent discussing the blooming of the crocuses. Even though it was usually one of those seemingly insignificant details, like the time the crocuses bloomed, that was the key clue for understanding the plot.

Mikko said he had read *Murder on the Orient Express* on the plane.

"When you know who the murderer is, you can concentrate on other things as you read," he said.

I asked what other things there were.

As Mikko considered his answer, I asked the servant to pour me only half a cup. I had reduced my coffee drinking as part of the diet I had started after getting the boot from Union Credit.

I asked if I could suggest a scenario. This situation we were in was like something straight out of a Christie novel. The only thing missing was a pompous Belgian stroking his mustache or an old lady knitting and asking odd questions in a sweet voice.

"Let's pretend that one cup of coffee is poisoned."

Veera glanced at her cup.

The servant said she would bring the dessert shortly. I said we could wait.

"No more games like that," Elise said. "Can't we do more word play?"

"What would Christie do?" I asked. "First, she would let the murder happen so the detective could show off his skill and to give the author a setup for the book and fat royalties from the sales."

Veera said that was how mysteries usually were. A murder happens so it can be solved.

"Why does it have to be so complicated? If one of us wanted to kill another one of us, why on earth would he use poison? He could just take the saber out of the display case and lop off the person's head. Poison is the coward's way. Using poison is a sign of insecurity. A person who uses a gun or a blade knows what he wants."

"No, he couldn't," Elise said.

"Couldn't what?"

"Take the saber out of the display case and lop off the person's head."

"Okay, so maybe the head wouldn't come off all the way, but he would still be dead. Russian soldiers didn't just wear those sabers in parades. They were made for proper killing."

"He still couldn't."

I glanced at the display case. The saber wasn't in its place. Had I left it on the buffet table? I looked. Not there either.

I didn't have time to wonder about the saber's absence, though, because Mikko stood up, walked around the table, and picked up my coffee cup.

"If you're afraid your coffee is poisoned, let's pour it out."

I grabbed the cup before Mikko could do anything to it. I said it was just a mental exercise.

Mikko snatched at the cup. I resisted. Coffee splashed on the placemat. Fortunately, I had only taken half a cup.

Veera ordered Mikko to behave himself and go back to his seat. Mikko obeyed.

"The servant poured us all the same coffee," Veera said. "If Rob's coffee is poisoned, then we're all going to die."

"True!" exclaimed Elise.

I admitted that it was a poor hypothetical.

"You haven't read enough Christie," Veera said.

The servant arrived with the luxurious chocolate cake I had fetched from the patisserie earlier in the day and offered it to Veera first.

I said that I generally read very few books.

"If the story is good, they'll make a movie in a few years. And then you don't just get the author's vision; you also see the results of the work of the actors, the director, the set designers, the sound technicians, and the special effects team. And besides, it's cheaper than a book."

Mikko said that reducing a novel merely to its story left out much of what was essential. He was having a hard time sitting still. I asked if he felt like some cognac. Instead of responding, he just stared at the coffee cups. I asked the servant please to upgrade us all with cognac before we attacked the dessert.

I reminded everyone that every era introduced new tools to the arts. Artistic forms went through a process of development, and each time period favored different narrative tools. Nowadays the preferred tool was the motion picture. A hundred and fifty years ago making movies had been impossible.

Mikko pointed out that photography hadn't made the other visual arts obsolete. I reminded him that the photograph had largely eclipsed drawing, though. No one hired a charcoal artist with a quick hand to sketch portraits of the executive board for their annual financial report. We just take pictures. Click. If Vincent van Gogh had lived today, he would have used an automatic shutter release to take thousands of digital pictures of himself. He would have taken a picture of himself at the same time every day and then stitched them together to show himself aging day by day.

"Only hippies treat sick people with herbs anymore now that we have synthetic drugs developed in the lab. Movies are the current apex of the storytelling industry."

Making books costs basically nothing, so we produce a lot of them. The direct result is that books are worse on average than movies, which we make fewer of. A story has to get past a whole series of gatekeepers before a production requiring hundreds of people and expensive equipment can begin. The movie industry follows a simple principle of the *survival of the fittest*. All you need for a book are a persistent author and too much free time.

The servant finished pouring the cognac. My intent was to close the conversation so we could move on to the treats.

*THE LANDSCAPE WAS the kind people call calming: the train moved through snow-capped mountains, here and there a herd of cows ruminating in an Alpine meadow like in an advertisement for chocolate. The perspective was slightly distorted by the window glass.*

*The landscape didn't make him calm, but it did dull his agitation.*

*He was starting to feel tired. He had awoken about thirty hours earlier and had been in a state of intense concentration ever since.*

*He couldn't give in to the exhaustion, because calm could lead to relaxation. He couldn't afford that.*

*Why couldn't he?*

*That question was too difficult to process. He could afford practically anything. Even if he got caught, he wouldn't die.*

*He might not even go to prison. There would be no way to find any evidence against him that could conclusively prove he was a murderer, or even a killer, but you never knew about the justice system. All that really mattered was whether the jury had reason to believe in your guilt. The pieces of evidence that would point to him were numerous. That much was clear.*

*The most incriminating was that he had fled.*

*Why was he running away?*

*The train passed the mountains. After them came another range of peaks.*

*The answer was simple: because he had fled to begin with.*

*It had felt like the only option. He couldn't stay in an apartment with three dead people.*

*He was fleeing his old life. He had lost the people closest to him, so he didn't exist the way he had before either.*

*The train hadn't met with any delays, so it would arrive in Salzburg in a little more than half an hour.*

*What would he do there?*

*That would be good to think about.*

*He didn't remember anything about Salzburg other than Mozart's house, which their student tour group had visited. That didn't help much—the composer was sure not to be at home. On a Sunday the small city would probably be quieter than usual, so only the cafés, the restaurants, and the souvenir shops in the old town would be open.*

*He would find a room in a small hotel, buy a glass of Obstwasser schnapps, and continue on tomorrow. That would be the most sensible. But he was driven to hurry on. He had become attached to this pace. He couldn't just be—he had experienced that too. He wanted to be in a big city where he could be anonymous. He wanted to be in a big hotel where the workers would change three times a day. The thought of getting stuck in Salzburg was oppressive.*

*He would continue on to Zurich. At some point he would have to go there anyway, so why not go now?*

*What would he do for the rest of his life? He rotated the silver cross in his fingers.*

*He would have to consider that as well.*

# Veera

Seeing my Mikko so full of power was a huge turn-on.

He could hardly keep still as Rob gave his pseudo-intellectual lecture on the evolution of artistic genres. All that was missing was Darwin's apes.

"Filmmakers know how to calculate whether a script is valuable enough to make it profitable to produce a movie. They aren't always successful, but over the mid-term there must be more successes than failures. Otherwise bankruptcy yanks incompetent producers from the stage. The funding structure ensures quality," Rob proclaimed.

Mikko sprang to his feet, screaming that Rob was disrespecting art.

Mikko leaned on the back of Elise's chair, then circled to the other side of the table, faster than he should have in his socks on the hardwood floor. At least, not with Mikko's head for alcohol.

This was the kind of man I wanted, a man with Mikko's brain and Robert's rage. Maybe I needed to make trips like this a regular thing for us.

I felt like shouting, "Kill him, kill him!"

I'm not sure whether I did or not.

Is it going to happen now? I wondered.

I was in ecstasy. I can still see those seconds. Not in the sense that they were the climax of my life, but they were definitely good enough to end up on the highlight reel that flashes before your eyes as you die. If that happens anymore.

So what happened next?

Mikko slipped past Rob toward the Thames. Luckily there was a window in the way. As he went, his hand hit Rob's coffee cup, which fell to the floor.

Unfortunately, it didn't smash into little pieces for effect, because it was so sturdy and well-designed. Finnish craftsmanship.

The coffee splashed on the floor.

Mikko jumped at the clatter like Peter Rabbit meeting Mr. McGregor.

It was a complete anticlimax.

Mikko was a man of anticlimaxes. Mikko, my Mikko! Oh how I loved him.

My sweet, obedient husband forgot all about art and Rob and how angry he was, and bent over to get the cup. What else would he do! The cup rolled across the wood floor toward the window, still spilling coffee. Mikko managed to step on it, lost his balance, and fell on his back.

Rob seemed a little baffled, as was I.

I assured Mikko that everything was okay. Threading my arms under his, I pulled my husband against myself. Mikko was still groping for the coffee cup when I sat him back in his place.

I said that everything was all right.

Although of course it wasn't. Rob was still alive.

# Mikko

ULTIMATELY I SUCCEEDED rather well. I was overwrought, so it just looked like an accident. What everyone would remember was my anger, not the coffee cup. Maybe they would even think it was funny. I was prepared to endure that if it was the cost of narrowly averting Robert's death.

The coffee spread all over the floor. The servant approached with a cloth and began sopping up the poisoned brew.

After returning to my place, I dried the coffee off my fingers using a napkin. I would have preferred to wash my hands, but that wasn't an option since I'd already used the bathroom trick.

I decided I wouldn't touch any food with my right hand.

I rubbed my thumb and index finger together even though I knew nothing was on them anymore. Better overly cautious than careless. I've had plenty of scoops that fell through during the verification stage. You have to be sure. Overly enthusiastic journalists just toss whatever rumors they hear onto the Internet, leaving their editors to squirm when other papers call and ask if the information is correct. The editors have to lie, claiming the information was crosschecked with independent sources, only to march down to the cubicle of the reporter in question after the call and hear that the "information" was nothing more than the opinion of some chronically attention-starved politician.

The servant brought Robert a new cup of coffee.

I mixed some milk with my own.

"You never take your coffee with milk," Veera said.

That was true. I hadn't drunk milk with coffee since my grandmother offered me my first cup. At the time I was less than ten years old, and more than half of the coffee was whole milk, with three sugar cubes.

"Whenever I drink coffee in the Shard, I take it with milk. The height of the building demands it."

That was just as correct a reason as any other would have been. I don't know why I wanted milk in my coffee. Maybe I thought it would calm me down. Maybe I wasn't thinking anything.

"Mikko never deviates from his routines."

On my plate was a thick slice of chocolate cake.

I also never ate gobs of fat like that.

The coffee was disgustingly bitter. I had to mix in several cubes of sugar to even choke it down.

I sipped some cognac. That softened the sharp flavor of the coffee and dulled my anxiety.

What a close call.

Relieved, I tossed back the lukewarm coffee in one gulp and the cognac in a second. Then I concentrated on the chocolate cake, even though all the fat was revolting. Saturated fat was poison for the body.

# Elise

WHEN THE OTHERS went in the library, I went in the kitchen. I had my reasons. My reason was Mikko. As we stood up from the table, Mikko told me the rye bread they brought was spoiled.

Mikko said, "Could you throw it away so no one eats it by accident?"

The servant was loading the coffee cups into the dishwasher. On the surface of the coffee pot I saw a nice looking woman with a mysterious smile. It was me. I couldn't think why I would be mysterious.

The bread sat on the island like a rock. A big, dark rock, like regret. A big regret. The kind that gets stuck in your throat and chokes you. That you can't get down no matter how hard you swallow.

It probably still smelled like rye, though.

I felt like tasting it. I hadn't eaten rye bread in a long time. *A loooong time.*

It wouldn't hurt anything if I tried it, would it? I was supposed to throw it away. Of course not in the garbage, in the compost, so the worms could fill their little bellies.

Did worms have bellies?

The worms wouldn't starve if I ate a little piece. The surface of the bread felt smooth under my fingers even though it was bumpily.

That probably isn't a word.

I didn't taste it. I know how to be strong willed.

I have a bit of a bad habit of saying that I'm something I wish I were even though I might not really be that yet. I see things like they should be.

Sometimes that causes problems. I might not have remembered to order the food even if I promised I would, then say I did. Robert has learned that not absolutely everything I say is true.

The world looks more beautiful that way. That can't be bad, can it? And if it isn't bad, it has to be good. That's why I'm a lucky girl. And I have a lot of reasons to be happy.

The servant asked, "Is everything all right, madam?"

I said, "Couldn't be better."

I tasted the chips. They needed cider to wash them down.

After that I didn't remember the bread.

# Robert

"DOES ANYONE HAPPEN to remember in what years the summer and winter Olympics were organized in the same country?" Mikko asked after we had stood up from the table and moved to the chairs in the library. Veera inspected the bookshelf as if she were searching for something. Elise had gone in the kitchen.

"The correct answer is no."

"Wrong answer," Mikko said "The summer Olympics have been organized in the same country as the winter games three times."

"The answer is 'no,' because no one happens to remember. If someone does pub quizzes and has heard the question before, they'll know the question and the answer. Or if someone remembers all the places athletes have shed their sweat, they can get the answer by running through everywhere the Olympics have been. In neither case do they 'happen to remember.'"

I realized I was quibbling like Mikko did.

I had learned to adapt my behavior to my clients. If a client seemed more interested in bantering than digging into the details of contracts, I was only too happy to drop some appropriate punchlines and load the table with whatever structured products gave Union Credit the best margins. If a client wanted to share his ideas about world politics, first I would feel out what he thought and then jump on board with an impassioned argument for his side. If the client was religious, I would become a fundamentalist for the sixty minutes I spent with him, whether it was in a glassed-in conference room or at a restaurant characterized by minimalistic decor and small portions.

"In 1924 . . . "

I asked Mikko if he thought I didn't know the answer to his Olympics question. He replied that it felt like that. Of course I knew. Maybe it had even been Mikko who posed the question to me long ago. Didn't he remember? We always used to ask each other questions like that after we'd memorized all the cards in Trivial Pursuit.

"Well, let's have them."

Mikko had already revealed the first. 1924, Paris and Chamonix in France. 1932, Los Angeles and Lake Placid in the United States. 1936, Berlin and Garmisch-Partenkirchen in Germany. Three seemed like a lot from the modern perspective, but a hundred years ago hosting the Olympics hadn't been a green light to print money. Perhaps holding both competitions in the same country had been thought of as the rule since three of the four first winter Olympics were organized in the summer hosting country.

"In 1928, Amsterdam hosted the summer games, and the winter games were in St. Moritz," Mikko pointed out.

He probably knew every host country by heart.

"Where were the games in 1972?" I asked.

"The summer games were in Munich, and the winter games were in Sapporo," he said.

"1956?" I asked.

"Melbourne and Cortina d'Ampezzo," he said. "Let me ask one too. How many times did Paavo Nurmi stand on the highest podium in the Olympics?"

I started thinking out loud as if I didn't know. Pretending to hesitate, I counted the medals one by one. What had happened in cross country in Amsterdam? Did they remove that race after Paris?

"There isn't some catch to this, is there?" I asked Mikko. "The team cross-country races in Antwerp and Paris. Was it that the whole team wouldn't fit on the podium and Nurmi had to stand on the grass?"

"No, no tricks like that," Mikko said. Tricks *like that*. Mikko was a professional manipulator of words.

I managed to wheedle him into confirming that Nurmi didn't participate in the 10,000-meter in Paris because the Finnish coaching staff had decided to let Ville Ritola win and then keep Ritola back from the five thousand so he wouldn't bother Nurmi there. And Nurmi didn't want to lose to a man he considered worse than himself.

"He was a man of principle," Mikko said.

"Obstinate. Finland went without a guaranteed Olympic medal."

"No, we didn't: Eero Berg took bronze," Mikko said.

"We didn't get the silver," I said.

"That went to Wide from Sweden," Mikko added.

"Nurmi won nine gold medals during his career, so."

A smile appeared on Mikko's face. It was his last smile.

"Yes!" Mikko exclaimed. "But . . . "

"But because medal podiums weren't adopted until the 1932 games, Nurmi never climbed to the highest podium a single time in his career. Before then they gave the bling to the coaches, who gave it to the athletes. When they remembered."

Mikko couldn't conceal his annoyance. Nor I my satisfaction. Mikko wasn't a client, he was a friend, so I didn't need to worry about his mood.

"Too bad such a great runner was so greedy."

I asked whether Nurmi ever even would have won the Southern Finland Regional Championships if he hadn't been driven by a desire to succeed.

"Success doesn't have to mean greed."

"The underlying impulse is the same," I said. "The hunger for victory is greed. Stinginess is greed."

"An artist tries to produce the best piece of art possible, not get the largest sales price."

"You're talking about artists who were born in rooms with central heating and receive two warm meals a day. Paavo Nurmi went to work as a twelve-year-old so his fatherless family who lived in a single room could have food."

I had studied Nurmi's biography after moving to London, because I had thought anecdotes about famous Finns would be good cocktail party fodder. I tried Nurmi, but no one knew who he was even though half of my clients claimed to be training for next summer's marathon. The other half had already moved on to triathlons. The occasional elderly private banker might know Sibelius was a composer, but there was no point trying any of our other great men. Except of course Kimi Räikkönen. *Yeah, Kimi, he's marvelous. "Leave me alone, I know what I'm doing."* The encapsulation of our national heritage into one brash Formula 1 driver was nothing if not efficient.

Mikko reminded me that Nurmi's greed led to his disqualification from the Los Angeles Olympic marathon. He exchanged the opportunity to win the crowning race of his career for the mess of pottage of paid exhibitions. According to Mikko, that was Nurmi's tragedy.

Actually Nurmi's tragedy was that he never became Finland's richest man. Pounding the track was the best way for the son of a carpenter to make money because he had a competitive advantage at it, unlike factory work. The same approach continued after his sporting career when he became a real estate developer. Careful cost control, strict project management, and good retail prices using the Nurmi name and reputation. He maximized profits just as he had maximized training efficiency in his previous career.

"He broke rules," Mikko said.

"He revolutionized convention."

"Nurmi was a tireless perfectionist."

"He worked like a machine. He didn't have any alternative."

Mikko admired Nurmi because he was a runner. I admired him because he was a professional.

# Veera

WELL, IT DIDN'T look as though Mikko was going to sink a dagger into Robert's heart. There they were swapping trivia again like little boys in the schoolyard. If Mikko and Rob had resembled teenagers at the dinner table, now we had definitely regressed to elementary school. Next it would be nursery playtime stomping in puddles.

Unless I prevented it.

I thought things through as simply as I could. Mikko had wanted to kill Rob. He had backed down in the bathroom and failed at dessert. So if Mikko wasn't up to it, I would have to step in. This wouldn't be the first time practical matters fell on my shoulders. Who fixed the broken gutter? Who nailed the baseboards back on? Mikko was only barely capable of changing a light bulb. Just so long as the kitchen stepladder was in its place in the closet and there wasn't anything on top of it. Like a roll of masking tape.

Rob's death capsule. He had been so sure of himself when he showed it off. Now he would get to find out how it really tasted.

I was holding a book about the *Titanic* published in commemoration of the hundred-year anniversary of its sinking. Clever idea, that, celebrating the deaths of hundreds of people. Just so long as it meant you could pack people's houses with a little more junk. The Wonder Ship proudly cut through the waves. It looked a little like Rob.

Interrupting the boys' sparring match, I asked how many smokestacks the *Titanic* had. They started thinking about it, but soon they were engrossed in reminiscing about *Trivia Three*, a quiz show that used to be on MTV3, and neither noticed when I left. There was no sign of Elise.

The ampule wasn't in the dining area where Rob had been showing it off. I tried to look carefully for it. I couldn't see very well. Even though I have a good head for alcohol, this time I'd had an awful lot on an empty stomach.

Sober I never would have thought of killing Rob.

Or if I had, I would have just cursed instead of plotting a murder.

Rob had said he stored the cyanide in his safe. Maybe the ampule was there. I stole into Rob's office. The lights of the city were enough to illuminate my dubious deeds. On the desk there were three monitors and two passports. Were Robert and Elise going somewhere? Why hadn't they mentioned it?

The safe stood on the floor. On the door was a numeric lock.

Four numbers or six? Six, of course. No more than that, though. Rob wouldn't be stupid enough to use ones or zeros or 123456. But the code would have to be relatively simple. Birth date? Not likely. ROBERT spelled out in numbers? Rob might be just narcissistic enough for that.

Birth date backwards?

Rob was born in October, on United Nations Day. Rob was proud that the flag always flew on his birthday.

It was pretty damn hard thinking of the numbers backwards. I pulled a flier out of Rob's paper recycling. On the cover was a photograph of a white stucco house situated between blue sea and blue sky.

I wrote the numbers in the margin of the flier with a ballpoint pen that had Rob's name on the side. 24.10.1976. So 670142. I pressed the six.

The door moved under my finger: the last person had left it open a crack.

So I grabbed the top edge of the door and pulled. The door opened.

*Voila!*

Awfully careless, Rob!

At that moment I didn't think of what should first have come to mind when a banker has left his safe door open: Was it on purpose? Did Rob want someone to take something from his safe during the evening? Or was Rob setting it up so that if a third party came into the apartment the next day they would think that everyone in the place had had access to the safe?

But, no, I didn't think of any of that. I just opened the door wide and started inspecting the contents.

On the bottom shelf were folders of various colors filling the entire space from bottom to top. The upper shelf was significantly more interesting. On the left edge were two stacks of bills: pounds, euros, and US dollars in wrapped bundles, and then next to them other countries' currencies in rolls fastened with thick rubber bands. Next to the cash were a few gold bars and a box that looked like a child's toy.

I knew I had found what I was looking for.

I opened the box. Two glass ampules filled with blue liquid were bound together by a small strap. Undoing the tiny clasp, I slipped an ampule out and felt a dose of death in my hand.

Death was normal for me. But killing wasn't. That was why my hand shook.

I leaned against the safe door to stand up and then took a swig from the bottle of cognac on Rob's desk. Some of it spilled. Luckily it landed on my skin, and luckily it was brown. Licking a finger, I wiped it off.

I had probably sat for an examination in a toxicology course and read everything relevant about cyanide poisoning. I remembered that the method of action of cyanide was based on blocking the production of ATP. When cells don't get energy, they fatigue rapidly—something like that. But in any case, the end result would be a quick death as Rob had described.

Poison, the coward's choice! Rob would get to experience personally the taste of defeat at a coward's hand.

I wrapped one of the ampules in a paper tissue and slipped it into the inner pocket of my purse. The other needed to be in my hand at all times. There weren't pockets in my dress, so I used my old repository for my house key and taxi money. In it went to the left cup of my bra.

I was just closing the safe door when I noticed the papers. They weren't on the shelf with the folders, but instead in an envelope upon which Rob had written the word "Contract" in ballpoint pen.

Two printed sheets of A4 explained in detail Rob's obligations to Elise—the size of her monthly allowance and other standard of living provisions—and Elise's obligations to Rob. The contract guaranteed significant financial benefits for Elise for as long as it was in force. Why had Rob written it? Could there be any other reason than that Elise had blackmailed Rob or that Rob feared blackmail?

Had Rob done something to Elise?

*Like to Maarit.*

I understood when I noticed the interior surface of the safe.

On the door two photographs were taped side-by-side. Each showed a smiling woman under twenty. The girl on the left was blond and wore a summer dress made of Marimekko fabric. The girl on the right stood in a school courtyard in a winter coat.

The woman on the left was Maarit, the one on the right me.

Rob didn't have a safe so he could protect his investment papers, he had a safe so he could hide his darkest memories. He wanted to keep them close but away from prying eyes.

He wanted to remember death. That was what he said. So he

would remember to live. He wanted to remember the death *he caused*.

I was sure of that.

So why was my picture there next to Maarit?

The thought sent shivers through me, and I didn't want to consider what I should think of it. I leaned against the door again to pull myself up. I didn't close it, though. Maarit watched me the whole way as I walked out of Rob's office.

The cyanide capsule weighed ten times its insignificant mass on my breast. The library clock gave one lonely chime.

*A SMALL MAN with a bushy mustache indulgently sucked a cigarette next to a cheap looking box of an office. The illuminated sign atop the office reported the name of the business as Hermanns Automobile. Presumably this was Hermann himself, because the gate of the used car lot was closed and locked.*

*He saw his chance in this Hermann.*

*The Salzburg train station had delivered disappointment. The next rail connection to Zurich wouldn't have departed until after six and arrived at midnight. By road the trip was a good 450 kilometers. But he couldn't wait.*

*Rental agencies would demand to see a driver's license, which would be recorded in their database. The digital age had made disappearing difficult.*

*He waved and called a greeting to the man, who was wearing a fleece sweater and fiddling with the antenna of a dark blue Škoda as he smoked.*

*The man pointed at a sign indicating that the business was open from Monday to Friday until eight, six on Saturdays, and closed on Sundays.*

*He yelled that he wanted to buy a car. The man waved his hand to tell him to go away, and replied something in Austrian German.*

*He responded to the man's wave by flashing a fifty-euro bill.*

"Auto kaufen. Gut bezahlen."

*The man lit another cigarette, unlocked the gate, and opened it slightly. He still couldn't understand what the man said, but the bill quickly disappeared into the sweater's zippered pocket.*

*The fleet of cars was aging and the prices commensurate. Which suited him just fine. In the toilet of the train to Salzburg he had counted the stacks of bills taken from the safe. There were just under ten thousand euros, and about the same amount in pounds. He also had the money from the ATM at Heathrow. In the roller bag were the gold bars, which despite their diminutive size represented not only a significant weight but also significant exchange value. He would sell the largest of the bars tomorrow in Zurich.*

*They walked side-by-side through the cars in the dirty lot.*

*He told the salesman he was on vacation with his children in Austria. Their car had broken down, but they had to get moving. The children wanted to see Vienna. That was why he needed a car on such short notice. It was really great the salesman had the flexibility to show him a vehicle on his day off.*

*According to the tag hanging from the rear-view mirror of one dark green Audi, it was a 2005 model with 132,000 kilometers and cost €5,500. Aluminum rims, fog lights, CD player and subwoofer. According to the stamps in the records, the car had received regular service and inspections. Some of the information might have even been true.*

*The small man extolled the car's virtues. It had been a family's second car and basically only driven in the summer. The rest of the time the Audi had rested in a heated garage.*

*The salesman went to get the keys.*

*He sat down in the front seat, turned on the car, and pressed on the gas, all the while keeping an eye on the carry-on bag.*

*He offered five thousand euros.*

"Gut bezahlen?" *the salesman said.*

"Ja, fünftausend, nicht fünfhundert. Unglaublich viel für diesen Wagen," *he said.*

*They shook on the deal.*

*He took the bills out of the bag. The man counted half of them before shoving the stack into the pocket of his fleece.*

*He sat in the car until the salesman brought a pile of documents. Without a glance he tossed them in the glove box.*

*The salesman asked him to pass along his greetings to the children and wished them a pleasant time in Austria.*

# Mikko

A GOOD QUIZ show question isn't too hard or too easy, and the answer has to be possible to deduce using solid common knowledge. An excellent question has some sort of twist.

Robert asked those kinds of questions. I was surprised because I thought the world of finance would have damaged his ability for honest competition. A successful capitalist doesn't look for victories; he looks for crushing victories. Tens of millions in profits aren't enough for them. The ultimate success and final goal of a business leader is the complete destruction of his competitors. Capitalism seeks the Treaty of Versailles. It doesn't have to care that humiliation sows the seeds for the next war, because the state of war is constant.

"How many smokestacks were there on the *Titanic*?"

That was a good question, but Veera had asked it, not Robert.

I tried to recall a picture of the *Titanic*. Closing my eyes helped, but it also increased my exhaustion. I had slept poorly the previous night, and the trip to London by way of Tampere had been trying. Also, this evening had been extremely long—especially taking into account the time difference. I struggled to stay awake. The dizziness from the alcohol roared in my head, the emotional storms of the evening pulsed in my veins, and my right leg was starting to cramp. I clenched my teeth.

Robert recounted his memories of the *Titanic*'s smoke stacks: fat, slightly slanted tubes. I remembered the coloration. They were mostly the same light color as the upper deck walls, but at the top they were painted black like the rest of the ship. The effect was impressive. Something you would never believe could sink.

"There were at least three of them," Robert said.

Veera asked if that was Robert's answer.

I pointed out that we should agree on the order of answers. The second to answer would hear the first response and would be able to change his own accordingly.

"If I answer first, is that a problem? You can copy me or not. It's up to you. If I answer right, you should know if I answered right."

Robert's suggestion was beneficial for me, but this was a question of fairness. Would Robert always answer first, or would we trade off? And what if whoever had the opening turn happened to get an abnormal number of easy questions? And what about numerical answers? If someone were to ask the diameter of the equator of Uranus, the second answerer would only need to guess whether the number was larger or smaller than the first attempt. That was assuming that with numerical answers whoever came closest received the point. So we would also have to agree whether that would be the case or whether the answer had to be exact. And what would be the error tolerance? Ten percent? And would answers containing lists be worth more than one point? When mentioning individuals, would the first name need to be included or would the surname suffice?

Veera said that she had only asked how many smoke stacks the *Titanic* had. She hadn't intended to organize a large-scale trivia spectacle. She didn't even have a beehive or a miniskirt.

I asked Robert whether he remembered *Trivia Three*. Now that was a proper quiz show with proper questions and answers. The winner prevailed by knowledge and insight, not by happening to guess whether one of the other contestants knew the answer or some other equally inane way like on the current TV quiz shows.

"You taped them so we could compete against each other."

"The questions usually had a play on words. Like this one. Do you remember? The question went: *Name that country. The capital city could be 'a place for money.'* Robert, you should know this one!"

"A place for money?"

"A place for money? Five point question. Asking for the country."

"The bolívar? Bolívar, Venezuela."

"That isn't the capital city."

"The Deutsche mark, no. Crown, pound, dollar . . . "

"No ideas? I'll make it easier: it doesn't have anything to do with a currency."

"Cash, coin, dough, scratch. Saudi Arabia. The capital is Riyadh and the currency is the riyal."

"What makes it a place for money?"

"There's a ton of cash there."

"Wrong answer."

Robert argued that it could be though. I said that it wasn't; I was looking for the answer that Jyrki Otila and Reijo Salminen had looked for on *Trivia Three*.

"Prague and the Czech Republic? Czech as in write a check."

"Nope, not that either. The Philippines. Capital city, Manila, as in an envelope."

Robert thought Prague was just as much a place for money as Manila. P as in place. Even the parking places were marked with a P. Prague, park your money, so a place for money. I reminded him that the judges only ever accepted the answer they were looking for.

"The original question might have been 'Name that country in the news.' Maybe the Philippines had been in the news then."

"Did they ask about Imelda Marcos's shoes?"

"The contestant knew the answer and got the five points, so they didn't give any more hints."

Robert argued that I couldn't remember quiz show questions

from twenty-five years ago. He claimed that the clue could have just as easily been "a man in Los Angeles."

It wasn't though. I remembered the question quite clearly.

"Let's call Otila," Robert suggested.

"Otila is dead."

"Let's call Salminen then."

"He won't remember."

"But he might."

"We're not calling him."

"You're just afraid you're wrong!"

I tried to convince Robert that we couldn't go bothering a retired quiz show host on a Saturday night. Salminen had to be asleep by now. Robert thought a retiree like Salminen could use some money. He would make the trivia sage an offer he couldn't refuse.

"*An offer you can't refuse*. Name that movie."

Robert had the phone in his hand.

"Where are we even going to get the number?"

"Hush!"

Robert turned the speaker on and set his phone in the middle of the table. Salminen answered. Robert promised him a thousand euros with value added tax on top if necessary for five questions. Salminen agreed. Leaning in to the phone, I asked about Manila. He didn't remember it, but agreed that it easily could have been a question from *Trivia Three*. It was the right style. "A man in Los Angeles" was also a possible clue for the same reason.

"What orchestra instrument played a leading role in the final scene of the Hitchcock film *The Man Who Knew Too Much*?" asked the voice from the telephone speaker. It was the same voice I remembered asking quiz show questions thirty years earlier. And I was sitting next to Robert just like then.

"Cymbals," Robert said.

Of course the answer was right.

"What British citizen is the only person to win both a Nobel Prize and an Oscar?"

"Bertrand Russell?" Robert whispered to me. "But why would he have received an Oscar?"

I said that I doubted any doctor, chemist, physicist, or mathematician had ever won an Oscar.

"Unless it's John Nash and *A Beautiful Mind.* Is there an Oscar for the person a movie is based on?"

"Nash received the Nobel Prize for Economics but not an Oscar. *A Beautiful Mind* did receive the Oscar for best picture, though, along with three in other categories," said Salminen.

"It's either the Nobel Peace Prize or the prize for literature. I has to be an author who got an Oscar for script writing," Robert reasoned.

We started going through the British Nobel Prize winners.

"Do we count the Irish? Playwrights? Shaw or Beckett?" Robert asked.

"Time is running out," said Salminen

"It has to be one of those two. I bet Shaw," said Robert.

"We say Shaw," I said.

"Right you are. Shaw's play *Pygmalion,* also known as *My Fair Lady* in its musical version, received eight Oscars, one of which was to Shaw for best original screenplay."

Salminen said that Shaw and Winston Churchill hated each other. Shaw had sent Churchill a guest ticket to the opening night of the play. He could also bring a friend, "if he had one," Shaw wrote. Churchill replied that due to other engagements he would not be able to attend the opening, but he would come to the following performance, "if there was one."

"What do Anton Chekhov, Mikhail Bulgakov, Arthur Conan Doyle, and Axel Munthe have in common besides being writers?"

I knew Chekhov and Conan Doyle were doctors. I waited to

see how Robert would react. His expression asked if I knew. I nodded. Robert motioned for me to speak.

"Were they all doctors?"

They were. Third point to us.

I realized that we had become a team. We weren't competing against each other; we were working together.

"Why don't the players on the Spanish national soccer team sing when the national anthem plays?"

"Easy. The 'Marcha Real' doesn't have any words," Robert said.

Fourth point.

"Finally, another film question. What fruit is an omen of death in *The Godfather*?"

*The Godfather* definitely counted as general knowledge. There was the novel by Mario Puzo, and the Francis Ford Coppola movie trilogy, with Marlon Brando and Al Pacino starring. That I knew, but I hadn't actually seen any of the films. From Robert's body language, I deduced that he didn't know the answer either.

We were both caught by the shameful fact that neither of us had seen *The Godfather*. That must have been more embarrassing for Robert than for me, because watching movies was de rigueur in the circles he ran in. Robert had to be happy he wasn't being humbled like this in a pub quiz organized by J. P. Morgan but rather safely in my company.

We had to guess.

Robert nodded at me to move away from the phone and whispered that based on the probabilities, a common fruit would be the best choice. There were simply more apples and oranges in the world than starfruit or kiwis. I wondered whether a more exotic fruit might be a better symbol from the standpoint of the film. Apples were so commonplace.

We landed on a grapefruit.

But the correct answer should have been an orange.

"Don Corleone is shot as he's buying oranges, and he dies in an orange grove. In *The Godfather: Part III*, there are nearly a dozen orange scenes before a death. At the end of number three, an orange falls to the ground just before Michael Corleone does. Unfortunately, you received no points for this question."

Robert said thank you and was just about to hang up when I remembered to ask Salminen whether he happened to remember how many smokestacks there were on the *Titanic*.

"I say there are three," Robert said.

"And I think there were more of them. So I'm saying four."

Without a second's thought the voice from the bowels of the telephone declared that there were indeed four funnels rising above the *Titanic*.

"However, only three of them were smokestacks. The fourth contained air vents."

# Robert

HEDGE FUND MANAGERS rely on algorithms and robots to make their trade decisions, but all I need is my gut.

And my gut told me the party was at its best, so it was time to end it. You have to know when to cut off pleasure. You have to turn longs to shorts when everyone else is telling you to buy and the economic horizon is clear save for a few harmless fluffy clouds.

The evening was definitely a success. There had been a little conflict, just the right amount of danger, and a lot of friendship. Relaxing into my armchair, I felt more satisfied than I had in ages. I had achieved the evening's objectives. If Mikko had thought I was a bastard when he came to London, now he only considered me stupid, simple, or deluded.

I had wanted to tell Mikko that I considered him a friend. I had said it as well as I knew how. The trivia competition had been the crowning event of the night, and Mikko didn't need to know that I had arranged the phone call with Salminen via email a week earlier.

Elise had put on some Finnish music: the ballads that had played when we were children, the rock songs we had been too young for. Elise threw her legs over the armrest of the couch and sang along. She knew the words well considering she was younger than the rest of us. When she didn't know, she hummed.

Elise fumbled for her glass, which was empty. Springing up, she proposed a toast to friendship.

That would be the perfect conclusion to the evening. I stood up and clapped my hands together.

Elise suggested cocktails. Veera asked what would be in them.

"Vodka, orange juice . . . "

The servant had appeared in the corner to take the order.

"No, not orange juice," Mikko exclaimed. "Oranges give me a rash."

"They do?" Veera asked.

"Sometimes."

Instantly the servant moved to the fruit basket and removed the oranges, placing them on the tray where she had been collecting the empty glasses and candy wrappers.

Veera thought something blue would be a better fit for a dark night like this. "Blue angels!"

"Who played the female lead . . . ?" Mikko began.

"Marlene Dietrich."

" . . . in the movie *Casablanca*?"

"You weren't going to ask that."

"But I did anyway."

"Bergman, but not Ingmar."

"I. Bergman anyway. The answer is accepted."

Elise asked the servant to bring four blue angels.

"This has been a wonderful evening," I said so everyone would know that what was coming was an encore, after which we would all go to sleep. Each in our own bed. In the morning we would order from the hotel restaurant since the servant would need a break.

"Next summer come visit us," Veera said.

"We were actually intending . . . " Mikko said. "We just need to arrange a time."

Then we spent a few minutes planning the following summer like people who have that option. We thought about what we could do in Helsinki. A picnic on Suomenlinna Island? The summer theater? Grilling in Mikko and Veera's backyard? What would we grill?

"Couldn't we rent a cabin for the summer?" Elise asked.

In the background, Judge Bone sang about a dark angel taking the birthday boy after too much cake and punch.

# Veera

THE AMPULE PRESSED against my left boob as if wanting to remind me that there it was near my heart. Not a loving heart pumping red blood full of oxygen. This was blue blood full of death.

The servant glided in from the kitchen. With both hands she carried a round steel tray bearing four glasses. She hadn't skimped on the blue liqueur or the flora: each cocktail glass had a curl of lemon on the rim. Vitamin C! Flavonoids!

I would break the cyanide capsule into Rob's glass and let him die of his own cleverness.

That sounded easy enough, but it wasn't. I thought about what would happen next. The servant would offer glasses first to me and Mikko, then to Elise. Rob would take the remaining glass. That had been the order all evening. How could I guess which glass would be left? Perhaps the one closest to the servant? But there were two. The glasses were like the dots on the number four side of a dice.

Bloody hell! I would have to do something. The servant was already approaching me, smiling like a house dog who had just been given a T-bone steak.

Turning toward the bookcase, I slipped my left hand into my bra. At first my shaking fingers couldn't get a grip.

"Mikko, you should help out. Veera has resorted to groping herself!"

Smart ass. You just go ahead and grin while you can.

Tucking the ampule into the crook of the fingers of my left hand, I explained that the underwire was pinching me. Then I turned back around and grabbed a cocktail glass. I placed my left hand on my hip so no one would notice its unnatural position.

I tried to avoid squeezing too hard. I didn't want to break the ampule and cut myself. I didn't want death leaking through my fingers onto the handwoven Persian rug on the library floor.

Mikko grabbed a glass, too. He looked a little pale. My husband seemed to have drunk too much.

Elise took a glass. She was singing along with the Hurriganes.

Rob and Mikko were reminiscing about past summers and planning how they would go see the places they remembered from their childhood when we saw each other in Finland. Was the climbing tree still where it used to be or had the parks department cut it down for firewood for the mayor? What did the equipment at the playground look like now?

My spineless jellyfish.

The servant stood next to the men. Rob let the servant wait. He was so far above everyone else.

I acted fast. I pinched the glass ampule between the nails of my thumb and middle finger as hard as I could. The top snapped off. No one noticed the sound it made because the stereo was screaming about being a roadrunner. Baby, baby indeed.

Blue liquid dribbled into the cocktail glass I had placed under my hand. The blue cyanide mixed with the liqueur without changing its color. A couple of drops splashed on the lemon, but none of us was in good enough shape anymore to notice unless we knew to look.

The poison tingled on my fingertips. Shards of glass pressed into my flesh. As I wiped my hand on the hem of my dress, I placed the glass back on the tray.

"I think this one has a little more," I said and took the other glass on the tray.

Mikko said there couldn't be any difference between them if they were made according to the recipe.

"Since when do you settle for less, Veera?" Rob said and took the final glass from the tray.

The servant turned and left.

"Only the best is good enough for me," I said.

That could be my final confession to Rob.

# Elise

*PURSE YOUR LIPS and put your back to the wind.*

Hey, I knew this song! It was Katri Helena.

I sprang up and said, "Let's dance!"

Katri Helena said we should walk a winding road, but instead we were going to dance.

Robert said, "First the toast."

I said, "No, we'll miss it. The song will be over soon."

Mikko asked, "Isn't it a recording? We can just play it again."

I said, "The song is playing right now. Katri Helena has something to tell us."

Where was the wind going to take me?

I wouldn't give up: "Quickly now! There's no time to waste."

I grabbed Mikko by the hips.

Left, left.

I said, "Now two with the right."

Right, right. Mikko followed.

I jumped against Mikko. My knee hit him in the butt.

When I jumped back, Mikko nearly fell.

Veera lined up behind me.

All three of us bounced while Katri Helena looked for peace in the wind.

I shouted, "Now jump."

Robert joined us as the tail.

Right, right, left, left. Forward. Backward. Forward, forward, forward!

The jumping was the best part. Forward, back, forward, forward, forward! Veera and Mikko jumped well. Robert was more following his own steps.

Mikko led the line into the foyer. I greeted the suit of armor and waved for it to join the dance, but it just stood there and stared. Stick in the mud! We bounced into the dining area. Then back into the library.

I didn't know about Katri Helena and the wind and finding peace, but I liked dancing.

Then came the final bounces. Whew. I wiped the sweat from my brow. Veera was panting.

Mikko said, "A little midnight workout."

Robert said, "A little *nachtmusik*."

I was really thirsty.

Mikko asked, "How many times was *Eine kleine Nachtmusik* performed during Mozart's lifetime?"

Haha. Mikko and Robert knew lots of things, but even I knew this one.

On the table there were four angel glasses. Which one of them was mine? That I didn't know.

So I took the one that looked fullest and was the bluest. Hehe.

Robert guessed, "Five thousand?"

Robert guessed wrong.

Sports causes dehydration. Dancing is a sport. I tossed the whole glass back in one gulp.

I said, "Mozart had to die before he heard the piece performed."

*Bong.*

*Bong.*

# Mikko

ELISE DIED.

The goddess incarnate collapsed on the wool carpet. Her cocktail glass slipped from her hand and banged against the cigarette table.

"Elise! What's the matter?"

Elise gagged. I never would have imagined such a sound could come from that mouth. It was as if an evil spirit had possessed an angel.

Robert was sure Elise was having a seizure.

I was just as sure Elise had been poisoned. That I had poisoned her.

"Elise, you weren't supposed to die!" I cried.

Because they were nearest to me, I grabbed her feet. I wrapped my arms around Elise's delicate ankles and held them tenderly. Elise thrashed as if she wanted to break free.

She was leaving this world, I thought. That was what the dying did.

I had poisoned Elise. I didn't understand how it had happened. I had got the strychnine out of Robert's coffee cup, and even if some had gotten in the air, strychnine didn't cause symptoms like this from inhalation. Especially this suddenly.

Had Elise eaten the rye bread? Because I specifically told her to get rid of it? Had Elise misunderstood?

"Elise, Elise!" I spluttered through my tears.

"Let's call an ambulance," Robert suggested.

Veera said there wasn't time. Cyanide caused death in a matter of minutes. And besides, she was a nurse.

Still breathing heavily, she knelt down and turned Elise's head. Then she stuck her fingers in Elise's mouth.

"Throw it up. Throw up all the evil," I whimpered.

"Do you have medicinal charcoal?" Veera asked.

Robert said no.

"The man who's prepared for everything."

Robert responded that this was exactly what he was prepared for: having an ampule of cyanide never would have meant anything if there were a package in the medicine cabinet that could bring him back to life.

"Bring water. Now!"

"Is it cyanide?" Robert asked.

Veera said she knew the signs of cyanide poisoning when she saw them.

"Sugar! Quick, sugar!" Robert yelled first in Finnish and then in English and ran into the kitchen.

Elise gagged cloudy liquid onto the floor and into Veera's lap.

"Bring water!" Veera yelled.

"What can I do?" I asked.

"Stay two meters back."

"Is it catching?"

"Two meters away."

I undid the belt of Elise's dress and the delicate zipper. Robert ran in from the kitchen with a bag of sugar. He explained that people had tried to poison Grigori Rasputin by putting cyanide in his cake and wine. Rasputin wasn't bothered in the slightest and asked the guitarist to play something jolly because he was in a merry mood.

"Don't get in the way!" Veera said.

"Glucose neutralizes cyanide," Robert argued.

"If the poison is already having an effect, her cells aren't getting any energy. They're being paralyzed. Bring water! We have to rinse out her mouth."

"Glucose makes cyanide harmless."

"Do you have pharmacological proof?"

I could hear the alarm and horror in Robert and Veera's argument. It was all I could do to breathe. My stomach clenched. I felt shaky. I didn't understand why they were talking about cyanide.

"No, it's strychnine," I said.

"Should we call a doctor?" Robert asked.

Veera asked Robert if he wanted to explain to a doctor how cyanide had ended up in Elise's drink.

"I'm sure you have a good explanation for it," Veera said. "Bring that water!"

I said that the poison was strychnine. Treating her for cyanide wouldn't help.

Her face, which was so beautiful, contorted in a revolting grimace.

"Elise, Elise, how can I help you?"

"Elise is my wife," Robert said and shoved Veera aside.

Elise is my love, I felt like shouting, but all I could do was cry.

Robert poured sugar from the bag into Elise's mouth. Her cheeks were stained with vomit, and lipstick has smeared across her face. Her lips twitched, and she thrashed.

Robert asked me to help. I held Elise's head in place. Enormous evil forces moved her body. My arms weren't strong enough to contain them. Robert snarled. Locking Elise's head between my thighs, I pulled her mouth open. Elise spat wet sugar. She was trying to say something, but she couldn't form the words.

Her expression screamed with agony.

"Elise, this wasn't supposed to happen this way!"

The sugar was gone. Elise rolled to one side and then the other. I released my grip. Robert stood up.

"She's dying," Veera said quietly, so quietly that it was barely audible over Elise's choking.

"No, really!" Robert yelled.

Elise rolled onto her back and struggled with the last of her strength.

"I love," she screamed, but it didn't sound like a confession of love. It sounded like the lament of an injured animal.

"So do I," I whispered. "All of you!"

Elise's face twisted into her last grimace. I did not feel like kissing it.

Elise gave up the ghost. The evil spirit left her good body.

# Veera

OH JESUS'S ECUMENICAL testicles. What an idiot I was! Of course I should have remembered that Rob is the one fortune smiles on most seductively. Always and without fail.

The pig even managed to wiggle out of this.

Elise's glass stood untouched on the table. The savage poison churned inside the wrong person.

It hadn't occurred to me that I would have to treat a cyanide poisoning victim, even though I knew this was what would happen.

There were probably antidotes to cyanide but no chance that I would remember them. Treating poisonings was a job for first aid workers. Active carbon was a panacea for oral poisoning, but we didn't have any.

When you're in the thick of things, you can't sit around trying to remember best practices. But I knew that if you can get the poison out of the body before it takes effect, then it can't take effect at all. We had to clean out her mouth. I scraped the roof of her mouth and behind her teeth. A shard of glass pricked my finger. Blood dripped from her mouth.

The way Elise was convulsing on the rug made it clear the cyanide had her in its grip. Every hundredth of a second worsened her condition and brought her closer to death.

After every hundredth of a second there was one hundredth of a second less remaining of her struggle. Perhaps it was immoral of me to attempt to draw it out. Helping people in distress was just in our blood in my profession.

They had sold Rob the real thing.

Elise vomited. Even though vomiting wasn't recommended as a treatment for poisoning, it wasn't any harm either. Anymore. I pushed my fingers farther back and tried to trigger the gag reflex again.

In addition to having to keep Elise alive, I had to prevent Rob from calling anyone.

How would I explain why there had been cyanide in Elise's glass?

There were probably a lot of other questions it would have been good to consider earlier too.

I told Rob he didn't want anyone here either. No, not even if it was his private physician and we swore him to secrecy. We didn't need anyone else interfering.

I had to shoo Mikko away from Elise.

Stomach acid gushed from Elise's mouth, but it was too little, too late to help. Only God the Father could bring Elise back to life now. Hopefully Elise believed in God. I didn't.

I had killed a person.

Rob came in with his bag of sugar. Be my guest and try, I thought. She's your wife after all.

I looked at the drunken men's hopeless fumbling and felt a sudden soberness.

And what if I had succeeded? How would I feel if it were Rob on the floor instead of Elise? What would I do in that case?

I would pull Rob's mouth open, shove my fingers in, and yell for activated charcoal because I would know that Rob wasn't going to recover. I would do everything I could to prevent what I had caused.

It wouldn't have felt any better if it had been Rob. Killing isn't what people are supposed to do.

Mikko blubbered hysterically. Rob gave up and kicked the empty sugar bag around the room. The white crystals sank into the Persian rug.

Mikko bent down to listen to Elise's gurgling, until she went silent.

When a person is dead, they're dead, and there's no way to bring them back.

I had killed the wrong person.

I had killed a person.

# Robert

WHEN SOMEONE DIES next to you, it reminds you that you could be next in line.

I increased my threat level. I sat down in an armchair where I could see Mikko huddled on the floor in the corner by the foyer and Veera, who smelled her own blue angel and then took a careful sip.

"There isn't anything wrong with the alcohol?"

Veera shook her head and swallowed.

"The poison was only in Elise's glass."

"How do you know?"

"Didn't you see how she downed that whole glass right before she collapsed?"

I pointed out that the two events could just correspond in time without any causal relationship.

Veera asked what I was getting at. I said I was trying to figure out what had happened.

"Your wife is dead," Veera said and then drank the rest of her blue cocktail.

"And you think it was cyanide?"

"You were the one who showed us the ampule!"

The cyanide ampule had remained somewhere in the dining area after we ate. My memory wasn't clear. Any one of them could have picked it up.

"Why did Elise die?" I asked.

This was an exceedingly important question.

Veera said it looked like suicide.

"But Elise has been saying all night how happy she was. Why would she take her own life?"

"Was she faking? Maybe she was happy because she had already made her decision and knew the end was near."

Mikko waved as if he were asking for a turn to speak. "Elise wasn't happy!" he said. "Elise would have been happy if everything had gone the way it was supposed to, though," Mikko said, but I didn't pay any more attention to him. Mikko was talking nonsense again. Elise's death had put him in a state of shock.

"Cyanide poisoning isn't the most pleasant way to die."

"Did Elise know that?" Veera asked.

"Maybe Elise wanted to experience how death would taste," I said.

"It didn't taste good."

Suicide or an accident seemed like the most sensible explanations. Why on earth would Mikko or Veera have wanted to kill Elise? I couldn't think of a single reason.

Standing up, I walked over to Elise. I didn't want to look at her face.

"We have a body here."

This was a problem we all shared, but it was primarily mine. Elise was my wife. The body was in an apartment controlled by me. Apparently her death had been caused by the cyanide I purchased.

I really didn't want the tabloids discovering that.

"That might hurt your career," Veera said mockingly.

I told her it wasn't in any of our interests that our party had ended in a person's death.

"Again." Veera said the word carelessly, but it nailed me to the wall.

"It isn't in your best interests, either," I said.

"What do you intend to do?" Veera asked.

"I'm asking what *we* will do."

"We have to put on a beautiful funeral for Elise," Mikko said.

I promised Mikko that we would. Then I asked Veera if the cyanide would show up in an autopsy.

"We have to destroy the body," Veera said. "Burn it, throw it in the Thames, bury it in the ground. Report Elise missing."

"Elise left in the middle of the party and didn't say where she was going," I said.

"We all thought she just went downstairs to buy some cigarettes," Veera said.

"Elise doesn't smoke," I said.

"Cocaine," suggested Veera.

"Nothing illegal," I said.

"So she was going out to buy milk in the middle of the night?"

"But what if Elise left earlier?"

"And we wouldn't have noticed anything? Wouldn't we have started calling her phone in concern? Start calling now!"

I didn't quite yet. First we had to think through our story carefully and only afterwards create the evidence.

We decided that we had gone to sleep but Elise had stayed up . . .

"The servant," Veera said.

"She will say precisely what I instruct her to say."

Veera asked if we should send her away. That was reasonable to say the least. The servant had brought the drinks, but even Elise's cries of agony hadn't made her come into the library. When I had gone to get the sugar, she had been washing some dishes that couldn't go in the dishwasher. When I'd asked for the sugar, she hadn't asked what I needed it for.

Which, on second thought, was rather suspicious. Quickly I walked into the kitchen. The servant was up on the step ladder putting a platter on top of a cabinet.

"Careful!"

The servant was startled, and her leg slipped. She reeled off the ladder and fell on the tile floor. The platter broke but only in two pieces.

The servant assured me she was unharmed. She said it had been careless of her, but that wasn't true. She was simply startled by me since I didn't usually come in the kitchen.

The servant also could have taken the cyanide ampule and broken it into Elise's glass. Actually, she had been the one with the best opportunity, since she had mixed the drinks. Wasn't it most likely that the person who had taken the ampule from the dining area had been the one whose job it was to keep that area clean?

Elise interacted with the servant much more than I did. Did they have some sort of conflict I didn't know about? Could the servant have killed Elise?

I looked at the slender woman. She seemed like a very unlikely candidate for a murderer. But Bernie Madoff had also seemed like a very unlikely swindler, and that was exactly why he had been able to bamboozle even professional investors for so many years.

I wanted to get rid of her. Even just for safety's sake.

"You can leave for the day. We can take it from here."

The servant resisted, but I assured her we would be fine. I asked if she had eaten anything. She hadn't. She was just disoriented from her fall. Packing the rye bread Mikko and Veera had brought into a plastic bag, I gave it to her. I encouraged her to have a taste of Finnish cuisine at home.

"But this is your bread," the servant said in protest.

I told her I had eaten more than enough rye bread as a child. "I like it best with pickled mushrooms, but it's good alone too. Especially when it's fresh."

The servant removed her apron, put on her jacket, and left carrying the plastic bag.

*THE ROADSIDE CAFE on the Autobahn A12 was reminiscent of a beerhouse: the TV blared a sports program and conversations were shouted. Apparently it was the only meeting place in the village. Assuming there was a village.*

*The men sucking on their beers glanced at him suspiciously, all looking as if they had dark secrets. A stranger had entered their midst.*

*He ordered a coffee and something to go with it that he guessed contained a lot of fast carbohydrates. He had managed to keep the hangover at bay so far, but that wouldn't last forever. At some point he would have to pay that bill.*

*Just so long as he could make it to Zurich first.*

*He had brought the iPad with him and now turned it on, although it didn't seem to jibe with the milieu, which seemed stuck in the previous century. To his surprise he found an open WIFI network.*

*He scanned the news—nothing. He checked the status of the flight from Munich to Helsinki. It was nearing its arrival time, if his time zone calculations were correct. He also would have liked to check his email, but would logging in leave a trail? Would it show where the login had occurred? Would he be revealing himself? He would have to figure that out. Until then he would have to keep away from it.*

*Isolation was cruel and unusual punishment. What had felt like carefree abandon on the train in Munich now was only oppressive.*

*Should he simply turn himself in to the police, tell them*

*everything, and explain that he had only fled out of a failure of judgment? He certainly wouldn't be the first person to go out of his mind after witnessing a tragedy.*

*People had just started dropping dead around him.*

*He would think about that tomorrow once he had slept off the exhaustion. His brain wasn't functioning in a way that allowed making big decisions.*

*His brain hadn't been working the night before either–none of theirs had–but that hadn't prevented them making choices between life and death.*

*He studied the remaining route on the map. Next came Innsbruck and then more autobahn to the west.*

*The weariness weighed on his neck. At a drug store he had found in Salzburg, he had purchased some headache medicine and already swallowed half the packet. His stomach was complaining about all the ibuprofen. Remembering the caffeine tablets he had taken from the mirrored cabinet in the bathroom, he searched for the bottle in his bag, and shook three out into his hand.*

*He had to continue driving.*

*He thought of a luxury hotel room with the soft, inviting bed where he could watch mindless shows on TV until he fell asleep.*

*He took two more caffeine pills. The Audi growled to life.*

# Mikko

THE WORST THING possible had happened. I deserved to be punished for my evil intentions, but why did innocent Elise have to receive the ultimate penalty?

I was a worm.

I didn't even comprehend what I had caused. Or how I had caused it.

I had been careless.

I didn't have any memory of having poisoned Elise's drink.

I couldn't have! Why would I have wanted to harm Elise? Had I thought that if I couldn't have Elise, Robert shouldn't either? Did I want to relieve Elise of Robert's torment and couldn't imagine any other way?

I hadn't done that, though. I couldn't have been that stupid.

But that didn't remove my guilt. I had started the game with death. A person who assumes the power of God must also bear the consequences. I couldn't.

"Elise, Elise!"

The only bright spot was that she had received such a large dose. Death by strychnine is horrible. Elise had died quickly.

Had she taken the strychnine from my pocket and mixed it in her own drink? How could she have done it without us noticing?

I lifted myself up enough to slip my hand into my front pocket. My fingers touched the plastic baggie. At least that was still there.

I pulled out the bag. All of the remaining powder appeared to be accounted for. So I hadn't killed Elise with strychnine.

And Elise hadn't killed herself with my poison either.

I crawled over to Elise's lifeless corpse.

"Oh, Elise, tell me what you did," I whispered.

I stroked Elise through her dress. Her skin was still resilient, but soon her body would stiffen and purple and red blotches would appear as gravity caused her blood to pool.

But in my memories, Elise would remain as she was the first time I saw her. To me she would always be beautiful. To me she would always be an angel.

My hand stopped on a strange bulge. It was an aberration on her smooth skin. The bulge was a tiny pocket in Elise's dress. I hadn't recognized it as a pocket because it looked decorative.

I shoved my thumb and forefinger into the pocket. My fingers found something hard and slick. I squeezed the object between my fingers.

It snapped and broke.

I pulled my fingers out. They were covered in blue, stinging liquid.

A pungent smell of almonds came from it.

# Veera

"VEERA, VEERA."

Mikko was whimpering next to Elise's body like a child who had hit his finger with a hammer.

Mikko showed me the fingers of his right hand.

"What now?"

The smell of almonds reached my nose. It wasn't coming from Elise's mouth, it was from Mikko's fingers.

"Why do you have cyanide on your hand?"

Mikko said there had been a cyanide capsule in Elise's pocket. And now it had broken.

"Elise's?" I asked, although it wasn't as if there were that many alternatives.

"Am I going to die now?" Mikko asked.

"No."

"But I want to die!" Mikko shouted and moved his fingers toward his mouth. He probably intended to suck on them. Unfortunately his coordination wasn't so hot at the moment, so his fingers just poked him in the cheek.

"Ow."

"No more bodies!" Lunging over to Mikko, I wiped his fingers on Elise's dress. "Rob, bring water!"

This time he obeyed and came running back with water in a Moomin mug. Why on earth were there Moomin mugs in Rob's house?

I washed Mikko's fingers and dried them vigorously.

I said the cyanide capsule proved Elise had committed suicide. Simultaneously I thought about how I would get rid of the ampule in my purse. Or had Elise taken it? But how would she have? My bag had been on the couch the whole time, and I had been sitting next to it except when we were doing the conga line. And why on earth would Elise have been digging in my bag, and why would she have taken the cyanide even if she had found it? Too many coincidences.

"That's exactly what it doesn't prove," Rob said.

"Elise had cyanide in her pocket? I think that's evidence of some sort of plan."

"Why would Elise have needed two ampules? If she had two ampules, why did she leave one in her pocket?"

"As a backup in case she failed with the first?"

After sitting Mikko against the wall, I collapsed on the couch in the same place where I had sat before the cyanide disaster. My purse leaned against the arm of the couch.

"Exactly. Of course," Rob said.

"What! Did you change your mind? Are you admitting you were wrong?"

"If the facts change, I change my opinion. What do you do?"

The facts hadn't changed. Rob's opinion had changed. He had realized something.

Should I be realizing something too? Whatever it was, I had to get rid of the other ampule even faster now.

What did the extra ampule signify? It showed that Elise had taken the ampule that Rob showed off at dinner and put it in her pocket. It didn't mean that Elise had intended to kill herself.

I shouldn't have thought so ill of the dead, but I did anyway: Elise didn't have the capacity for planning more than five minutes ahead.

Had Elise meant to kill someone else? Me? Rob? Mikko? But why?

I didn't understand what I was supposed to realize, but I understood that it was in my best interest to cut off any further discussion of Elise's death.

So I changed the topic back to how we were going to get rid of the body. It was definitely in my best interest that it be handled quietly and quickly.

"It would be best to bury Elise's body somewhere very out of the way," I said.

"How are we going to get her out of here? There are security cameras everywhere. We can't just put on her coat and lead her out."

"Fold her over and put her in a furniture box," I suggested. I fumbled with the zipper of my purse without looking at it. The zipper was made for someone with small hands who had only been drinking water. It was not made for opening after a long dinner party. Every purse was the same. Maybe the designers had teamed up to develop an alcometer disguised as a clothing accessory.

Rob asked if we were going to cut her in half with a saw. He said that sounded smarter than going at her with a carving knife. And really it all depended on what kind of boxes he had. Surely something was left over from the move.

I got a hold of the zipper. I squeezed the purse between one buttock and the armrest. Hoping to cover the sound as I slid the zipper open, I pointed out that a used moving box might not bear the weight.

"Yes, the box would have to be sturdy," Rob said.

"It would be unfortunate if a leg fell through the bottom while we were hauling it through reception."

I got the purse open. My fingers found lipstick and a credit card.

"Better to take her in several trips," I continued.

"Every trip down in the elevator increases the risk of being seen and someone asking questions."

"You can just tell them you're taking furniture to decorate your summer house."

"For our winery in Hungary! I'll say that Elise has already gone on ahead. Or should we send the body by DHL to some out-of-the-way place? There are men from courier companies in the building constantly."

The tissue packet had come open. I pinched it enough to feel that the ampule was inside.

I told Rob that was a good idea. "Get us a little swig of something to celebrate!"

Rob was of the opinion that we ought not to increase our inebriation because cool consideration required cool heads. I called him a pussy.

That worked.

As I pulled the ampule out of my purse, wrapped in tissue, I looked for a place to hide it. Behind a book in the bookshelf? Right next to me were a dozen Agatha Christies with dark bindings in a row. Rob was certain never to touch them. A cleaner would find the dusty ampule during the next cleaning of the shelves and throw it away.

What would actually happen now? Would Rob remain living in this apartment or would he move elsewhere? Use his money to find a new piece of ass?

I stood up with the packet of tissues in my hand.

"Do you have a cold?"

Rob hadn't gone in the kitchen. He stood at the other end of the bookshelf where there appeared to be a drinks cupboard behind a hidden door.

I explained that the smell of almonds was making my nose run.

Rob asked if Finlandia would do.

"Just so long as there's no ice."

# Robert

THE SECOND AMPULE solved it. This definitely wasn't suicide. I had only brought one cyanide ampule downstairs. The two others I had locked back in the safe.

Elise could have taken the ampule I showed off at dinner and done something careless with it. That could have explained her death.

But it didn't explain a second ampule.

Elise didn't know the code, and neither did the servant. Had Mikko seen it when I opened the safe while the women were in the sauna?

Or had I left the door open? I tried to remember: Mikko had been doing something by my desk when I got out the passports. I was startled because I hadn't noticed him move over there, into my personal domain. I had pushed the door closed with my foot.

I didn't have any memory of the lock motor engaging.

If that was the case, that I hadn't locked it, anyone could have taken something from the safe during the evening without the others noticing, because there wasn't a direct line of sight to the door from the library. Mikko had been in there while I fetched the cognac. Had he only been pretending to sleep? But how would that have helped him get the cyanide? Elise could have visited the safe just as easily while Veera and I were downstairs. Veera could have gone while we were in the sauna, as could have Elise . . . No one could be eliminated from the list of suspects, and no one was any more likely a culprit than anyone else.

I continued sizing up the situation. I needed a comparative advantage. No one was going to win this game anymore, but I needed a way to come out ahead.

And not get killed.

First there was the possibility that neither of the ampules in Elise's possession had been the one I brought to the dinner table. In that case, Elise would have had to go in my office, open the safe, take out the two remaining ampules, put one of them in her pocket, and break the other into her glass.

I couldn't come up with any explanation for why Elise would have come in the library with the ampules if she had wanted to kill herself. Why wouldn't she have broken one in the office right after getting it? Why would she have waited to commit suicide at the end of the night?

And what if Elise had grabbed the ampule I brought to dinner but decided to put off suicide for some reason? Why would she have gone to get another ampule?

This meant that Elise had not been in my safe. And that Elise had not committed suicide.

That meant that Mikko or Veera—or the servant, who moved unnoticed from room to room and easily could have visited my office—had killed Elise. One of them had purposefully retrieved the cyanide ampule in order to murder.

That also meant that there was still one ampule somewhere. Either the one I had shown at the dinner table or the other one the murderer had taken from my safe.

Because if someone had gone in my office and taken one ampule of poison, why wouldn't they have taken both?

If the murderer was the servant, the ampule had either left the premises or was lurking somewhere for its next victim. If the murderer was Mikko or Veera, the cyanide was definitely here.

It was extremely likely the ampule was still somewhere. I had to keep up my guard. And not just for myself but also for Mikko or Veera. One of them was probably innocent.

"Do you dare accept a drink I offer you?"

"Why wouldn't I?" Veera asked, squeezing the tissue in her hand. She had stood up to sneeze and was startled when she saw me at the bar cabinet.

"And Mikko? Would you like a glass of vodka? Or I have something milder, say Blue Curaçao?"

Mikko declined.

"Are you afraid I might poison you?" I asked

"Would you poison me? Why would you poison me?"

This was a classic deductive problem. Everyone in the room could have already been through the same train of thought as me. Everyone who had come to the same conclusion knew that there was likely a murderer in the room.

"I'm sorry. Bad joke. Well, would you like something?"

I was the most natural suspect. The ampules were mine, and I could get into the safe easier than the others.

Anyone innocent would suspect I was guilty. And the culprit would be motivated to cast suspicion on me because I was the most likely murderer. The culprit would use their rhetorical skills and convince the other of my guilt.

I was at a disadvantage, but I was ahead of the others because I was probably the only one who had thought this far. Veera wasn't at her best in multidimensional thinking. And Mikko was seriously drunk.

Next I would have to decide how to make use of my head start. Would I try to figure out who wanted to murder Elise? Or did I just need to try to survive?

I interpreted the nodding of Mikko's head as assent, even though it could just as easily been a sign of drowsiness. I poured healthy splashes of vodka into three cups and closed the cap. At least at drinking I had a comparative advantage: I had the most weight and muscle mass, and I was used to drinking regularly.

I looked at Mikko. He was rubbing his fingers on his jeans. Was he trying to wipe away the guilt?

I looked at Veera. She was standing next to the couch squeezing the tissue as if seeking security from it.

One of these two people had killed Elise.

But why?

# Mikko

I CAME TO to see Robert waving a whiskey glass in front of me half full of something clear.

"Your drink, sir!"

A sip told me it was vodka. I emptied the glass.

A moment of clarity followed. I pushed myself up along the wall. I saw a cocktail glass.

I saw two cocktail glasses. I saw two cocktail glasses with blue liquid.

I understood what I didn't see.

I didn't see Veera's glass or Robert's glass.

I saw three glasses. Two were on the table, placed there by me and Elise. On the lower shelf of the bookcase next to Veera was a third glass, which was empty.

On the table in the corner where Robert had stood before we started our conga line, there was no glass. Robert's glass lay broken next to the base of the bookcase.

Elise had taken Robert's glass from the table.

"Hey! That glass . . . " I said, waving toward it.

I lost my balance, falling against the wall and hitting by elbow.

"Would you like to order another already?"

Robert laughed, jauntily sashaying back to get the bottle.

At the same time Veera bent down and tossed a wad of tissue under the couch.

The tissue came to rest on the floor, but something else rolled out.

Robert had paused with his hand on the neck of the open vodka bottle. Veera cleared her throat.

"What was that sound?" Robert asked.

"Did I drop my lipstick?"

It hadn't sounded like lipstick rolling. Veera groped under the front of the couch. Robert did the same on the other side.

I guessed what they would find.

Robert straightened up first. He raised the glass capsule full of blue liquid to the light as he might examine a bill for signs of counterfeiting.

"Veera, do you know how this looks?"

"No, Rob, you should think how this looks. This looks like that cyanide ampule has your fingerprints on it."

*When there isn't anything else to do, try the truth.* That was the advice I gave my interviewees as they squirmed trying to invent answers to my questions that would give the most favorable picture of them. As they waded deeper and deeper into the swamp with each lie, finally getting stuck up to their waists, I offered them those words as an almost friendly gesture. *What if you tried the truth?*

The smart ones followed my advice. The real crooks invented more lies, which my colleagues and I would tear down over the following weeks. The smart ones got off with a single, quick crash.

No one had to say that to me. Good sense dictated it.

"Robert, Veera!"

I stood up, leaning on the wall. I managed to stop time as great orators do with their mere presence.

"Behold a man. A guilty man. Blame me, but see the man inside."

"Mikko," Veera said, but I silenced her with my eyebrows.

Placing my feet shoulder width apart, I balanced my weight on my heels. "All of this is my fault," I said. "But grant me an opportunity to explain. Duty and justice are blind to friendship.

A journalist has a duty and a right to resist pressure or persuasion that attempts to guide, prevent, or limit the dissemination of information. What guides the journalist guides humanity. Friendship cannot stop a man from doing what is right. From doing his duty."

Veera looked at me with intense concentration. Robert shook his head.

"Robert, my friend."

"Yes?"

"I confess. I intended to kill you."

Breathing deeply, I collected my strength. I prepared to recount in detail how I had prepared for my task and built myself up to carry it out. I outlined what I would say. I would tell about purchasing the strychnine, about the rye bread. Afterwards I would chastise Robert for his inhumane treatment of Elise, but that would not be the climax of my oration because . . .

Before I could release the air I had inhaled into my lungs, I heard a clap.

As I raised my eyes, I heard another clap, and a third, and between them a dry laugh.

"Excellent performance," Robert said, lazily slapping his hands together.

"Excuse me?"

"Good story. What happened next? You soiled yourself and asked Veera to help?"

"I . . ."

"Do you really think I'll believe you could have murdered me? That you were man enough for that?"

I lost my grip on the situation and my strength. My leg cramped, and my muscles wouldn't obey my instructions.

"If you were capable of killing me, you would have. You had so many opportunities. You could have done it the proper Finnish way and knifed me when we were in the office together."

I groped behind me for the wall. A wave of cramping seized my arms.

"You could have bought a gun and shot me. Why didn't you do that? You didn't dare."

The wall was farther away than I'd thought.

"You didn't dare, Mikko. You aren't man enough."

I lost my balance.

Veera walked toward the foyer. I saw her out of the corner of my eye as the world went sideways. I fell.

"You made your wife do it. You've always been like that."

My left arm bent painfully beneath the weight of my body.

"I know you. You have intensity, but you're a coward. I'm not afraid of you."

When I felt the vomit coming on, I crawled to a nearby yucca plant. I got hold of the pot. A slimy yellow liquid gushed out onto the dirt.

# Veera

HE WHO LAUGHS last, laughs best. And that wouldn't be Rob.

Rob was laughing now—a hollow, mocking laugh.

God damn you, don't you mock my husband! Not here, not now!

I marched into the foyer, hearing behind me Rob's dry laughter and Mikko's vomiting.

I was nauseated too, but not quite as concretely.

I found the right door on the second try. The bathroom lights went on automatically when I stepped over the threshold. Humidity beaded on my face.

The champagne sword was still in the towel basket. Pulling it out, I wiped the blade on a damp bath towel. I saw my profile in the mirror. Black dress, red lips and cheeks. I grimaced at the mirror and took a firm grip on the sword. My credibility increased.

The sword felt like a weapon. I didn't think of it as an elitist bottle opener any more.

Stepping into the foyer with the sword in hand, I swung it a few times to the left and right. The weight made it swing in wide arcs. It would have been good to hold it with two hands, but only one fit in the knuckle guard.

"Mikko, you should become a lay preacher if the reporter gig runs out. Isn't the media industry in trouble?" Rob was saying. "Or a business coach. You wouldn't believe how many trainings I've been to. Some have been okay, and there have been some of these supposed coaches who could barely get a word out of their mouths. They still earn their keep, though."

Rob told stories like a washing machine salesman. I stopped in the doorway to listen, waiting for the right moment. Mikko was still bent over the yucca plant.

"You'd be fair to middling at least. Read a couple of articles, and I'm sure you could lecture for forty-five minutes on any topic. Then you have the participants do a couple of exercises using logo pens from your consulting firm in notepads printed for the course. Then break into pairs to debrief. That's five minutes times two, which is more than one fifth of the time you have to fill for your fee. Didn't you want a fresh drink? I think the last one already came up and out."

Rob grabbed the vodka bottle. He poured with his right hand, watching the liquid slosh. His left hand held the glass.

Now was the time to strike!

I had to go around the couch, and Rob spotted me. Confusion and fear flashed in his eyes. Rob realized this wasn't an appropriate moment for comedy anymore.

"God damn you, don't you mock my husband. Not here, not now!"

I struck. The blade of the saber swung and hit the side of the couch. Quickly I pulled the blade out of the leather and slashed at Rob again. Rob jumped back. He still had the Finlandia bottle in his right hand and the vodka glass in his left.

"Veera, you're insane! You could kill someone with that."

"What do you think I'm going use this for? Does this look like a bread knife to you?"

"Ok, what are you trying to do?"

I let the sword slice the air. Rob backed up.

"Veera!

"Careful not to spill!"

I swung back from left to right. A swordsmanship class would have been useful, but how are you supposed to know what life is going to throw at you?

*It doesn't matter if your form is perfect. Just so long as you feel it!*

That was what my Body Combat trainer said. That's what this was—a fight—although not with punches and kicks. Instead I was using a meter-long butter knife. And the music wasn't Nightwish; it was a jaunty polka.

Just so long as you feel it! Exactly!

I rushed at Rob, driving him into the corner between the bookcase and the kitchen door. And Rob didn't have any option but to go where I led him. Even someone much stupider than him would have figured out by now that I wasn't waving the saber just to work my upper back. These swings had a purpose and a target. I meant what I was doing.

"Veera, stop!"

Did Rob think I was a child who obeyed if you just said no?

I flicked my wrists, flourishing the sword. The tip bounced like the nose of an excited dog ten centimeters from Rob's chest.

"Don't do anything sudden!" he shouted.

"Why do I feel like you're the one who shouldn't make any sudden moves?"

I poked the sword toward Rob, who pressed himself closer to the wall.

"Veera."

It was Mikko, whose voice was a muffled whimpering.

"Don't I seem to be the popular one now? I've got men yelling at me from both sides."

"Hey, come on. Put the sword away," Rob said.

"Because Uncle Robbie told me to?"

"You're going to put the sword away because you're a sensible, intelligent woman."

"Oh! Previously known as a brainless fuck buddy."

"Let's talk this through calmly."

"Veera," Mikko said.

"Don't you interrupt. Rob and I are in the middle of something," I yelled, and flicked at Rob's shirt with the tip of the sword.

"Let's sit down and talk."

"The sword will handle the small talk for me," I said and raised the saber to strike.

*Bong.*

The chiming of the grandfather clock filled me with power.

The stroke of the saber sent dark shards of wood flying from the bookshelf. The blade hit the glass and smashed it. Rob moved nervously like a part-time amateur goalie suddenly dropped into a World Cup final penalty shootout.

I raised the sword over my right shoulder and swung again.

*Bong.*

Rob retreated from under the blade. I adjusted my grip and swung again.

Rob extended the vodka bottle between both hands to block the attack.

*Bong.*

The blade clanged on the bottle.

Pushing back against the sword with the bottle, Rob edged sideways out of the corner. When I drew the sword back, Rob threw the bottle at me.

The bottle spat vodka in my face and on my dress before banging to the floor and rolling across the hardwood until it came to a stop against Mikko's foot.

# Robert

I COULD SEE it in her eyes: Veera was serious. Even though her eyes were clouded by the fog of alcohol, behind them burned a rage. I had learned to recognize fear, rage, and greed. That was as much my craft as the mastery of any arcane derivatives instrument.

Veera was a decisive woman. She was a woman no one except someone like Mikko could survive living with.

Veera had poisoned Elise. Now she wanted to kill me. Why she wanted to do it didn't matter. I didn't take time to think about it, because words weren't going to stop Veera. I had to defend myself. I had to fight for my life.

I managed to escape to the kitchen. I slammed the door shut behind me, but that would only slow Veera down for a moment. The kitchen dumbwaiter? How quickly could I get into it and down to the hotel kitchen?

I discarded that plan. I wasn't the running type. I don't wriggle out of difficult situations, I solve them. Retreat is not a defense. Attacking is.

I pulled the drawers open. I hadn't been in the kitchen very many times. This was the servant's space, and I respected her territory. Objects banged against the sides of the drawers. Scissors, spoons, forks, napkins, spices, freezer bags.

A saucepan hung from a hook on the wall. That would work as a shield. Didn't we have a filleting knife? I was sure we did, but where?

Veera burst through the door. Grabbing the pan, I swung it against the sword. Bang. The sound wasn't as interesting as in the movies or as clipped and efficient as in a fencing match. It was just a bang, metal on metal without a hint of style.

When I protected my upper body with the saucepan, Veera aimed her blows at my legs. The sword was longer than the saucepan and handle. She had a reach advantage. The sword slashed the thigh above my knee, splitting the fabric and causing searing pain.

My advantage was that I knew this place. With my left hand I grabbed whatever I could from the table and threw it at Veera. She didn't have anything to shield herself. I forced her to retreat.

Veera flailed with the sword, but I bore down on her. I grabbed a pot off the counter for a helmet. It fit just right on my head.

The initiative had shifted to me, and I was able to keep Veera out of the sword's range. She moved back into the library.

I was running out of little things to throw, but I had to keep up the barrage. What next? The poker and shovel! They were next to the fireplace behind Veera. That would be my goal, even though the distance was three meters with the couch and cigarette table in between. Next to me I spotted a flower vase, remote control, and chocolates. First I threw the vase. Veera dodged, and the vase exploded on the floor as she swung the saber toward me. I crouched, taking cover and grabbing for the remote control. With all my might, I threw it at Veera's shin. A hit! Veera groaned in pain, and the cluster bomb of chocolates I threw next made her balance fail.

I jumped over the back of the couch toward my goal. The ash shovel I ignored, but the three-pointed coal poker could stand up to the Russian soldier's sword.

I rolled onto the couch. The saucepan ended up under me, and the rapid motion freed the pot, which clattered under the cigarette table.

"Don't try anything!" Veera yelled.

But I did. Lunging toward the fireplace, I just barely reached the tool stand and tipped it over. I lay half on the couch, half of the floor and reached for the ball on the end of the poker.

Veera's blows shredded the couch. The rhythm of events wasn't measured in seconds but in tenths.

When I got a firm grip on the poker, I turned and swung it backwards as hard as I could. It hit the glass table, which shattered like a car windshield.

Veera jumped when she saw that we were now equally matched. I still had one foot on the couch, but I also had the element of surprise on my side. My position had improved relative to Veera's, and in a fierce competition psychology and trends mattered. If two companies are competing and one is on the ascent and the other in decline, the first will grow stronger and the second will grow weaker more quickly that it should seem at first glance. Two words: Nokia and Apple. I was Apple, and Veera was the one whose market share was falling and profits collapsing.

Veera was quick to react. I admired her. I mean it. She immediately understood that the power dynamic had changed and that she was under threat.

Veera made a break for it.

"Robert, don't," Mikko wailed. He was back on his feet but hunched over, holding his stomach.

I didn't have time to chat. I had to catch Veera and neutralize her, because Veera was dangerous not only to me but herself.

I heard a clatter from the foyer. Veera had disappeared.

I turned my back to the one wall that had no door and listened. All I could heard was Mikko's groaning in the library.

"Veera," I called.

Veera hadn't left in the elevator. I'd stand guard. She couldn't get out of the apartment. Veera would have to crawl out of her hiding place eventually.

I waited for a few seconds and then a few seconds more. Then I chose an active strategy. That's how I work. Passivity will get you index returns and a slow, painful death. Neither held any attraction for me.

I opened the door to the walk-in closet, also watching my back. Veera couldn't have gone far.

Nothing collapsed on the floor from behind the door.

"Veera!

I turned on the light. With the poker I moved the clothes aside and made a couple of pokes at the larger winter coats. On the upper shelf there was nothing but the cardboard boxes containing hats and gloves.

The bathroom. The lights came on when I triggered the motion sensor.

"Veera!"

Nothing moved. Nothing indicated that Veera might be hiding in the bathroom or sauna. I went in anyway.

Clearing my way with the poker, I moved farther into the bathroom. I listened for Veera's breathing.

When I went to open the sauna door, I heard Veera's voice behind me.

"You aren't as smart as I thought."

Veera wasn't mocking; she was just making a statement. She stood at the door, filling the opening. The sword pointed at the floor.

"Coming in here was stupid," Veera continued, and now her voice was full of self-satisfaction.

I spread my arms. The poker banged against the edge of the sink.

"You didn't realize the light wasn't on in here even though it turns on by itself."

"You won," I said, but I didn't mean it. In the capital markets, satisfaction is the enemy of success. Why wouldn't the same be true in love and war?

To get out of this, I had to make Veera think she had the upper hand. "Rob, there was no way I could have been in here. You walked in like a defenseless little animal."

Calmly I stepped toward Veera, feeding her sense of satisfaction by agreeing and cursing my own stupidity.

Until I was within poker range.

Then I struck.

With an explosive wrist movement, the poker swung at the middle of the sword. Veera's grip on the hilt failed, and the sword fell to the tile floor.

"Hands above your head! Turn around slowly and walk to the library. If you don't remember the way, the poker will remind you."

*THE BEAT OF the bunny hop played in his head. Each downbeat rattled his skull. He surprised himself occasionally by whistling the tune. It irritated him.*

*They had done that dance when the evening had been at its best. Right after that Elise drank her poisoned draft.*

*If only he could turn back time and stop Elise from drinking from that glass! If that hadn't happened, everyone would still be alive. They would have spent today in London, together or separately, and have planned their next meeting.*

*And now—everything was gone.*

*He thought about what he could have done differently. Not much. With the information he'd had then, as they'd been hopping along to that dance, he couldn't have known he should do anything differently.*

*After he'd left the cafe, the brakes of the Audi had started making an unpleasant sound. Luckily the road was dry and the traffic light. The driving conditions were almost perfect.*

*His own condition wasn't, though. He was bothered by guilt over the things he could have changed.*

*He had just passed Innsbruck. There were still a couple of hours left to drive.*

*He was horribly tired. The caffeine tablets didn't seem to be helping. On the contrary, after taking them he had become even more exhausted. Was all the strain of the past twenty-four hours going to crash down on him at once?*

*Staying in Innsbruck would have been sensible, but he wasn't going to turn around.*

*He thought of that soft hotel bed again. He would choose a luxury hotel and hang a "Do Not Disturb" sign on the door.*

*Where was the wind blowing him?*

*He turned on the radio to drive Katri Helena out of his head.*

# Mikko

LIGHT ORANGE LIQUID came up my esophagus. The peas and carrots served at dinner colored the topsoil and the stem of the yucca plant.

The second round of vomiting made me feel significantly better. I could move again and the cramps subsided, but the acid still burned my mouth.

The sounds of Veera and Robert's battle had faded. I hoped they had made peace, but even more I hoped for water. Gingerly I walked into the kitchen and turned on the faucet, but then I remembered the bottled water served with dinner. I found the refrigerator concealed behind massive stainless cabinet steel doors, with water bottles lying on the bottle shelf like vintage wines.

After rinsing my mouth out with spring water, I drained the bottle in two swigs. The cold water gave me chills. My body was shaking again.

Taking another bottle, I returned to the library.

At the same time, Veera marched into the room from the other direction with her hands on her head. Robert was prodding her in the back with a poker. In his left hand, Robert had the champagne sword.

Robert asked Veera to sit on the sofa. "Time for a serious talk," he said and sat down next to her.

Veera said that threatening someone with a weapon was a natural point of departure for a serious adult conversation.

"Mikko!" Robert exclaimed. "Could you please take these implements?"

He shoved the sword and poker at me. I asked if he was sure.

"We all know that Mikko is fair and trustworthy. He wouldn't hurt a fly, right?" Robert said to Veera.

I said that I appreciated the trust Robert was showing me even after I had been the one who came to the party with the intent to kill.

"Okay, fine. Mikko, take them," Veera said.

"Take good care of them. For all our sakes," Robert said.

Shaking with cold, I sat down on the opposite couch and leaned the weapons against my leg. Robert asked Veera to explain in her own words why she had killed Elise and then threatened him with a sword.

"I'm the guilty one," I said, interrupting.

"Shut the fuck up!" Veera yelled.

I said I understood that given my past intentions, Veera and Robert had every right to hold me in contempt, but even so I hoped that I could cast some light on the motives for my behavior and thereby receive even a portion of their understanding. Of course I had no expectation of any explanation alleviating the reprehensibility of my intentions. I would leave it to Veera and ultimately to Robert what actions they would initiate against me.

"If you haven't noticed, Elise is the carcass, not Bob," Veera said.

"We have a bigger problem," Robert said with a deep sigh. The statement and sigh sounded like a closely linked pair, which he had probably used on many occasions in conference rooms at Union Credit.

"You didn't finish the job," Veera said and sprang up from the couch and rushed toward me.

Veera seized the poker and champagne sword, letting out a

string of vile curses when the blade of the sword cut her hand. She stood between the couches, pointing both weapons at Robert.

"Veera!" I screamed.

Then I felt my legs cramp again. It wasn't just from the cold.

"Well, what now?" Robert said with resignation and lifted his hands lazily toward the ceiling.

"First, I'd like you to apologize," Veera said.

"I'm sorry," Robert said.

"No, not a banker's apology. With real humility."

Veera emphasized her dissatisfaction by advancing the tip of the sword and the prongs of the poker so close to Robert's chest that if he breathed in, they would make contact.

Robert held his breath. He was afraid.

So was I. I flexed my toes, willing the cramps to subside. "Hey, Veera, would you please give me those weapons?"

My wife didn't seem to hear. She held the poker and champagne sword steady and stared into Robert's eyes.

"It would make this much easier if I knew what I'd done wrong. Why do I deserve death or torture? What am I supposed to apologize for and to whom? Why are you threatening me?"

"Our division of labor is that Mikko does the thinking and I take care of business," Veera said.

Then I moved.

My hill training and standing long jumps had paid off, giving my thighs explosive power. Exerting all the force I had, I lunged at Robert with both hands outstretched and knocked him to the ground. Then I shielded him.

"I don't want everyone to die!"

"Everyone has to die. Few things in this world are as certain as that. In our religion even God came to earth to die," Veera said. "Get out of the way so there won't be any more extra bodies."

# Veera

WHY DID MIKKO have to go and get in my way?! He didn't leave me any options. I had to try to get around him.

Despite his drunkenness, my husband reacted quickly. When I moved to the right, Mikko went in the same direction. When I tried to go under, Mikko shifted down and covered Rob's body.

Still I thought I could get past Mikko. I lunged to the right and struck at Rob.

Mikko was faster. It was his own fault the sword hit him in the side.

Mikko's shirt ripped like the veil of the temple. Those Marimekko shirts with the vertical stripes are made for fat old ladies, not joggers like Mikko. On him it was nearly a sail.

Mikko screamed and moaned, even though the saber couldn't have gone very deep.

Of course when his human shield crumpled Rob jumped onto the couch cushions, leapt over the back, and then ran away.

I took off after him. Mikko would survive his scratches but not if Rob got away and Mikko's murder plot failed.

I knew I wouldn't survive if Rob was still standing at the end of this, anyway.

Rob's question was actually a good one. I didn't know why I was killing him. But I trusted that Mikko knew. Who can you trust if not your own husband? At least when your husband happens to be a man like Mikko.

It was like being a soldier in Mikko's war. The Cossack doesn't trouble his mind with why he has to kill. Contemplating the reasons was the concern of the generals. They carry the brass and the responsibility.

I played a Body Combat song in my head as I ran, even though the record player was blaring Irwin Kostal.

I preferred The Prodigy to *The Sound of Music* for what I was doing now.

I caught Rob in the foyer. He was waiting for me. To protect himself, he had only an umbrella he had grabbed from the stand, a golf course type with a bank logo on it, which would work well as a lightning rod in the middle of a fairway but was a Barbie toy compared to a cavalry sword.

"Apparently you want to lose."

"I had to give you a handicap."

If I had doubted before, now I knew this shithead deserved to die.

Using the weapons in stereo was difficult. Eeny, meeny, miny, moe. I chose the sword. It was made for killing, while the poker was for moving logs. So I tossed it in the corner. It bounced on the floor.

I grabbed with my left hand outside the guard and swung from behind my head like a splitting maul.

Rob dodged. The sword blade sank into the wood floor right where a few hundredths of a second earlier Rob's foot had been.

Jerking the sword free, I quickly swung it back and to the right where Rob had jumped. I didn't look where the blade was going. I had to guard my flank.

The sword hit the umbrella.

"This seems familiar somehow," Rob said. "Have we done this before?"

We fought. Left, right, left!

The umbrella bent with every stroke. Red scraps of fabric fell onto the floor and became a slipping hazard.

Mikko appeared at the library door. He had taken off his dress shirt, under which was a cotton T-shirt from a charity run, which matched the Marimekko. On his side was a dark patch that Mikko was applying pressure to with his hand.

"Do you see what you've done to Mikko?" I shouted at Rob.

"Me? I wasn't the one who stabbed him!"

Rob breathed heavily between each word.

"If you hadn't started this game, no one would be swinging any weapons around."

Mikko begged us to stop. "Veera, none of this matters. Elise is dead."

"Yes, yes, but Rob isn't!"

Then Mikko confessed everything.

Usually my husband speaks with great deliberation, pausing for effect and considering the stress he places on each word, but now the words came in a flood. Mikko told us about his meeting with Elise and hatching his murder plot, but he did so as if reading a telephone book as quickly as possible. As if his time was running out.

Rob and I continued sparring, but the pace slowed and the blows softened. We wanted to hear what Mikko said. We wanted to understand his words.

"I loved Elise. More than I ever loved you."

Those words I picked out of the torrent, and when Mikko burst into sobs as he said them, I believed.

I mean, my God!

Mikko, my Mikko! And that plastic bitch!

I decided it was all Rob's fault.

Let him be guilty! For all of it!

I wound up for my next swing as far back as I could.

To hell with them! To hell with all of them!

I took two jumping steps, focusing all my strength on the blow. I pulled air in and squeezed my hands around the hilt.

The sword didn't swing. It had stuck in something that gave a metallic rattle. Whatever it was gave way a little, but wouldn't let go and then pulled me backwards.

I lost my balance, and when I fell, I knew nothing good would come of it.

That was my final thought.

Well, no, that wasn't. My final thought was that Rob had been right. Downstairs in the hotel room had been our last time.

# Robert

VEERA DIED WITH style. That was the kind of end I would hope for myself if I had to choose an accidental death.

In mid-attack, Veera toppled into the suit of armor. She banged her head on the thick metal of the thigh. A hollow boom came like a death knell, and the small but strong spikes of the armor sank into her skull.

Simultaneously the sword came unstuck from the breastplate. The weapon launched out of Veera's hand, rotated around its center of mass in the air, and plunged into her chest, where it remained.

Veera didn't die from the sword but from the head injury. The sword just rounded out the artistic effect. It was the cap on the column, the lime slice on the margarita, the bonus payout in the structured product.

The armor rocked, off balance. When it fell, it crashed against the chest of drawers upon which sat the flowers Mikko and Veera had brought. One of the long, white lilies fell across Veera's stomach.

An exceptionally fine exit from the stage.

Except that Veera didn't exit the stage, she just lay on the foyer floor with her mouth open. She looked the same as I remembered her from our London trysts, when I had woken at four o'clock unable to sleep because of the alcohol and gazed at her in the dim light filtering through the blinds, wondering if everything should be different.

"Now we have two bodies," I observed to Mikko, who rushed to give Veera mouth-to-mouth. "Do you think your breath smells bad enough to wake the dead?"

That was tasteless. Perhaps it was my way of coping with shock.

I left Mikko to his breaths and compressions. I removed my suit jacket and sweaty collared shirt. I poured myself a stiff glass of vodka. Then I sucked the alcohol over my gums so it would go to my head more quickly.

I breathed through my nose.

When I returned to the foyer, Mikko was still bustling around Veera.

"Veera is dead," he said.

"Yes. As I said, now we have two bodies."

The problem was fundamentally a practical one. I asked Mikko how he intended to deal with it.

"I imagine we should call the police," Mikko said.

He wasn't up to serious brainwork. I motivated him by reminding him that he was to blame for the whole mess. Without his murderous plot, he and Veera never would have even traveled to London. The women would still be alive. It was a bit much to expect me to figure out how to deal with his mess all on my own.

"Everything is my fault," he said.

"Yes, it is. So stand up and lend a hand!"

Removing the saber, I grabbed Veera under the armpits. Whatever else happened, we had to get the body out of the foyer. That was at least somewhere to start.

I waited until Mikko realized what was going on and took Veera by the legs. We dragged the body to the bathroom. Veera's rear end slid across the floor.

"What do we do?" I asked. "Veera was your wife after all."

Mikko stood next to the shower, not contributing in any way. With his hands against the wall, he breathed heavily. His head hung down.

"You promised to love each other in good times and in bad until death do you part. You're a free man now. Not that Veera took your marriage vows very seriously."

Was that twisting the knife in the wound? Mikko had every right to be heartsick, but didn't I, too? Mikko's wife had died, but so had mine. And besides, I hadn't just lost my wife, I had lost Veera as well. Mikko had taken Veera from me twenty years ago, but up until now I had been able to borrow her. That option had expired now too.

"It was an excellent trick claiming you were in love with Elise," I said. "It worked on Veera. You were just unlucky that Veera reacted so strongly and things turned out the way they did."

"Veera died."

"Yes, that's true, but you did everything you could."

"It's true." Mikko groaned.

"Yes, it's true. She's dead as a doornail."

"I loved—"

"The last act of service you can do for your dearly departed is to help me dispose of the bodies. And I'm expecting some degree of initiative on your part. This will only take a few hours."

"I loved Elise."

"I think you have your women mixed up, but it's all the same. They're both dead. What do you think? Axe? Saw? It's just too bad Veera is dead. Her professional skills could have been useful. What's it like cutting human flesh? Are there some places that will bleed more than others? What would a professional do?"

"It wasn't a trick. Elise and I were supposed to run away together once you were dead."

Mikko still had energy to spin a yarn. I asked where they had met. As I did I shifted Veera's limbs into a more compact position.

"At the Kämp Hotel in Helsinki," Mikko replied and then recounted his story without lifting his eyes from Veera's feet. Occasionally a grimace flashed across his face.

"It must have been a misunderstanding," I said.

Mikko began to shake.

"I'm sorry! I don't mean to be rude, but think it through! You and Elise!" I exclaimed. "Well, in any case, let's get to work. Should we get Elise in here, too, or should we just start with Veera? And should we take their clothes off before we start chopping them up? You can select your weapon of choice. Cleaver, saw, saber, or drill? We don't have an ax."

Mikko turned his torrent of vomit toward the floor drain in the shower. I averted my eyes.

That's how I am.

# Mikko

AFTER WIPING THE acid from my lips, I rinsed my gums with cold water. My left arm was still cramping. I pressed my arm against the sink.

I promised to help Robert as soon as I had rested a bit.

"Try not to be too long about it."

"I don't think I have a choice."

"Fifteen minutes?" Robert asked and then left the bathroom without waiting to hear whether I agreed. He was a boss. He gave instructions.

What was left in the mirror was a gaunt man with bloodshot eyes. He shook his head, but his cheeks didn't sway and his hair didn't fly.

When I tried to leave, I tripped over Veera's shoulder and fell, landing on her chest. I begged her pardon.

" . . . for everything."

I didn't know what I should be most sorry for. That I had cheated on her? Or that I had planned to murder Robert? That I had caused her and Elise's deaths?

I felt as if Veera forgave me. Her blood stuck to my trousers. It seemed like she was marking me with her approval.

I dragged myself to the guest room. I took my jeans and T-shirt off and put them on the back of a chair so I wouldn't soil the bedspread.

Twenty years had passed since my last hangover. Robert had

suggested that we spend that weekend together, just the four of us: he, I, Veera, and Robert's girlfriend at the time, Maarit. We drank a lot of alcohol, in twenty-four hours nearly as much as I had drunk in my entire life up till then. My feelings swelled, and I experienced joy but also anger. I became irritated with Robert and left the cabin before the others. I went home to sleep and woke up the next night to the phone ringing. I waited for someone to go answer it. I let it ring until I remembered I was home alone. When I got up to get it, my head reeled, and the ringing stopped before I made it to the entryway. Instead of going to the phone, I went to the bathroom and hung my head over the toilet with my eyes closed.

It was horrible.

The next day Veera called and told me Maarit was dead. Maarit had stayed at the cabin alone when Robert and Veera returned to the city to see a movie. During the night Maarit suffocated.

The caller during the night must have been Maarit. If I had made it to the phone, would Maarit still be alive? Why had Maarit called me instead of the emergency number?

I felt guilty. Veera and I never spoke of Maarit again after that. I never told anyone about the call during the night. And after that I had never drunk more than three servings of alcohol at a time—not until tonight.

The cramps moved from my thighs into my knees. Soon both legs convulsed, and I couldn't straighten them.

These didn't feel like hangover symptoms. No, these were more characteristic of strychnine poisoning.

Had I breathed in enough of the powder to kill? Why hadn't I washed my hands after overturning the coffee cup? Had I poisoned myself?

The thoughts hit me like jolts of electricity as my muscles suddenly contracted.

This was the moment of death, the moment when I realized

that easing the symptoms was only postponing death. How the strychnine had entered my system was irrelevant now. Wasting the final hours or minutes of my life contemplating causes and seeking explanations was futile.

I sobbed, crying out loud against the bedspread. I pulled a pillow out from underneath. Venting my disappointment into that was softer. The pillow smelled like Veera. Only a couple of hours earlier we had made love with uncommon pleasure on this bed.

Veera was no more, and soon I wouldn't be either.

I was only getting what I deserved. Death was the perfect punishment for me.

Death might even be a relief since life after the deaths of the two most important women in my life would have been a nightmare anyway. I might have been sentenced to prison for attempted murder. That would have been just. I had attempted to commit murder.

Now I was going to avoid all that unpleasantness. The postmortem on this night would fall to Robert alone. He would survive, and he always knew how to explain things the best.

I lay on the bed, taking deep breaths and staring at the white painted ceiling. In the corner was a hairline crack. In a brand new building.

Staring at the ceiling was nearly the most inane thing I could do with my limited remaining time.

People should think ahead about what they'll do if they know they only have an hour or less to live. Otherwise when the moment comes, precious minutes will go to waste. What happened to me will happen to them: I thought about why I had wasted so much time in my life. Why had I used so much time on slogging through jogs that didn't improve my fitness and just irritated me? I could have used that time reading books—good books, not the bad ones I had struggled through even though I knew they weren't going to get any better. Why had I sat in editorial meetings doodling even though I could have walked outside and enjoyed the sun on the shore of the bay? Why had I stood in line at the Lidl next to the train station for macaroni and yogurt because they were a few cents cheaper there?

Time hadn't felt as valuable then as it did now. But I couldn't have those moments I wasted to replace the ones I had left.

And which were now even fewer.

Fewer and fewer and fewer.

I was using my time wrong, and that distressed me. There was no way to preserve it.

I knew my end would be terrible. I had chosen my poison so it would cause as much agony as possible. The pain could be ameliorated with strong painkillers, but I didn't have anything that strong. Robert probably didn't either.

The cramping would only get worse.

I would have to end this myself. That much mercy I could show myself.

Should I empty the strychnine pouch into my mouth? That many times the lethal dose was sure to kill me, but it would still take time, although I hadn't been able to find any information on how long death would take and what the dying process would be like exactly. Strychnine deaths were described in the literature, but research on the action of strychnine in the human body was sparse. "For understandable reasons," one source said as if giving a dry cough to indicate it was a joke.

I could pull a plastic bag over my head.

No, suffocating was also a slow, agonizing way to die.

I couldn't get the windows open. And I couldn't stand the thought of the fall from this height, which would last several seconds. And I didn't want the attention that splatting on the street would bring. Jumping from the tallest building in Western Europe was sure to draw headlines. I would end up on one of those true crime TV shows where the hosts compensated for their lack of skill by talking loudly and focusing their word choice on maximum shock value.

I'm the one who puts things on the front page. I'm not supposed to be there myself.

I could get the sword and slash my wrists open. Or would the jugular be better? How long would that last? At what point would I lose consciousness? When would the pain end?

Robert was right: it would have been easier if we had Veera's expertise.

Why didn't I have a gun? Why didn't Robert?

That was a life lesson. Keep a pistol on your person. Used properly, even a small caliber weapon would do.

I started typing a text message to Julia. Now there was no need to be concise or abbreviate. The message could go in several parts for all I cared, since they would end up on next month's bill. The executor would have to deal with every eleven-cent one of them. That would actually save Julia on estate taxes. She was going to end up in the highest bracket because not only was she inheriting a house that was in the clear, she was also getting my savings. My stock portfolio was larger than most might guess, several hundred thousand euros: Kone and some other machinery manufacturers who were capitalizing on the Asian market, YIT Group, two major construction machinery providers, Kesko, Fortum, and UPM, which I had bought cheap during the financial crash.

*Think about what you'll do when you know you're about to die. Spend 15 minutes on it today.*

*I love you. Dad.*

Was that too lovey-dovey? I erased the love part. Then I wrote it again.

The text fit easily within 160 characters. I tried to imagine how I could make the message longer, but I didn't have anything else to say. I sent the text on its way and turned off the phone.

Robert was in the doorway rocking from the balls of his feet to his heels and back, his upper body bare.

"Feeling better now? Any ideas? We can handle this together, right?"

He had the nerve to bother me while I was dying.

"You don't seem fighting fit, but some hair of the dog should help."

Robert went to get the vodka bottle, which was less than half full now. He poured some into an untouched water glass that was on the nightstand at my side. On the other side was Veera's glass, which she had drunk bottled water out of just after we settled in.

"Okay, let's take a little break, but would you mind if I took a shower? In here, I mean," Robert asked.

"It's your shower."

"I'd leave you alone, but the big bathroom is . . . occupied."

Without any further discussion, Robert went into the bathroom, took off the rest of his clothing, and started singing a Robbie Williams song as he showered.

I grabbed the bottle. Alcohol was an old approach to anesthesia. I would have to drink it fast to get the best dulling effect on my nerves and mind.

*The suitcase strap.*

I had rolled the red and blue belt up next to our suitcase.

The curtain rod. Wouldn't hold my weight. The metallic decoration on the ceiling. The hook holding it would definitely work.

Robert sang, and the water gurgled. I grabbed the luggage strap and tested. You tightened it using two metal buckles. They slid nicely just so long as the strap didn't bunch up. The fabric was stiff and had a coating, though, so it wasn't likely to snag. Why had we brought this one rather than the newer Samsonite strap with the ABS buckle?

The sounds of the shower died, and the singing ended. I hid the strap under the bedspread. Taking a stiff swig of vodka from the bottle, I stashed it next to the foot of the bed on my side where Robert wouldn't see it.

Robert returned wrapped in a bath towel.

"I feel like a new man. I'm going to go change into some work clothes before we get down to business. What do you think? Can we get the girls carried down in one piece after all? We're both strong enough. It's just thirty kilos a piece. Elise at least would fit in a garment bag."

I interrupted him, telling him that many things separated us. We had different views on social issues. But we were still friends. We had a shared history. We had shared the most important moments of our lives.

"You are my only friend," I said. "I never would have become who I am without you. I became a better person because you were you."

"Because I'm evil?"

"Because you're different. I can't imagine a better conversation partner. I've learned a lot through you about life and people."

Robert pointed out that I had spent much more time with Veera than with him.

"Women are mercurial. The only real friendship is friendship between men. Pals. Buddies. Well, okay, buddy, let's get to work!"

I asked for another fifteen minutes, to which he agreed.

"Rob . . . " I said as he was still at the door. "Forgive me."

Robert waved his hand. "You could never do anything I wouldn't forgive you for."

I realized that I had called Robert "Rob." For the first time in a quarter century.

Fifteen minutes was my final deadline. I never missed a deadline. The few times an editor had come knocking on my door asking for an article were only because they hadn't had the patience to wait to read what I was writing.

Fifteen minutes. I had a luxury problem because I was able to choose the mode and place of my death. I wasn't going to end my days wrapped in the white, detergent-worn cotton sheets of a hospital bed.

I moved the chair onto the bed. I had to put books under the legs so they wouldn't sink into the mattress. In my backpack I had *Murder on the Orient Express* and Lord Byron in the suitcase for the flight home. Veera's purse provided a Jo Nesbø paperback. Under the fourth leg I shoved a travel guide Veera had insisted on bringing even though I had said we weren't going to need it for a two-day trip in a city we had visited before.

It turns out I had needed it after all. Veera had been right, as usual.

I missed her so much.

Maybe I would see her in a few minutes on the other side.

That was a strange thought because I didn't believe in life after death. I don't understand where that hope might have come from.

Balancing, I climbed up on the chair, easily reaching the chandelier. It appeared to be an antique, not one of those composite reproductions they use to give apartments a vintage appearance. It hung from the ceiling on a sturdy hook.

Getting the chandelier off the hook only required strength, not coordination. I pushed with both hands, and it slid over the edge of the hook and whumped down on the bed.

The mattress released a burst of air. Robert probably hadn't noticed the sound, though.

Climbing down, I turned the bed so the edge was more or less under the hook. I rebuilt the chair stand and swung one end of the luggage strap over the hook. I pulled. The strap was good quality. The threads didn't rip even though I had worked a hole through the strap with a pair of nail clippers. Veera had brought those too—amazing, practical Veera!

I only had a few minutes left of the time Robert had promised me.

I made a loop with the strap. The noose was quite high. I would just need to push off. From the force of that, the chair would fall back onto the bed. The noose would tighten around my neck and cut off the blood and oxygen to my brain. In a few seconds, I would be unconscious.

Nighttime London spread out before me. Lines of lamps along the roads, a few windows in the high rises still lit.

I didn't see the darkness, just the lights.

I was privileged to be able to choose the last thing I saw. The view was beautiful. Some people paid thirty pounds for the opportunity to get to see London for an hour from the Shard's viewing platform. I got to see it for the rest of my life for free.

I placed the noose around my neck, but then I stopped to gaze at the world. The world was ugly, but there were beautiful sides to it.

Then I took my head out of the noose and climbed down onto the bed. I drank another mouthful of vodka.

Should I write a goodbye letter?

I heard a clattering through the door. Robert was probably arranging things in the foyer, but he would be coming soon. My time was running out.

Quickly I got back on the chair and pushed my head through the noose.

Steps and whistling came from the foyer.

The melody was Bon Jovi. "It's My Life" was the song, I think.

Veera had hummed the same tune earlier. Was that a coincidence?

I didn't have time to think about it. Robert had decided for me when I would have to find the courage. The time was now or never.

*Bong.*

*Bong.*

*Bong.*

*Bong.*

# Robert

FIRST I NOTICED that the bed was out of place. Then I spotted the chair toppled on the bed.

From there my eyes moved up and to the side, and I knew what I would see next.

I'm used to surprises and I know from experience that the improbable is possible. I have practical experience with this because I've made millions on uncertainty.

That doesn't mean that I'm numb to surprises, though. I just know how to deal with them better than average.

When Elise had started convulsing and writhing on the library floor, I began processing how to respond to the new situation. I evaluated our positions and planned my tactics as I always did when unexpected information rattled the capital markets.

When Veera grabbed the sword, I wasn't even surprised.

But when I saw Mikko hanging from the ceiling with his head resting unnaturally on his right shoulder, I stopped. My brain stopped too.

Mikko had been a part of my life for as long as I could remember.

I had never considered that he might have suicidal thoughts, but getting into his head had always been difficult. And I may not have tried as fervently as he had to understand my thinking.

I remembered what Mikko had said when we had just talked after I came out of the shower. He had said something about friendship, which I had interpreted as an outburst of emotion caused by the intoxication and traumatic experience. I couldn't recall the words, only the tone, which was serious, as Mikko always was.

I hadn't understood that those words were a eulogy.

Mikko didn't do anything on the spur of the moment. Had he planned all this from the beginning? Had he come here to die?

Had he really also come to kill me?

I walked over to him. I didn't want to check his chest. Not long could have passed since his hanging. Mikko might still be alive, but his brain had certainly sustained permanent damage. It was better not to take him down. I chose mercy not only for Mikko but for myself, and above all for Mikko and Veera's daughter.

Turning my back to the body, I faced the city and then lowered the blinds.

Then I closed them.

In the dimness Mikko's naked body looked almost beautiful. I closed the door after me. I went and turned off the stereo in the middle of "Black Sun Rising" by Juice Leskinen.

I sat down in an armchair, but I couldn't bear staying still. I walked past the dining table to the window. I didn't look out; I looked down.

There were already three bodies. It was easier to move one than three. I didn't even have an assistant anymore.

The decision came quickly. When the facts change, a man has to change his plans so they lead to the desired outcome. He has to work with the available options.

I had to get out of the apartment. The rest I could think through later.

I grabbed a roller bag from the walk-in closet. The door to the safe was open. Maarit and Veera stared at me as I emptied the cash, the gold, and the file with my most important papers into the suitcase.

The cyanide ampule box was empty. One had killed Elise.

Another had turned up in her pocket. The third must be somewhere on the library floor amidst all the mess. I didn't want to look for it even though the chances of needing it were greater now than ever before. The aftermarket value of the suicide option had risen, even though death felt like anything but a scarce commodity at the moment.

I would need as much money as possible. Circling the apartment, I gathered anything easy to transport that I could turn into cash. I grabbed both passports from my desk.

Could I take a phone with me? Would they be able to track my credit card?

I was proud of how logically I was able to pose these questions to myself.

When the suitcase was full, I wiped the smell of the bodies off my skin with a wet towel. I chose underwear, socks, and a casual shirt in a colorful checked pattern. Dark blue jeans and a relaxed sports coat. The shoes were dark brown Clarks, which were well broken in and wouldn't cause any blisters even if I had to use them for quite a while.

I rolled the bag into the foyer. After calling the elevator, I decided to say goodbye. It was an irrational act. I should have hurried away.

Life is irrational. It was irrational that there were three corpses in my apartment.

I didn't turn on the light in the guest room. Mikko hung peacefully. He had died as he had lived: alone. Alone, even though I had been close-by.

I closed that door and opened another.

Veera lay in an unnatural heap. The bloodstains on the bathroom floor were a reminder of dragging the body and the violence of her death. On Veera's neck a small, silver piece of jewelry glinted, the cross she had received from her godparents when she was confirmed and which she had worn ever since. I turned her head and unfastened the chain. I dropped the stylized cross into the front pocket of my coat.

The bathroom stank of vomit. I turned down the floor heating. It was already lower than normal. Then I turned the heat off completely.

The medicine cabinet door was open. Would I need anything from there? I grabbed the bottle of caffeine tablets. The next day could be long.

Elise's face was grotesque. I had dragged her into the middle of the room while Mikko rested. I covered her face with couch pillows. No, they wouldn't stay. Running to the bedroom, I pulled off the bedspread and rolled it up to take back and drape over Elise's corpse.

In each room I turned off the lights before leaving. None of the machines would be on in the kitchen, and it didn't matter if they were. None of the faucets were dripping, and if they were, let them.

Finally, I returned to the office and took the photographs from the inside of the door to the safe. I folded them and placed them in my wallet, which I put in my inner pocket. It pressed against my chest as I entered the elevator.

I approached my journey at six meters per second, not knowing where I was going. I was used to that.